Book 1
Sophie O'Brion Mysteries

The Vacant House

Tamara G. Cooper

DEDICATION

To all my boys
I love you bunches and bunches

Also by Tamara G. Cooper

Brothers of Texas Trilogy

Who Killed Brigitt Holcomb?

Rosie Won't Stay Dead

Deception at Fairfield Ranch

The Vacant House

1

Frantic barking woke me.

I'm sure most people would jump out of their beds at such a commotion, hearts pounding, hands shaking as they tried to turn on their flashlights to see what evil had invaded their neighborhood.

But not me.

Calmly, I rolled over and reached for my phone. It was 5:45—the paperman was running a little late. Since I had only about a minute to get downstairs, I tried to muster up a sense of urgency, but another sleepless night left me groggy and irritable and thinking, "Oh, just let him win this time." But I couldn't. The fierce warrior rose up inside me, and I tossed the covers, grabbed my robe, slid my tired feet into slippers, and shuffled across my bedroom. My dresser mirror revealed an extra in a zombie movie watching me as I passed by. "You're up early," I mumbled to my reflection, ran a hand through my mussed hair, and dreamed of coffee as I stumbled down the stairs toward the front door.

Samson the German Shepherd was racing up my steps with the prize within reach when I grabbed my newspaper and shook it at him. "Ha! Ha! The human wins again." Even with having to race Samson most mornings, I would never consider switching to the on-line version of our town's paper. The residents of Forman Falls, Texas, were fiercely proud of the *Gazette*, and we didn't want to lose it. Besides, I loved the feel of the newspaper in my hands.

As did my next-door neighbor on my left, Jennie. Usually, she opened her screen door at the same time to get her paper, and we grunted at each other—two cups of coffee, minimum, were necessary for either of us to form meaningful language before sunup. But this morning, the only part of Jennie's anatomy that appeared was her hand, dropping like a giant spider from the bottom of her door. It hopped around, landed on her newspaper, and both hand and paper

1

disappeared up. When her front door slammed, I glared at Herman Farnsberry's house across the street.

It appeared my good neighbor Jennie actually believed Mr. Farnsberry's lies about me.

My sweet neighbor two doors down on my right called last night to tell me the latest gossip: that I was being accused of killing Farnsberry's cat and tossing him into the toilet of the vacant house, directly across the street from my home. "Did you do away with his cat, Sophie?"

"Of course not, Mrs. LeGraff. And even if I did, I wouldn't have chosen the vacant house's potty for his reveal. I have more imagination than that."

So, on this hot and mucky East Texas morning with the sun peeking above the trees lining our beautiful street, I marched myself over to Mr. Farnsberry's house and knocked on his black wrought-iron screen door. I crossed my arms, tapped my foot, and rolled my eyes when he didn't answer. He's an early riser—the lights were already on in his kitchen and dining room—and I had no qualms about knocking again, louder and longer.

A piece of paper slid between the door and the screen frame. *Do not trespass or I will call the police.*

Oh, puh-lease. "Mr. Farnsberry?" I leaned over to see better, resting my forehead against the thick mesh of the screen door with my eyeball almost touching it, but I couldn't see a thing. "Mr. Farnsberry, I did *not* kill your cat."

Another sheet materialized. *My finger is poised to dial 9-1-1. Please leave.*

"This is ridiculous. I wouldn't do what I'm being accused of! I'm a respectable, decent, *caring...*" Hmmm. "Okay. A *reasonably* caring woman who wouldn't hurt a fly much less a cat. All right, yes, I *would* hurt a fly but never a cat. For heaven's sake, let's be reasonable here."

A third page slid into view. *Dialing.*

"Oh, all right!" I tapped his screen with my newspaper—not very hard; it was more to satisfy the urge to tap *him* for not giving me a chance to defend myself. I stomped down his steps and stalked toward my house. But before I reached it, Samson the Paper Snatcher, with a snarl and a bark, raced up to me and buried his teeth in my paper.

"Oh, no, you don't!" I yanked and did some snarling myself, but Samson won the tug-of-war and ran like the wind toward the vacant house.

I raced after him, shouting at him to drop my paper and drawing, I'm sure, the attention of most of my neighbors when I screeched. I could well imagine what they were saying: "There goes Sophie again, after another animal."

When Samson slid under the vacant house, I fell to my knees and squinted into the dark netherworld only a dog could love. There he sprawled, his teeth still imbedded in my daily news. Flies swarmed all over his stinky paradise.

"Give it back, you thieving fleabag."

He dropped the newspaper in muck that looked and smelled like a mixture of dung, mud, and decomposing bodies. "Great, Samson. What self-respecting person would want that paper now? Bad dog! Bad dog!"

"Is there a problem, ma'am?"

I bumped my head when the man spoke behind me. I didn't recognize his voice but was sure my robe-draped derriere didn't present a welcoming picture. I rubbed my head and squirmed around, but my right knee landed on something sharp. "Oh!"

I jerked and placed both hands in the tall grass as I lifted my knee and set it on another spot that didn't bite me. Then I sat back and looked up at the man. I couldn't make him out with my hair in my face and the rising sun behind him. I could see he was big—tall, like the Jolly Green Giant looking down at me.

"Are you okay, dear?"

Across the street, Mrs. LeGraff stood in her yard, waving her newspaper at me. I sent her a thumbs-up with my best six-o'clock-in-the-morning smile and then turned my attention back to the man, his question still hanging in the air.

I tried to stand but by now, both my feet had gone to sleep. I grabbed the window ledge and pulled myself up and endeavored to look dignified despite wearing my most comfortable robe with a couple of missing buttons and one pocket ripped and hanging on for dear life. My right foot started to wake up—oh!—and I needed to stomp it. I wanted to say, "No, there's no problem," but I only got the word "No" out because when I lifted my foot, my house slipper slid off, and I couldn't stop myself in time to *not* stomp it. My foot landed on a protruding tree root, and I yelped and danced on one foot, tried to grab my hurt foot, tumbled forward instead, and landed squarely on my face.

"Ma'am, are you hurt? I'm Officer Burke Maguire with the police department. Can I help you up?"

Well, dear Gussie!

What was *he* doing here?

I turned my head just enough that I wouldn't be inhaling grass or bugs. "Thank you, but I don't need help." I tasted blood. I wasn't about to get up and present a bloody face to *him*, of all people. "Was there something you wanted, Officer?"

There was a long pause before he said, "Are you Mrs. O'Brion?"

My mother, an Irish hippie-wannabe who married Murphy O'Brion, named each of her children after long-dead Irish relatives. None of us had the same last name. I was the youngest. My name, Sophie MacIvey, came from a great-great-great-aunt who, I learned, discovered not only opium on a trip to London in the 1890s but the scandalous nightlife. I legally changed my name to O'Brion right before college.

I didn't correct his use of the word *Mrs.* "Yes?"

"We've had a complaint from Herman Farnsberry that you killed his cat."

4

Samson the Betrayer barked as if he sat in the 'Amen Corner' at church. I heard Burke rustling in the grass, and then he grunted. Was he looking under the vacant house?

"Is there any reason I should be concerned about this animal being hurt or killed?"

Oh, for crying out loud. "Of course not." Since my mouth had grass and dirt and, for heaven's sake, *blood* in it, I spit and spit again. "Samson stole my newspaper. I was just, um, just…"

He cleared his throat—or was he stifling a laugh? "Were you trying to get your paper back?" he prompted. I could hear the chuckle in his words.

"Absolutely not. It's ruined now, as you can see—and smell." I sniffed for good measure.

"So, you were?"

"Fussing at him. The dog doesn't possess one stitch of good manners."

It sounded as if Burke stood and took a few steps away from me. A page flipped.

"Where were you yesterday between eight-thirty a.m. and one-thirty p.m.?"

"In my home."

"Were you at home the entire time?"

"Yes. I didn't leave at all yesterday. I usually don't." Well, great. Just paint me pathetic.

"Can anyone verify your whereabouts yesterday from eight-thirty to one-thirty?"

"No. I didn't talk to a soul." Pathetic, pathetic.

He was writing again. "Why do you think Mr. Farnsberry named you as his cat's—" Here, he stopped, flipped a page. "—as Yoda's murderer? Do you two have a history of disagreements?"

"Who? Yoda and I?"

He chuckled. At least he still had a sense of humor. This could work in my favor.

"I meant you and Farnsberry, but you can tell me about your history with Yoda if you'd like."

"There is no history between me and the cat. We were just acquaintances and rarely spent time in each other's company." I made it to my side. Ouch, but my knee hurt.

"Ma'am, I'd be happy to help you up."

"I don't need to get up."

"All right. Then, uh, you and Farnsberry have a history?"

"He was my principal in middle school and has lived in this neighborhood since then."

I heard him shuffling something. "Thanks for your time, Mrs. O'Brion. I'll be in touch." He walked away from me. A door slammed. A car started. He drove away.

Finally.

"Oh!" I sat up, shivered, and frantically brushed any bugs or spiders off my robe and out of my hair. Samson's cheerful bark brought me back to my newspaper, and I bent over and looked him square in the eye. "You can keep my paper, Samson, but if you ever set your teeth on another newspaper of mine—" At this point, I had the good sense to lower my voice. "Well, you heard what happened to that cat!"

Samson whined, slithered through the stinky gook, and buried his nose in it. When he came up, he had something in his mouth. I quickly grabbed the window ledge and stood, clearing a wide path when he wriggled out into the sunshine and deposited the glob near my feet. "Oh? A peace offering from your grimy world? Not accepted, buddy boy."

But my inquiring mind had to know, so I picked up a twig, stabbed at the muddy lump, and moved it around. It was a necklace, with two pendants and a cross on it. I maneuvered the chain onto my stick and hurried home.

♦

The necklace soaked in my kitchen sink while I showered and dressed. I carefully washed and rinsed it and turned over one of two tear-shaped pendants. *Sharon* was engraved on the back of the gold one. I didn't know anyone named Sharon, but the necklace was stunning. I was sure those were real diamonds imbedded in the gold pendant; the other pendant was silver with what looked like rubies and emeralds in it. Someone had spent a lot of money on this necklace.

In the middle of the two pendants was a cross, simply made of wood with no jewels.

I placed the necklace on a paper towel on my table/writing station near a window. I was on a deadline with my next book, and I needed to get my mind off Samson, my newspaper, the necklace, and Burke Maguire. I shoved the cat murder to a back burner in my brain, too, until the local news van drove slowly by around ten o'clock as if the driver expected to find a toilet-paper-draped cat collar dangling from my front porch. Bertie the editor would be thrilled to have a crime to report in her newspaper, especially one involving me.

When the van drove by again, I stepped out onto my porch, smiled, and waved at the driver. He slammed on his brakes, leaned over to see me better, and then kept going, without answering my greeting.

About ten minutes later, someone knocked on my front door. I checked outside as I passed the row of windows in my living room. No news van in sight or a vehicle of any kind.

I looked through the peep hole.

Burke Maguire again! What *now?*

I took a deep breath and opened the door.

He chuckled as if he'd caught me pilfering cash from the church collection plate. "Well, Sophie, it *is* you. You clean up real nice these days."

So, he'd known it was me earlier and hadn't said a word. But who could blame him? I probably looked wild enough to have killed a cat and contemplated the same for a paper snatcher. "Is this an official call? You think I killed Yoda?"

He reached for the screen door.

I hesitated a fraction before I pushed it open.

We faced each other for an awkward moment, and then he stepped inside, looked around, and joined me at my big front window. He had certainly grown since high school, was a good two inches over six feet, and he'd filled out.

"I'm walking the neighborhood, talking to folks."

"Slow day for crime?"

"Even if the accusation is absurd, I have to—"

"You think I'm innocent?"

He looked into my eyes without blinking, without humor, and actually seemed to see me. His features softened. "Unless your character's changed drastically over the years."

"Well, it hasn't. I didn't kill Yoda. Although, there were times I wanted to—"

He held up his ringless left hand. "I don't need to hear a confession about your desire to off Yoda."

"Not the cat. His owner."

He chuckled. "Or Mr. Farnsberry. You tormented him no end in middle school with all your pranks."

"I was a writer in the making, honing my plotting skills."

"Is that what you call it?" He quickly sobered. "You live across the street from the vacant house. Have you noticed anyone playing there lately or snooping around?"

I looked out at the old, two-story clapboard. All the windows were boarded up. Tall weeds hugged the concrete steps leading up to the landing under the scarred front door. Rusted hinges dangled on the door jamb, the only thing left of the screen door ripped off by Halloween ghouls years ago. Old chipped paint covered the house. It was an eyesore but for the large back yard surrounded by lush greenery hanging over its fence on all three sides.

8

"It's still a favorite haunt. Kids play football. Girls play dolls on the landing. Oh, and a couple kids sneaked out from around back night before last."

"What time?"

"Around one o'clock." The question in his raised brows caused me to add, "I couldn't sleep. The thunderstorm cooled everything off, so I enjoyed the quiet on my porch."

"Do you know what they were doing?"

This time, I raised *my* brows. He knew good and well what they were doing. When we were in high school, it was a favorite place for kids—including me and Burke—to sneak onto the property and steal a kiss or two. "For the record? Enjoying the stars."

The corners of his mouth lifted as he scribbled a few words and turned the page. "Would you write down all the kids' names for me, please? And their addresses, if you know them."

"They don't live on my street, and I don't know their addresses." But I wrote down their names and handed the notebook back to him. "Oh. And Mr. Farnsberry."

"He told me he was there last week."

"Not last week. Two days ago."

"He didn't mention that. Did he go inside?"

I shook my head. "It was right after sundown. The oddest thing, though. He looked under the house with a flashlight."

"Probably searching for Yoda."

"He was holding Yoda."

"You're sure it was him?"

"Yoda was a distinctively gargantuan cat. It was him all right."

A dimple appeared when Burke tightened a corner of his mouth. "I meant, are you sure it was Farnsberry?"

"I watched him until he went inside his house."

"I'll ask him about it."

"Right. And be sure to tell him that Sophie O'Brion, his cat's alleged killer, ragged on him."

"I'll keep my source a secret." He studied the page of names. "One of these kids could have killed Yoda."

"That's preposterous."

"Who, then?"

"I haven't given it much thought."

"Maybe you should. You're the only suspect who—" His gaze settled on the necklace spread out on my writing table. He drew the paper towel close to the edge and leaned over. "Sharon?"

"Samson gave this to me as a peace offering for stealing my newspaper."

"How could he afford it?"

Despite my resolve to keep this strictly business, I laughed.

Burke chuckled, picked up the necklace, and thoroughly examined it. "This is high quality and expensive. Gold, rubies, diamonds, emeralds." He turned it over several times. "Where did Samson stash this?"

"In his palace." Burke glanced at me, and I shrugged. "Just a joke between us, Officer. Palace. Under the vacant house. Same thing."

"So, you don't hate animals."

I looked heavenward and steered the conversation back to the necklace. "Maybe Sue at the jewelry store can tell us something about it."

"It couldn't have been under the vacant house for long because it's still in remarkably good condition. Mind if I take it in and call Sue?"

"You're thinking there's a crime here?" I handed him a sandwich baggie, and he slipped the necklace inside.

"I don't know. I'll check to see if it's been reported missing." He walked to my front door and turned around. "It's good to see you again, Sophie."

I opened the door and the screen and said the first stupid thing I thought of: "Thanks for coming by. Be safe out there."

He walked outside and stood quietly as he scanned the

neighborhood and then headed for his patrol car.

As he drove off, I stepped onto my porch and watched his vehicle until it turned off my street. Burke Maguire, standing on my front porch again after twelve years. The thought made me sad, and I walked inside and shut the door.

◆

Thirty minutes later, I received a call from Edna Conroy, a lady in her mid-fifties who attends my church. "Why, hello, Miss Edna. How are you today?"

"I had nothing to do with killing Herman Farnsberry's cat, that's how I am."

Well, well. "How did you get mixed up in this mess?"

Edna sighed. "Missy, my cat, and I paid a friendly call on my old friend Herman and his not-so-friendly, mentally-disturbed cat. My Sunday school class is visiting backsliders, and I never leave my Missy alone at home. It makes her nervous." She sniffed. "I had considered leaving her in the car, you see, because I intended staying only long enough to say, 'Hey, how are you, we miss you at church, dear friend, so come back soon and have a nice day.'"

Edna hardly took a breath. "But it's much too hot in the car. The second we walked inside Herman's house, my sweet Missy jumped onto my shoulders. Do you know *why* she jumped up there, Sophie?"

I stifled a snicker. "Yoda?"

"He practically flew into my arms to get at her. Well, she was so upset, she crawled onto my head—and me with a new hairdo from Suza's just that morning. My sweet Missy isn't a tiny cat, so can you just imagine what she did to my hair? Her nails were clipped a few days ago, thank the good Lord, but still."

"Missy's adorable," I answered diplomatically, but the cat isn't a whit adorable. She's fussy and ill-tempered and wouldn't know a meow if it licked her. She snarls like a dog and sometimes barks like one, too.

"And then," Edna continued, "I was about to lose my balance, when Yoda ran up my dress—"

"Your dress!"

"On his way to my head where my sweet Missy was clinging for dear life. Herman grabbed Yoda, whose claws were concreted to my dress, and he ended up pulling all of us over, onto his not-so-soft carpet. To top it off, my dentures fell out. I was absolutely mortified."

"Oh, my goodness, Miss Edna. Were you hurt?"

"Thankfully, no. I landed on Herman. But my sweet Missy was so upset, she scratched Yoda. They got into a fight and I screamed and dialed 9-1-1 and that nice young police officer came over—oh, what's his name—the new one that just moved back here?"

"Burke Maguire."

"And what a nice man. He happened to be in Herman's neighborhood when the call came in. I will admit this, Sophie: if someone hadn't done away with Yoda, I considered putting him at the top of my list. He gives—gave—felines a bad name."

"Well, Miss Edna, I'm glad you're okay, and I appreciate the confession. It'll be our little secret."

Another suspect in the mysterious demise of Yoda couldn't keep my hair from needing a trim. I told Edna that I had to leave in one minute if I intended to make my appointment on time.

On my way to Gladys' Hair Lair, my phone rang. *Unknown Caller.* I answered it anyway. "Hello?"

"Sophie?"

"Burke."

"In the last few years, has Herman Farnsberry exhibited hostility toward you?"

"How did you get my phone number?"

"It was on file."

Hmmm. "Just a sec." I pulled into the salon and quickly saved his number to my phone.

"Any hostility, Sophie?"

"Mr. Farnsberry and I aren't close, but I don't growl at him when we run into each other, and he doesn't growl at me. Why?"

"I'm trying to establish intent. I can only come up with your middle school pranks."

"You think he'd accuse me of killing Yoda because I pranked him a few times?"

"A few times?"

"All right, maybe more than a few. Burke, have you verified that Yoda is dead? Have you seen a body?"

"Why would he lie about his cat dying?"

"He shreds my reputation on his word alone?"

The silence between us pounded with my question.

Good gracious. "I have an appointment, and I'm already late. Let me know when you find Yoda stuck up a tree or hiding behind a sofa."

2

With my hair trimmed and styled and not in a ponytail for a change, I drove home to find Samson and his Pekingese friend, Moocher, fighting over a tennis ball in my front yard. This was a perfect opportunity to show my neighbors how in tune I am with the animal kingdom. I scooped up the sticky-wet ball and threw it. While the dogs raced after it, I ran inside, holding my hand up like a surgeon waiting to be gloved, hoping none of the disgusting drool on my fingers dripped onto my clothes. After scrubbing my hands, I grabbed clear, disposable gloves and hurried back to the porch.

Samson growled at me with the ball proudly displayed in his mouth. He wagged his whole body with his chest on the ground and his rear in the air. Ah, now, isn't that just the cutest thing? I tugged on the ball, but he wouldn't let go. "Okay, you sticky-fingered pile of dog hair, drop the ball."

He did. I straightened up, glanced around the neighborhood, mustered a big smile, and threw the ball again. Both dogs darted after it. Moocher returned it this time and happily deposited it at my feet.

"That's more like it. Now both of you go party at Mooch's."

I smiled endearingly at them and threw the ball as hard as I could. It landed in Jonas Whitworth's yard, Moocher's owner and the neighbor on my right, in between me and Mrs. LeGraff.

My phone rang. I raced inside the house, shucked the gloves into a trash can, and grabbed my cell phone. Burke again. "Hey."

"Hey. Do you remember Farnsberry's wife disappearing nineteen years ago under suspicious circumstances? She was never heard from again."

"No, not at all."

"Guess what her name was?"

"Uh."

"Sharon."

I gasped. "Sharon? Did he kill her?"

"Couldn't be proven. No body. Insufficient motive. Solid alibi. Spotless background check."

I switched the phone to my right ear. "She probably ran away from the old coot."

He chuckled. "Maybe. But I'm taking a closer look into her cold case. Thought you'd like to know. I'll be in touch."

I hung up at the same moment my front door slammed. "Is the cat lady home?"

I smiled. Must be lunch time.

Growing up, I'd always wanted a sister. When Terri Smaller moved to Forman Falls in sixth grade, she landed the job. One major flaw in her character was that she was a rules keeper, and I was not. Her naive nature galvanized me to be as outrageous as possible. I didn't really need an excuse to be shocking, but as cheering sections go, Terri couldn't have been better at it. I tried to get her to take the lead in our pranks several times, but she'd just frown at me, shake her head, and say, "You go on. I'll be right behind you."

The day we found a freshly-dead frog on the school parking lot was the day I knew we would be soul mates forever. It was the last week of middle school, and Terri decided to stuff the icky frog remains behind the toolbox in Mr. Farnsberry's truck. "A parting gift for our principal," she said.

I was so proud of her.

"Sophie?"

"In the kitchen," I yelled back. "Just finishing up making donut holes."

She appeared, this tall, gangly, brown-and-bug-eyed jewel of a friend and tossed her purse onto a chair. "You're not going to believe who moved back to Forman Falls!"

"Do I get three gues—"

"Robert! I just found out this morning."

"Oh, no. Are you okay?"

"No, I'm not okay! He broke my heart! Why did he have to come back here? There are plenty of towns in East Texas for him to set up shop in but, no, he has to come back here to torment me some more!"

"It's been years, Terri. You're over him. You have Stan now."

"But what'll I say to him if we run into each other? I'd just want to punch him and get it over with."

"Okay. You need a script, something like: 'Hello, Robert.'"

"'You heart crusher.'"

"Terri, you have to take the high road. Just say something like: 'Hello, Robert—'"

"Go back into the swamp you crawled out of."

"All right. We'll dig a hole. You push him in. No one will ever find his body." I stared at Terri, waiting for her to come to her senses.

She pouted and picked up several donut holes. "I like it."

"I'm sure you do. Just say, 'Hello, Robert. Good to see you again' and walk off with a little smile. Leave him wondering why you're smiling. You can do that. You're over him, remember?"

"Not really. I mean, how do you get past that kind of hurt?"

"You don't, but you learn to live with it."

"You should know. So how was it, seeing Burke after all these years?"

"Fine. I've moved on, as you well know."

"And what in the world is Mr. Farnsberry doing, accusing you of killing Yoda? He's getting back at you for all the mischief you pulled on him in middle school. I wonder what he has planned for *me.*"

"That's ridiculous and you know it."

"These are ridiculous," she mumbled with a mouthful of donut holes. "Wish they'd put some weight on my hips."

"At least I have hips."

"With an extra ten on them."

"Curvaceous, O Jealous One."

"So, Burke dropped by to see you. What did he want?"

"He came to talk about Yoda. He thinks I'm innocent."

"Smart man. Sometimes." She tossed another donut hole into her mouth. "Really, how was it, seeing him again?"

"It was okay. Doesn't bother me at all that he came back. By the way, did you ever hear anything about Farnsberry's wife disappearing a couple summers before we entered middle school?"

"Disappearing?" Terri stopped chewing. "Is she dead?" Her bug eyes widened. I loved it when she did that. "Did he kill her?"

"I don't know. It couldn't be proven. His record was spotless."

"Except for getting away with killing his wife and maybe his cat?" Terri lifted her brows. "You should investigate." She glanced at my wall clock. "Gotta go. Stan's coming over tonight to watch a movie, and I need to straighten up the living room and look for a murder weapon for Robert." She gave me a hug. "Just wanted to check on you, what with Burke coming over and all."

"I'm glad you did."

She popped two more donut holes into her mouth just before she grabbed her purse and waved. "Tell Burke I said hey."

◆

That night, I couldn't sleep, which wasn't unusual. It's difficult for me to turn off my brain, and tonight, it was working at breakneck speed. I tossed the covers off, picked up my phone, and made my way toward the kitchen. Just as I stepped through the door, something thumped against my back door. I froze and dropped to the floor. My yard boasted a tall privacy fence with locks on both entrances. No one should be in my yard!

I'd never been afraid of the tall windows in my kitchen, but right now, they looked like two huge pairs of tinted glasses from the '70s that could easily hide a pair of eyeballs staring right at me. I attempted to crawl to the lower cabinet doors, but my legs screamed, "We are not crawlers!" so I bent over and charged my way to the counter.

I huddled there, a shaking mass of muscles and bones, my teeth clanging so loud, an intruder would have no trouble at all in locating the source of the signal.

A good three or four minutes crept by before I convinced myself that I should get to the door and see if anyone was in my yard. Since I didn't want to be trapped in my kitchen all night imagining all sorts of hideous and tortuous storylines, I slowly opened the door.

The nightlight beamed from the back of my yard, but I couldn't make out anything in its soft light. I pushed on the screen door. It wouldn't move. Then I flicked on the back porch light and saw the lump that prevented it: a gift-wrapped box with the words "Rest in Peace" written in bold black letters.

I gasped. "Yoda?"

I slammed the door, locked it, and had no qualms whatsoever in pulling a totally scaredy-cat move: I called Burke.

He came not ten minutes later, wearing jeans and a tucked-in T-shirt sporting a picture of a fist and the words, "Second to None!" on it. In the corner, in smaller letters, a logo boasted, "Marine Extreme." Serving his country as a Marine definitely explained the short cut of his blond hair, the bulging muscles under his T-shirt, and the fine shape of the rest of him.

"I'm sorry to drag you out here so late."

"I was still awake." He squatted next to the box and shined his flashlight down the steps, into the grass. "Did you check your gates before you went to bed?"

"They're always locked, and I never go through them. We do have a crime here, right? It isn't legal to put this box on my porch, on my property, is it?"

Burke stood, looked around the yard, and studied the box.

"Are you going to open it?"

"I'm getting to it. Here." He handed me his flashlight and slipped on gloves. "Shine it on the box." He took off the bow, and then gently opened the taped sides and slid the pretty paper off the box without even tearing it. I admire anyone who can do that. I certainly don't have that kind of restraint or patience when it comes to wrapping paper.

Burke took the top off the box. I shined the light inside; it rested on an envelope duct-taped to a red brick. The words "Sophie O'Brion" were written on it in straight, block letters.

Burke slid a sheet of paper out. I leaned over him and mouthed the words: *"Reference the number below for a complete makeover at the Crockett Mall and lunch for two at the Original Mexican Taco Station."*

"Depending on the restaurant, Sophie, lunch isn't a crime."

"But who sent it? What does 'Rest in Peace' mean?"

Oh, no. Terri sent it.

Burke turned it over. "It might be a veiled threat."

"Only for my wardrobe." I shook my head and looked heavenward, disgusted with myself that I'd dragged him out here in the middle of the night for one of Terri's pranks. "My best friend did this. She thinks I need a makeover." And she knows about my hidden gate and where I hide the key.

"Maybe. But I'm checking your gates anyway." He walked into the darkness with his circle of light crawling and jumping around the yard. While he was gone, I called Terri. No, she said she wasn't sneaking around my yard and no, she hadn't left the envelope.

Then who put it there? I may be a well-known author but here in Forman Falls, Texas, I have very few close friends, and none of them would have done this except Terri.

Burke reappeared and said, "Both were secure."

Then whoever did this knows about my ivy-covered gate. I could count on one hand the people aware of it, and only one—Terri— knew where the key was buried. I hugged myself and rubbed my arms when Burke picked up the box, opened the screen door, and stepped inside. Was he leaving already?

"Check out the reference number in the morning and try to get

19

some sleep."

Sleep? Out of the question. I was too spooked. Being a mystery writer meant I could control scary things and write them into a story where I wanted. When creepy things happened in real life, I was nothing short of a spineless wimp. "Thanks for coming out. I really appreciate it."

He walked toward the front door, opened it, stepped onto my porch, and glanced around my sleeping neighborhood. Then he nodded twice, said, "Call me if you need me," and left.

I watched him drive away, so grateful I hadn't fallen to my knees and begged him to stay and keep the monsters away. I had never been good with monsters. They liked me too much. But tonight, by golly, monsters were not welcome, no matter how much they enticed me with new wardrobes, great Mexican food, and spooky story lines.

I took myself to my bedroom, turned on the two table lamps, the overhead light, the computer light and the bathroom light. I couldn't even focus enough to start my computer and enter a world I'd created where monsters roamed freely, pillaging and plundering and planting clues.

So, I opened a romance. And kept one eye on the book and one eye solidly on my bedroom door.

3

My accuser, Mr. Farnsberry, visits his younger sister every Thursday. This isn't earth-shattering news unless you're a twenty-nine-year-old woman recently dubbed the Elm Street Cat Killer. If I could just get inside Mr. Farnsberry's house and rummage around a bit, I might find something that would break this case wide open, like, say, a cat named Yoda, skulking around the house, alive and cantankerous.

Mr. Farnsberry pulled out of his driveway and onto Elm Street. His sister lives one hour north in Mapleton, Texas. He usually spends two nights at her home and returns on Saturday. Ample time for me to pilfer, ample time to snoop, and ample time to get caught by a nosy neighbor and spend a few nights in jail.

But I was a desperate woman. Madge Simmons, the town gossip, had filled me in on what people in Forman Falls were saying about me. I was hurt that the tide could turn against me so suddenly. Harming a cat was near the top of my Most Despicable Behavior list.

When Mr. Farnsberry's black SUV turned right at the end of our street, I glanced at the clock. Ten o'clock tonight. That's when I'd make my move. I had twelve hours to go.

My cell phone rang. Burke, finally.

"We found a fingerprint on the box, Sophie. It was yours."

Mine? "But that's impossible. I was too afraid to touch it." I was grateful now that I'd followed through my senior year in high school with our police campaign, "Your Fingerprint Could Save Your Life", and let them print me. At the time, my principal said, "You never know when someone will suspect you of doing something, and you'll have to prove them wrong—or prove them right," he added with a quick grin.

"How did *my* fingerprint get there?"

Burke's answer was to say nothing.

21

Okay. "Someone came into my house and took that box." Which was a terrifying thought. "What about the wrapping paper? Any fingerprints there?"

"None. Did the box look at all familiar to you? Was it in your house?"

"I don't know. I was intent on what was inside. I mean, I didn't notice—" I didn't notice? I'm a mystery writer. How many times has Sgt. Kipke, of my award-winning Jack Kipke series, preached that the smallest detail is important in a crime scene? And my first experience with one in real life had me acting like an amateur.

"I'm just saying…" I sounded so lame, I wanted to cry. "Wait a minute, Burke. It's just a box, for heaven's sake, and I didn't put it there. Someone was in my house. There's the crime. What about the note? Any fingerprints on it besides mine?"

"No. Did you check the reference number at the mall?"

"I did. Judy told me it was from a man she didn't recognize, so I tore it up and tossed it. I don't know any men who would give me such a gift."

"Have you noticed anything missing in your house? Do you want me to come over and check it out?"

"I've done that. Everything's here." I was so frustrated, I sank into my sofa and closed my eyes. "Bad things come in threes, Burke. First, Yoda. Now, the box."

"You're superstitious, Sophie? I don't remember you being afraid of anything when we were growing up. Just be careful, stay out of trouble, and there won't be a number three."

I thought of my plans to sneak into Farnsberry's house—I could be working on number three tonight. Maybe I shouldn't do it. And maybe I should. Who else was going to help me get out of this mess?

"I'll be careful," I said, hung up, and slid the phone into my pocket.

♦

Every time I looked at my watch, it told me to think this thing through and forget it. But, of course, I don't listen to watches.

I could get caught, but who would find me? I'll walk down the sidewalk, turn right, cross the street, turn right again into the alley— which nobody uses but the garbage men—and make my way into Farnsberry's back yard. I'll carry a flashlight, so I don't have to turn on any lights in his house.

My first priority once I was inside? Make sure all the curtains were closed, so no one would see my light. But what if someone did see it? What plausible excuse could I have for being inside his home?

Terri. She was reasonable to a fault. I'll ask her to go with me, and if she doesn't think it's a good idea, I'll let it go.

"Oh, Soph, it's perfect. Wear black and a ski mask. I'll bring flashlights and stand watch or help you search. We can do this, girl!"

So much for Terri being reasonable.

"All right." I gulped. "Be here at ten. We'll head out then and hope this rain stops by then."

"The rain's a good cover. Anything on the box?"

"I'm thinking the man who put it there is a deranged fan. Unless, of course, you got a friend to go to the mall and buy this to, you know, give me a thrill. From a man and all that."

Silence answered me.

"All right, all right. Ten o'clock tonight. Be on time."

♦

Farnsberry's back door was locked. "Great. Now what?" I adjusted my itchy ski mask and looked around. Next door, the tall night light from the vacant house's yard cast a misty glow that crept over the wood privacy fence into Farnsberry's yard like a wandering ghost. Sprawling trees blocked the light from the rest of the yard.

"You have got to be kidding." Terri jiggled the knob again.

"You're the mystery writer. You didn't consider his door might be locked?"

That stung. "I thought we'd waltz right in. No one locks their doors in Forman Falls."

Terri huffed. "What's Plan B?"

"There is no Plan B. Let's check to see if a window's open. Don't use the flashlight. Someone might see it."

Secured screens graced every window in the back. Terri whispered, "No way am I going to rip a screen off. I just had my nails done yesterday."

Something brushed past me. I jumped and tried to thumb the flashlight on, but my cell phone buzzed in my pocket and I fumbled the light and it thudded to the ground. I grabbed my phone and looked at it. Burke! Why was he calling me so late? I almost rejected the call, but he'd think it was odd I didn't answer and may come to my house to check on me. Okay, time to do some really good acting. A little breathlessly, I said, "Hello?" I took several steps into the darker side of the yard—with Terri glued to my side—away from the house and any listening neighbors. I hoped my wobbly voice didn't give away the fact that I was about to commit a crime.

"Sophie? What's wrong with your voice?"

"Oh, hey, Burke." My heart rate soared as I tried to keep my voice at a level pitch. "What's up?"

"Where are you?"

"Just, uh, visiting a friend. Look, can I call you back in a little bit?"

Terri grabbed my arm like a vise. "Sophie, look!"

Her terrified tone sent chills all over me. I ended the call and spun around to face Farnsberry's house. The back door was open! "Someone's inside, Terri. Maybe—"

The door slammed shut.

And opened again!

I gasped, clutched Terri's arm, and ran. We tripped over each other's feet and landed in wet grass and mud. We slipped and sloshed, trying to get back up, but ended up falling again. Suddenly, we were caught in the beam of a flashlight. I turned around but couldn't make out anything except the bright light traveling down my attire and settling on my masked face again.

"What are you doing here, Sophie?"

Burke! What was *he* doing here? "Are you following me?" Which, of course, made not one whit of sense since Burke apparently got here first. The light disappeared. Footsteps moved closer to us. Whew, but it was dark on this side of the yard.

"Farnsberry asked me to keep an eye on his place while he was gone." Burke's hand nudged my shoulder and slid down my arm. He gripped my elbow and yanked me up. I slipped backwards. He reached around me and tugged me against his chest.

But he quickly released me as if I had scalded him and held me away with stiff hands and arms. "Are you just looking for trouble?"

I felt a little lost. His arms had been so strong and warm, and then, he'd pushed me away—like old times. "I-I'm looking for a way to clear my name," I said as I helped Terri to her feet.

"Hey, Burke. It's, uh, Terri Smaller. If we leave right now, will you not press charges?"

He shined the light on her face for a second or two. "Only if I see your skinny rears out that gate right now."

Skinny? He called my rear 'skinny'?

"Done," Terri said. "I am so gone." She grabbed my arm. "Come on, Soph."

I wriggled out of her hold. "Two more minutes. I'd like a word with Burke."

"Well, I'm leaving. No way am I explaining tonight to Stan. We haven't been dating long enough for this." She turned on her flashlight and walked to the back gate. It opened and then shut with a clunk.

"You have five seconds to get it said."

"You don't have to sound so—"

25

"Four."

"But I need to—"

"Three."

"Fine. I'm done. Are you going to arrest me?"

He blocked what little light sneaked into the yard. I couldn't see his face at all. But I could sure feel the disappointment in the silence between us. He huffed out a breath. "Not tonight. Don't trespass again, Sophie. We may go back a ways, but I won't hesitate to arrest you." He shined his light on the gazebo in the far corner of the lot. "Sit with me. We need to talk."

"No, we don't." I ripped off my ski mask. "I'm going home." I was not in the mood for a chat with him.

"That wasn't a request."

I took a deep breath and blew it out. Resigned, I said, "All right. We'll talk."

Warm night air wrapped around us as we walked to Farnsberry's gazebo, situated where the night light couldn't reach it. Surrounded by lush greenery, I knew his neighbors couldn't see us because I'd tried to peek into this yard in middle school and couldn't find a single spot that afforded a view. If anything, it was denser now. A closed-in feeling crept over me. It would be so easy for a serial murderer to hide in those bushes behind us and slit our throats before we could say, "Hey, pretty spooky out here tonight, isn't it?"

I fumbled for the flashlight switch and turned it on. The bright beam swept the bushes and shrubs and crawled up the trees around us. I didn't care that the neighbors might see it. I didn't want to lie here for two days gasping for breath in a pool of blood with Burke dead beside me.

My light hit the bushes.

"What are you doing?"

"Looking. Serial murderer. Hiding."

Burke chuckled. "Your imagination never shuts off, does it?"

"It's a gift." The light rested on a mound with a makeshift cross

26

stuck in the ground. Yoda's grave? He really was dead? I turned off the light.

"One of my jobs as a police officer is to protect the citizens of this county. Herman Farnsberry is one of those citizens."

I looked heavenward. "I know, in theory, that what we intended to do tonight was against the law, but we weren't going to hurt or take anything. I was just going to—"

"Criminal trespass."

Criminal? Oh. Well. When he put it like *that.*

"Sophie, you have to let me do my job. I don't need or want your help. You're going to get yourself in so deep, you won't be able to salvage your reputation."

I sighed, deeply. He was right, but I wasn't up to admitting that to him just yet. "Do you have any gum?"

"Gum?"

"I think best when I'm chewing gum."

"And I think best when I'm chewing pecan pie. How about getting some with me at Glen's Grill? They close in about an hour. We can continue this discussion there."

What? Did he just ask me out? "You don't have to sit here and guard the fort all night?"

He chuckled. "I'm not officially here. I was doing this as a favor because Farnsberry and my parents lived on this street for years and were friends. So, pecan pie?"

Okay. Just... okay. One, we need a place to sit this late at night where we can talk.

Two, Glen's is the only place open.

Three, if we take up space at one of Glen's booths, we should order something.

Four, it is not a date, and it is not meaningful.

I cringed before I said words I never, ever thought I would say to Burke Maguire again: "I'll meet you at Glen's in ten minutes."

"I could take you," he chuckled, "after you change your black

27

B&E clothes."

Oh, wasn't he cute? "Thanks, but I'll meet you there."

♦

Strange, that Burke Maguire was smiling at me and standing just because I had walked into the room. I didn't know what the look on his face meant—was he pleased as punch at something or was he about to tell me a joke?

His dimples flashed. "Is this table okay or would you prefer a booth?"

"I think I'd like a booth."

We slipped into the nearest one. I caught our resident gossip, Madge Simmons, grinning at me from across the room. Of all the people to see Burke and me together at this late hour, Madge was the worst.

"Officer." I greeted Burke as loudly as possible to let Madge know that this was an official meeting.

"Mrs. O'Brion."

"Miss." Even said softly, the word blared the news that I was alone. I don't know why I corrected him. My life needed to remain a closed book to him.

"Miss?" He blinked and stared at me as if his mind searched through his mental dictionary for the correct definition of that little, awful, accusing word. "As in, never married?"

Humph.

I picked up the menu. "I haven't eaten here in—" *Years*, I was going to say. Glen's had been a favorite haunt in high school, and Burke had been a huge part of those memories. I could still see he was staring at me, so I raised the menu. I studied it as if the cure for insomnia was written in code on it.

"What happened to MacIvey?"

I recited my last name's sordid history and then lifted my menu, so

28

I could read the bottom of it better. I'd left my reading glasses at home.

"Find any gum in your purse?"

I smiled and perused my menu until Burke said, "If gum helps you think, you should have some on hand in case you decide to break into someone else's home."

"'Someone else' isn't out to get me." I put my menu down. "You're not going to let it rest, are you?"

"Not until I have your promise that it won't happen again."

"No deal."

"Well, at least you wore gloves. That was smart. No fingerprints."

"And a mask. Don't forget the—oh, no!" I'd done just that, forgotten my mask. It was in Farnsberry's back yard. "Burke, I left my mask at the gazebo." I grabbed my purse. "I have to go get it."

"Not without me."

We stood, and Burke tossed a five on the table just as our server approached. "Sorry, Millie," he said. "We have to run. We'll be back in a few."

I hated that Madge Simmons lifted her brows as we darted past her. At the door, I looked back at her, and she sent me a slow smile and a nod. I shook my head and rolled my eyes at her and walked out the door Burke was holding open for me.

I looked up. A full moon was out, and all that was left of the rainstorm were thin clouds here and there in the night sky.

Sneaking into Farnsberry's back yard a second time that night wasn't nearly as much fun with Burke beside me. The air was still warm and sticky. Not even a hint of a breeze ruffled the many leaves surrounding us as we stepped up into the gazebo. I felt around for my ski mask and found it. "Here it is, safe and—"

I shrieked. Something had moved against me!

Burke grabbed my shoulders. "What's wrong?"

"S-Something touched my leg." I stepped out of his hold and yelped again.

Burke lunged and came up with—

"Just a cat."

My jaw dropped. "A cat? In Farnsberry's yard? He only had one cat, and he's dead. There's no way another cat could get in here with the privacy fence and all this vegetation."

Burke flicked on his flashlight. We looked into the cat's eyes.

"Holy cat, Officer Maguire! Yoda has risen from the dead!"

We both turned in unison toward the mound in Farnsberry's yard. Yoda jumped out of Burke's arms and ran for the back door.

"Then who's buried over there?"

"Let's find a shovel." Burke shined his light on a storage shed. "Whatever we find, we'll have to re-bury."

"Understood."

Five minutes later, metal hit metal. Burke eased a box out of the dirt and lifted the lid. "Well, well," he muttered.

I leaned over and gasped. "Is that a human jawbone?" The words sent chills all over me. "Number three, Burke. The cat, the box, and the jawbone."

"Sounds like a grade B movie."

"But whose bone is this?"

"Farnsberry knows. He had no qualms burying this and saying his cat had been killed."

"Are the bone and the necklace connected somehow?" When Burke didn't answer me, I added, "Maybe there's a grave right here on Farnsberry's property."

Burke swept the yard with his flashlight. "No evidence of digging. Cats don't usually dig up buried things."

"But dogs do. Samson gave me the necklace." I gasped and touched Burke's arm. "They *are* connected, Burke. What if this bone is Sharon's, and Samson found it and brought it to Farnsberry, since Sharon used to live in this house? Her scent is still here. Samson's owner, Jim Peters, walks Samson every day in the national forest—it's just on the other side of Farnsberry's fence, you know. What if

30

Samson found Sharon's grave? Hmmm, would you call it a grave or a final resting place? Well, yes, it would be a grave if someone actually *buried* her body and didn't just toss it into a culvert or—what? Why are you grinning at me like that?"

"I can see why you're a good writer."

"You've read one of my books?"

"I've read all of them." His expression became serious again. "Let's bury this. With Yoda getting out, I'll have to tell Farnsberry that I saw his cat, that I know he lied about Yoda dying—"

"And that he falsely accused me."

He placed the box in the ground, covered it, patted it down.

"One thing is bothering me, Burke. Cats love to sit on windowsills. Why would Farnsberry ask you to guard his castle with Yoda inside? You could have seen him or heard him mewing."

"You're suggesting he wanted me to spot the cat?"

"Yes, but why?"

"I have no clue. Come on. Yoda's sitting by the back door. I'll grab him. You open the door."

♦

On the way to Glen's, Burke called in two hamburger meals with pecan pie. Millie greeted us with them when we sat at the same table. We were alone in the restaurant, which meant no Madge Simmons to report our every move. When I unwrapped my burger, my mouth watered when I smelled grilled onions, jalapenos, meat, and pickles. I was starving and didn't care who saw me gulp down that first delicious, fat-loaded bite. Oops. The onions. I sure didn't want to be the only one eating them. "Do you have onions, too?"

He grinned like a little boy anticipating a double-loop racetrack on Christmas morning. "Can't eat a Glen's burger without onions." He took a bite and groaned in pure pleasure. At least five seconds passed before he opened his eyes. "Better than I remember." He reached for

31

his napkin. "I'll talk to Samson's owner, Jim Peters, in the morning."

I nodded, ummed into my second bite, and covered my mouth. "I have a theory, so don't laugh." I swallowed the last of my bite and sat forward. "Say Farnsberry killed his wife, Sharon, and buried her in the Davy Crockett National Forest or somewhere close by. Even nineteen years after her death, Samson recognized her scent and took her bone home. Then Farnsberry, shocked and afraid after finding the bone on his front porch, buried it and concocted the my-cat's-dead story. But why? That's the part that doesn't make sense. Why say his cat's dead?"

Burke thanked Millie when she placed our drink refills on the table. "You know a lot about dogs, Soph?"

"Research. One of my books was about a woman whose dachshund saved her from a serial murderer. Samson's a German Shepherd. His sense of smell is incredibly strong."

Burke swallowed his bite, wiped his mouth, and seemed to study me for a few seconds. "If Farnsberry did kill his wife, then you need to keep quiet about your theory. We don't want you to be his next victim."

"Are you making fun of me?"

"Not at all. If he killed once, he could kill again, especially if his secret gets out."

"But why tell everyone his cat had been killed? He could have buried the jawbone in the yard without anyone ever noticing, but then he puts a cross on top of it? If someone came to visit, he'd see Yoda inside, then he'd see the cross outside. Doesn't make any sense at all."

"I'll give you that one."

"And the necklace. Was she buried with it? That would be good to know. We have to—"

"We?" Burke's face became grim. "There is no we, Sophie. Let me do my job. I'll do my best to keep you safe."

I couldn't believe my ears. "You're kidding, right? After everything we've been through tonight, you expect me to just step aside? No way." I sipped my sweet tea and set it down with a thunk.

"Yes, way. Stay back, and I'll let you know what I discover."

Stay back? Hmmph. Now the man was dreaming.

◆

Even after such a long day, I couldn't sleep. My brain simply would not shut down.

Why had Mr. Farnsberry lied about Yoda? Why had he buried the jawbone, unless he knew who was missing that jawbone? If he didn't know the owner of the jawbone, he would have called the police and reported the find.

And why blame me? Surely Mr. Farnsberry hadn't held a grudge against me all these years for a few childish pranks. And if he did, why wait so long to get back at me?

4

Morning came too early when the newspaper smacked my screen door and just about scared me out of my skin. I'd slept on my sofa downstairs, hoping that a change of venue would help me fall into a deep sleep. I stumbled to the front door and opened it. A soft rosiness covered the morning and signaled that the sun would appear soon. I had experienced this softness many times after sleepless nights and stood still for a few minutes, enjoying it and hoping my neighbor Jennie would appear, but she didn't.

I did have a visitor, though. I grabbed my paper just as Samson raced up my stairs, barking wildly as he danced around my legs. I was sure there were some people in Forman Falls who would be thrilled to see such a spectacle this early in the morning, but I was not one of them. Samson did another jig, raced across my porch, and then looked over his shoulder and yelped at me. He obviously wanted me to go with him somewhere. "To that old stinky palace? No, thanks, buddy boy. Not today."

But he continued barking and giving me that come-hither dance. So, dressed in my ratty robe *again,* I followed him to Mr. Farnsberry's home and discovered an older woman wrapped in a shawl, standing on his porch, looking bewildered and shaken.

"Hello, ma'am. Do you need some help?"

It was far too warm to wear a shawl in Texas in September, even this early in the morning, but the woman clutched it tightly near her throat and said, "My brother. Is he here?"

Uh. "Your brother? Herman Farnsberry?"

At his name, some of the confusion left her eyes, and she seemed to breathe a sigh of relief. She let go of her wrap, and one side slid over a bony shoulder and rested in the crook of her left arm. "Where is he?"

"Are you Miss Ingrid?" I smiled, trying not to look confused myself. He had left for Mapleton yesterday to visit her.

"Ingrid Atchison. I went back to my first husband's name. He was my favorite. Have you seen Herman? It's not like him not to come see me. Every Thursday, written in stone."

"Yes, ma'am. Do you want to go inside? Do you have a key?"

"Yes, dear, I do." She fumbled in her purse for it.

I hoped that my motives were pure, that she needed help and I wanted to help her. I held out my hand for the key, a little giddy at the prospect of being able to snoop in Farnsberry's house again with the permission of his sister.

As the key landed in my hand, a car pulled up behind me. Drat that Burke Maguire! And drat the neighbor who had called him!

As Burke topped the stairs to Farnsberry's porch, his gaze flicked to my hand as it closed around the key, then he smiled at Miss Ingrid and said, "Ma'am." Turning his attention back to me, he said, "Sophie, may I have a word with you?" His well-aimed I-know-what-you're-up-to look was followed by my I'm-just-being-a-good-neighbor shrug.

"A moment, Officer. Let me help Miss Ingrid into her brother's home."

He looked at Miss Ingrid. "Officer Maguire, ma'am. Is your brother expecting you?"

The older woman looked up at Morgan County's handsome, well-built, blonde, blue-eyed policeman, and a coquettish smile graced her lips. I couldn't decide if I should chuckle at this turn of events or pinch Burke for gaining the upper hand.

"I came here to find Herman. Have you seen him, Officer?"

Burke lifted his what-is-she-talking-about brows at me.

I nodded and explained, "He left yesterday morning to go to Miss Ingrid's home in Mapleton, but he never arrived."

"I see. Ma'am, could he have stopped somewhere on the way?" He held out his hand and snapped his fingers at me. I wasn't about to give up the key. I deftly slid past him and unlocked the door.

"He never has." Miss Ingrid stepped inside and moved to the sofa. "Oh, my goodness." She swiped a finger across a lamp table. "I'll tackle this dust after I've rested a bit."

"Yes, ma'am. Have you tried his cell phone?"

"He's not answering, Officer."

"Maybe the battery's dead. Maybe he forgot to recharge the battery."

Again, she smiled up at Burke. "He is getting on up in years."

Samson appeared at the screen door and barked.

"Oh!" Miss Ingrid wilted into the sofa, gasping and clutching her shawl again. "I don't like dogs. Please send him away."

I started toward the screen door to do just that when Burke said, "I'll get him," opened the door, and stepped outside.

"May I have some water, dear?"

I turned back to Miss Ingrid. She did look a little pale and a lot dry.

Outside, Burke said, "What's this, boy?"

I was torn between watering Farnsberry's sister and getting to the porch to find out what treasure Samson had brought us today. I rushed into the kitchen, found a glass, filled it, and passed it to Miss Ingrid on my way to a touchdown.

Once outside, I whispered, "What is it?"

Burke opened his pocketknife, placed the blade under a long bone, and looked at the rounded end.

I leaned over. "Is that a human femur?"

"That would be my guess," he muttered. "I think it's time to ask Samson—"

At the mention of his name, Samson barked and jumped, Miss Ingrid squealed, I startled and got twisted up in Samson's feet and fell against Burke's shoulder and slid down into his arms.

"—where he found this bone."

I landed no more than two inches from Burke's face. I was at such an angle that my feet couldn't find purchase, nor could I move my head. Good gracious, but the man's arms felt like steel. He didn't push me away this time. His mouth was so close to mine that I could have nibbled on his bottom lip if I'd—dear Gussie, but his aftershave just about overwhelmed my senses as he gazed into my eyes.

"Are you okay, Sophie?" Whispered, like a breeze.

Oh, mercy. Speaking was out of the question. I didn't even know if I could nod, but I attempted it and succeeded, slightly, slowly.

He stared into my eyes for another three seconds. I couldn't breathe. Then, suddenly, he stood, his hands clutching my waist. Shivers raced up my back and over the top of my head and down my face to my collarbone. I hadn't had a man touch me like this since… hmmm… since… well, a long time ago.

Samson barked several times, forcing my focus back on him and not on the fact that Burke still had one of his hands on me.

"How will you find the bone?"

"I'll let Samson show me."

"I'm going with you."

"I don't think so. This is official business now, with a body."

"Body *parts*. And, Officer Maguire, you can't stop me from walking with one of my favorite dogs." I looked over at Samson and smiled at him. "We love walks, don't we, boy?"

Burke snorted, and his hand tightened on my waist. "*My* and *favorite* are adjectives you never use when referencing the noun *dog*."

"How would you know?" I made the mistake of glaring up at him.

His blue eyes softened. "I remember, Sophie." He stared at my mouth. His gaze moved up my face and did a quick search of my eyes and then drifted to my mouth again.

Whoa, boy. No chance of *that* happening! Those days are long, long gone.

I pushed away from him, well out of his reach. "I'll get my hat, spray, and net." I glanced down at my disgusting old robe. "And I'll get dressed."

He nodded. "I'll meet you at your house in twenty minutes."

Most people going on a hike in Texas would never leave without head protection from the hot blaring sun or using bug spray or netting for the mosquitoes and other flying insects. But what about protecting myself from Burke?

I turned back to Miss Ingrid. I had no clue what to do with the woman. I grabbed Burke's arm and shoved him to where Miss Ingrid couldn't see us. "What are we going to do with her? We can't just leave her here. Farnsberry's supposed to be at her house."

"I need to call in Farnsberry's disappearance and the human femur." He walked to his patrol car and got in. After several minutes, he got out and walked toward me. "Do you know anyone who could sit with Miss Ingrid?"

"Mrs. LeGraff lives two doors down from me. I'll ask her." I peered into the screen door. "Miss Ingrid? You remember my neighbor, Bonnie LeGraff, across the street? I'm going to talk to her, and I'll be right back."

"All right, dear. Herman should be along soon, I think."

"Yes, ma'am." I walked down the steps with Burke and lowered my voice. "Don't even think about leaving without me, Maguire." I sent him my most wicked, squinty-eyed look. It had simply slipped out. Growing up together on this very street, we used to tease each other with these hideous, piercing looks. It was too late to stop now. "I'll hunt you down and—"

He grinned at me. "You always were more bark than bite."

"And don't compare me to a dawg, Deputeeee!" I marched off toward Mrs. LeGraff's home while Burke chuckled behind me. I turned around and bared my teeth at him.

Which made him hoot and *woof!* at me.

I laughed out loud and kept walking.

◆

Well, bless Mrs. LeGraff's heart. She took our dazed Miss Ingrid

38

under her wing and offered to make her sweet tea. The two ladies, arm in arm, walked toward the kitchen to see if Herman had 'decent brew' on hand as I slipped out Farnsberry's front door.

"Ready?"

Burke nodded. "Ready."

Our first stop was Jim Peters' home.

Jim had moved into the old house down the street about two years ago, but he kept to himself. That's the kind of neighbor I appreciate. I had wondered a time or two how he made a living, but I didn't care enough to ask anyone.

His garage was open, with an old 50's-style car's nose poking out into the daylight. Burke walked up to the legs that seemed to sprout from under the driver's side and called out Jim's name. When he answered, Burke asked him if he and Samson had hiked in the national forest lately.

He scooted out from under the car and wiped his hands on a cloth. "We do almost every day. Why?"

"We think he might have found a shallow grave out there."

"A grave?"

"Wondered if you'd mind if we went on a hike with him in a few minutes, see if he could lead us to it."

"He'd love that." He snapped his fingers at his dog. "Come here, boy." Samson nuzzled Jim's leg and then his entire body wagged on his way over to me.

We left, and Samson happily followed us.

When we reached the patrol car, Burke opened the back door, and Samson eagerly jumped in and plopped down on the seat as if he'd been promised a steak and a cat if he'd show us where that body was buried.

Burke picked up the bone. "Here, boy." Samson sniffed it and would've grabbed it with his teeth if Burke hadn't been quick. "Show us, boy." Then Burke tossed it on the floorboard, got in, and we headed out.

We drove around the corner. Samson barked. We both turned around, and there he sat with the bone in his mouth as if he knew exactly what we wanted from him. "Good boy," I said and turned back around. Samson's paws appeared beside my shoulder, and he licked the side of my face. Ew! I swabbed my cheek and admirably refrained from snarling at him. "Is he trying to tell us something?"

Burke pulled over, got out, and opened the back door.

Samson jumped out and raced into the woods behind Farnsberry's property. We followed. Well, Burke followed. Following involved sprinting, and this writer does not sprint anywhere—unless, of course, a band of pillaging pirates was after me and even then, I might not be able to actually *sprint*.

I quickly put on my hat and netting and slipped the canteen strap over my head. I shuffled behind them. I really needed to commit to the ten-mile drive to Crockett and use my three-year-old gym membership at least once. I always intend to use it, so that counts for something. I tried to fast-walk to catch up to Burke and Samson, but I lost them.

I was about a hundred yards from where we parked when an empty wheelchair caught my eye. A foot near the chair seemed to shoot out of a tree. I sneaked up on that appendage and discovered it was attached to Muriel Wainwright's leg. She was lying on a blanket, looking up at, uh, at… "You all right, Muriel?"

"Oh, hey, Sophie. See that squirrel way up there near the top of that tree?"

I didn't see a thing.

"He scampered up there with something in his mouth. An earring or a ring." She lifted her brows at me. "Interesting, huh?"

I'd say. "Wonder where he got it." Even though I tried for 'casual', the excitement of the find came through my words and sounded anything but. "You come here often, Muriel?"

"Almost every day. So does Samson, Jim Peters' German shepherd. He disappears for hours in the national forest while Jim and

I talk. Something mighty interesting to Samson in those thousands and thousands of acres."

Hmmm. "Has he brought anything out?"

Her right eyebrow shot up. "Other than the necklace and the femur?"

"You've seen them?" But Muriel hadn't mentioned the jawbone.

"Wouldn't surprise me if he's found a grave. My father and I discovered one in the national forest years ago, but we were lost and couldn't tell the police where it was. Maybe Samson found it. He sure was protective of the necklace and the femur. Wouldn't even let me near them."

I needed to find Burke and tell him. "Are you okay alone out here?"

"Oh, sure. I'm strong." She squeezed the bicep on her arm. "My brother drops me off, picks me up after I call him." She patted her fanny pack. "And I have a gun."

Uh-huh. Well. "See you later then."

"Tell Burke hey for me."

Oh, brother. Was that a glint in her eye? She and I had been friends throughout our school years. She knew Burke and I had been best friends until high school when we began to date seriously. But he left me twelve years ago, Muriel. "Will do," I answered cheerfully and hurried back to where I'd last seen Burke and Samson.

They were long gone, and I had no idea which direction to shuffle in. I took a deep breath and yelled, "Burke?" No answer. *"Burke?"*

I searched the trees in front of me. Surely, they'd left some prints in the dirt, but the ground yielded nothing that I recognized as boot or paw prints. Maybe I'd pick up their trail a few yards inside the grove.

But what if I didn't? What if I got lost?

What if dark fell and I was all alone and there was a serial murderer watching me, hoping I'd fall into his trap because he'd already killed Burke and Samson and he was just waiting for me to make a mistake so he could slowly slit my throat and watch all the

41

blood drain out of me and into the hole he'd dug for Burke and Samson?

A shiver raced up my spine. All right, mystery writer. This is no time to get creative or queasy. Either go in or go back.

I glanced over my shoulder at Muriel's resting spot, but she was gone. She knew where I was going, though, that I was looking for a grave. She could tell someone where to look for me.

"Burke!" I screeched one more time, but when he didn't answer, I made my way into the waiting woods. My heart objected, thumping its way into my dry throat and pounding so hard, my whole body shook as if I were hugging an old washing machine.

I stood and listened. Everything was too still.

Had Burke and Samson scared all the animals away when they stomped through here?

Or… had the serial murderer?

Okay. That's it. Go home. Let Burke do his job and get out of here, you little scaredy-cat.

No, no. I just need to turn off my imagination. I can—

Footsteps!

I gasped. My head jerked to the right.

Pounding footsteps!

The serial murderer was running straight towards me!

I darted behind a tree and held my breath, hoping he wouldn't see my bottom sticking out from the tree like a pregnant woman's belly.

The footsteps stopped. "What are you doing, Sophie?"

Oh! Burke! I was so glad to see him alive.

I straightened, cleared my throat, offered him what I was sure was a very silly, wobbly grin. "Oh, nothing. Just waiting for you or Samson to show me… to come back and… to—"

"I lost him."

Hmmm. "I have a membership at the gym in Crockett. I can bring a guest but only once. After that, you're on your own."

Burke blinked at me as if I were a lunatic. "I kept up with him."

"Uh-huh."

"Right beside him. Swift as the wind."

"Uh-huh."

"Until he slid down a ravine and disappeared in underbrush so thick, I couldn't see the ground." He sniffed, looked around. "Next time, I'll come prepared for bushwhacking." He took off his hat and wiped his forehead. "Where'd you go?"

"I spotted Muriel Wainright lying on a blanket. She saw a squirrel carrying what looked like a piece of jewelry up a tree."

"So now we're chasing squirrels?"

I couldn't help but laugh. It was all so ridiculous. "Now you're taking me to Mr. Farnsberry's house, so I can check on Miss Ingrid and see if the prodigal has returned."

And snoop when opportunity knocked. I still had the key.

♦

I think I slept a few hours that afternoon because it was dark when Terri opened my bedroom door.

"You wanna know what I think?"

"No, Terri. It's late and I just want to go back to sleep."

She pulled off her shoes and sat on the edge of my bed.

I tugged the covers over my head and mumbled, "Go home."

"You see?" Terri snuggled into my leg, a sure sign she was settling in for the long haul. "I think it's time for us to get away from here. I have two weeks' vacation coming up, with all kinds of points for hotels and plane rides. You could furnish the rental car."

"I don't want to think about anything anymore." I reached for her hand and squeezed it to let her know I appreciated her efforts. My efforts to look around Farnsberry's house earlier had been fruitless. Miss Ingrid wasn't one to sleep during the day. "Oh, no, dear. I'd never get any sleep at night if I did." So 'rest' meant her eyes were closed but her ears were perked for any sound telling her that Herman had arrived or that someone was snooping around her brother's home.

"Let's go somewhere exotic, Soph, like Hawaii or Cancun. Enjoy the beach, some sun. Get away from all this stress."

"I'd love to, but right now, I just want to sleep. We'll talk about it later." The phone rang. It was Burke. "Samson's at my door. The bone isn't with him."

I sat up, frowning. "He buried it somewhere?"

"Probably. It was our only unburied link to the grave and Sharon Farnsberry."

"The jawbone. We'll have to—"

"Don't tell me. Just do whatever you need to do. Call me later."

"All right." I hung up, threw off the covers.

Terri was in my face. "What? What are you doing?"

"What are *we* doing." I slipped into my black pants. "Samson lost or buried the femur, so we have to get the jawbone. Burke's law enforcement, and he won't go over there and dig up the jawbone again. You need to get dressed. In my second drawer is a black pair of pants for you if, of course, they'll stay up on your skinny bones."

◆

"Remember." My voice was raspy when I leaned over Terri. "We don't want to scare Miss Ingrid to death. Don't talk, cover the flashlight, and follow me." I slipped on gloves, picked up the shovel, and sneaked into the blackness of Farnsberry's back yard. One light was on in the house, probably the room Miss Ingrid was staying in. Fine time for a full moon. All she had to do was lift her curtain to spot us.

When the shovel hit the ground, I sucked in a breath and looked at the lighted window. Terri did the same and didn't move for a few seconds.

"Okay," I mumbled and kept digging. The shovel hit the box. We both squatted to retrieve it when Miss Ingrid's light went out.

"Szzzzttt."

"I saw it, Tare. Move to where she can't see the flashlight."

She did. I opened the box and gasped.

The jawbone was gone.

And in its place was a piece of paper with the words: "Well, would you look at that. Wonder who took the bone?"

The flashlight went out as I fell back on my bottom. "Terri, what is going on here?" I grabbed my forehead and rubbed. "Why would Mr. Farnsberry swap the jawbone for this ridiculous note? Come on." I carefully picked up the note on a corner and stuffed it into my pocket. "We need to let Burke know what we found."

I quickly reburied the box, and we hustled out of there.

We crossed the street, and Terri said, "There's Burke. I'll leave y'all to it. Keep me posted."

He was waiting in front of my house in his patrol car. Terri waved good-bye as I slipped into the passenger seat and showed him the note. "Who took the jawbone and who wrote the note? It doesn't sound like Farnsberry, or is he trying to misdirect us?" I rubbed my temples. "I can't think. I can't think."

Paper rustled. Something nudged my arm. "Here."

Gum. He'd bought me gum. I smiled and put it in my mouth. "Thanks. I might need to mention that I get a little sassy when I chew gum."

"Get? Aren't you sassy most of the time?"

On a smile, I slipped the wrapper inside my pocket. "He'll put it back, you know."

"What?"

"Farnsberry saw us, Burke, when we dug up the jawbone the first time. He's playing some kind of game with me, and he'll put it back in the box and bury it a second time. I doubt we'll ever see it again. At least we still have Sharon's necklace."

"I'd bet the farm it's gone, too."

"I'll go check."

He grabbed my arm. "Not alone."

"All right. We'll go together."

When I opened my front door, the hairs on the back of my neck tried to stand up but they were trembling too much to do it. "Someone's been here," I spoke quietly, sniffing the air and growling. "He was smoking in my house, and I'm allergic to cigarette smoke!"

Burke squeezed my arm and tugged me behind him. He slid his gun out of the holster. The night light in my back yard provided a dim glow through my curtainless windows as Burke lifted his weapon and stepped into the large, open room housing my living room, dining room, and kitchen. I looked up at the twelve-foot ceiling to see if anyone was hanging from the fan.

"Stay," Burke breathed in my ear.

"No," I breathed back.

He stepped into the living room. I wanted to grab a loop on his belt, but I had the presence of mind to know that that would throw off his aim. I listened to anything that might seem different in my house, although I had trouble hearing anything with my heartbeat pounding on the drums of my ears.

Leading with his gun, Burke glanced around and walked carefully down the hallway. I followed him into each room, then the garage, but we found nothing.

He flipped on the main light and muttered, "Clear." This was so surreal. I'd written this very scene in my books but had never experienced it.

Still holding his gun, he nodded toward the stairs and disappeared up them. In moments, he returned with his weapon holstered. He walked straight for the table where the necklace had sat. *Had sat* being the operative words here.

"It's gone, Burke. As is every piece of evidence we had on the grave. Maybe there's a fingerprint on the table."

"Only in your books." He stooped, tugged out plastic gloves, slipped them on, and shined a flashlight on the carpet. "Is this yours?"

He handed me an earring, and our fingers touched. I almost fumbled the earring as heat warmed my face. I've written that, too, and had never experienced the prickly feeling that comes from such a touch. I turned my back to Burke, pretending to see better in the light coming through the window. "I lost this yesterday."

Behind me, he sighed. "Then we have absolutely nothing."

And absolutely nothing meant we were back to square one.

5

Of course, word got out that Herman Farnsberry was missing.

But the morning after Miss Ingrid's arrival, she let Yoda out on the front porch. "I simply cannot abide cats," she told Mrs. LeGraff. Neighbors spotted him and informed law enforcement that the cat was alive after all. My notoriety as the Elm Street Cat Killer diminished in light of the unbridled truth that Yoda had used one of his nine lives to escape my deadly plot against him.

But what about Farnsberry? Where was he?

Their attention turned to his whereabouts and the part I might have played in his disappearance. Honestly, did these people believe I'd dispose of Herman Farnsberry simply because he'd wrongfully accused me of killing his cat?

"Why, yes, honey," Madge Simmons advised me three days later at the grocery store just after it opened. I'd hoped to avoid people leading with their noses at this early hour, but there she was, one of the best talebearers in East Texas. "You're a famous writer. Everybody knows you have such a vivid imagination."

"And that translates into murder?"

"Well, if anyone could pull it off—" She giggled. "—it would be you."

I smiled tightly as I shoved past her. Of all the ridiculous things to say. I write about imaginary mysteries. I don't create real ones! I paid for my groceries and made it home in record time. Just as I finished putting away my groceries, my doorbell rang. Terri and Burke stood at my front door with 'uh-oh' expressions on their faces.

"What? What's happened?"

Terri deferred to Burke, who stepped inside my house and grimly looked around. He finally looked at me. "We found Farnsberry's car in a ditch twenty-three miles east of Mapleton on Highway 22. Paint was found on the driver's side. Looks like he was run off the road."

"Okay."

"He wasn't inside."

"Okay."

Burke stared into my eyes, cocked a hip, and placed his hand on his gun. "I'd like to look at your car, Soph."

"Which one?"

"You have two?"

"My Mustang for in town; my full-size SUV for long trips."

"The one that's red."

My mustang.

My jaw slid into a you've-got-to-be-kidding drop, and I shook my head. Terri rushed to hug me.

"T-Terrie, I'm really scared now. Someone is out to g-get me."

Frowning, Burke nodded. "Let's have a look at your car."

Terri nudged me forward. "Come on, honey. We'll do this together."

"But I haven't been out on Highway 22 in weeks."

Burke took my arm. "Then you have nothing to hide."

Nothing except the grotesque dent gracing the passenger side bumper of my Mustang. A swatch of black paint only added to my guilt. "That dent wasn't there yesterday. I pulled my car into my garage around two this morning. It was dark and I... I didn't..."

Notice. Again. And I hadn't noticed this morning at the grocery store.

Burke squatted beside my car. His fingers caressed the dent, the black paint. He leaned into the wheel covering with his flashlight and when he stood, his expression was dour, his mouth tight. "I'll have to take your car in, see if the paint matches Farnsberry's car. You have maybe three weeks before the results come back. It won't be good news."

He turned to leave but stopped. "Don't think about going anywhere, Sophie, or trying to investigate this on your own."

49

Terri rubbed my arm. "Go on, Burke. We'll be here all day."

He looked at me as if he wanted me to confirm this bit of news, but I didn't. No way was I going to stay with Terri and mope around the house, waiting on news that yes, my car was the one to force Herman Farnsberry into an early grave and that yes, they had a jail cell at the state prison with my name on it.

Hmmph. The very idea.

♦

"Look!" I motioned Terri over to my front window and peeked out the lace sheers. "Miss Ingrid and Mrs. LeGraff are walking toward Mrs. LeGraff's house. We can get inside Farnsberry's house and maybe find out where he's hiding."

"Whatever gave you the idea he's hiding somewhere?"

"If he was injured in that wreck, there would be a body and blood. Burke said there were neither. Farnsberry walked away. He hid his tracks, too. Maybe he has an accomplice helping him."

Terri's answer was to roll her eyes at me and say nothing.

"Farnsberry and his partner in crime are probably laughing at their good fortune that no one saw them pull this little stunt."

When Terri opened her mouth to ask the obvious question, I said, "I don't know why he's hiding. I don't know why he killed his wife or lied about Yoda dying. None of it makes sense. But that's why we need to get inside his house." I rubbed my forehead where a headache brewed. "I don't have much time to figure all this out."

I glanced outside again just as Mrs. LeGraff's screen door shut behind the ladies. "Okay. They're in the house and if I know Mrs. LeGraff, she'll keep Miss Ingrid over there all afternoon." I took Terri's hands in mine. "Please, Terri. Trust me with this. I know I'm right."

"What if Burke comes by?"

"He won't. Our county doesn't have the tools to analyze paint or

50

blood. They'll send the samples to a bigger lab. He's done with this for now. Let's go out back. No one will see us."

"Oh, all right. I don't know why you can talk me into things that I know are wrong. That's a major character flaw in me."

"This isn't wrong. You'll see." I opened the door and almost jumped out of my skin.

"Howdy, Miss O'Brion. I'm Officer Sheenen. You ladies intent on going somewhere?"

I wanted to wipe the grin off the young policeman's face, but I smiled instead and tried to think of a suitable story. I squinted up at the sun. "We thought about, uh, sunbathing, in the buff. Care to join us, Officer?"

The young man turned beet red and caught his tongue in his teeth. "Uh."

"And you will notice, Officer, that both my gates have locks on them. Officer Maguire has the keys. Unless you're prepared to join the party, I'd suggest you check in with your boss and see if babysitting two naked women is part of your job description." I smiled sweetly and tried really hard not to laugh at his discomfort.

"Yes, ma'am. Just a moment, ma'am."

I twisted my blouse's top button while Sheenen made the call. He stumbled past us, muttered, "I'll be out front in my patrol car," and slammed the front door.

"Good work," Terri laughed. "How do you plan to get us out of here and across the street in broad daylight?"

I wiggled my brows and grinned. "Follow me to my chest of wonders."

Thirty minutes later, Terri and I, dressed as two old women sporting wigs, aging make-up, brown dresses and umbrellas against the sunshine, walked out the vine-covered, well-hidden gate at the back of my property. My props from organizing the Forman Falls Community Theater helped disguise us as we shuffled down my alley to the main street walkway. We turned left, walked across Elm Street, and entered the alley behind Farnsberry's home.

It was simply too easy. We opened the back gate to his property, opened his back door, and opened the door of the room Miss Ingrid was using and waltzed right in.

And, there, on her nightstand, was a cell phone.

I grabbed a washcloth from the bathroom and picked up the phone. Under 'Recent Calls' were the names Madge, HF, Bonnie, Frank, and Edna.

Terri nodded. "Okay. 'HF' is her brother, Herman. 'Bonnie' is Mrs. LeGraff. 'Frank' is probably Edna Conroy's latest squeeze, Frank Zagorsky."

"I'd forgotten about Frank Zagorsky. What's his story?"

Terri moved aside the curtain at the window and peered outside. "Never been married. Lived in Europe. Handsome in a Jack Palance sort of way. Do you remember Jack Palance? Did that one-arm pushup at the Academy Awards years ago? Anyway, Frank Zagorsky's been seeing Edna Conroy for a few months now. That's about all I know on him."

"Could Madge be our Madge Simmons? I mean, how many Madges are there these days? Look, Terri. Farnsberry called Miss Ingrid this morning, and they talked for twenty-seven minutes. We need to show this to Burke." I wrote down HF's cell phone number and the others and placed the phone back where I'd found it. I opened a drawer. "Search for anything that tells us something about Ingrid or Herman."

We moved into the dining room, nosed around the china cabinet, and found nothing.

At first.

"Here," Terri said and handed me a small daybook. "This looks interesting."

I quickly opened it. The day after he left for his sister's house, he'd written: *Ingrid here for a few days.*

"Interesting that he'd known his sister would be here, worried

52

about him disappearing." I tapped the daybook on my hand and sucked in a breath when a voice spoke near the front door.

"I'm so sorry your head's hurting, Ingrid. Here, let me get the door for you. There, now."

Mrs. LeGraff!

I signaled Terri to head for the kitchen and the back door. We slipped outside and scampered across the backyard. "Don't look back, Terri. Just run!"

We made it into the alley. The gate latched behind us. I breathed a sigh of relief, bent over, and came up laughing. We'd done it! In and out of Farnsberry's, and we hadn't gotten caught!

But Terri wasn't laughing. She was looking past my shoulder, her gaze moving from me to whatever she'd spotted, with an expression that shouted, "Oh, no!"

My smile wilted. I slowly turned around.

A patrol car was parked not twenty feet from where we stood.

My stomach dropped. How did Burke—?

I popped up my umbrella and put my back to him. "Just walk, Terri. No, don't look at him. Just walk. We're old women, remember. Maybe he doesn't know it's us."

"Yeah, right."

"Slowly, slowly." Behind us, the sound of an engine turning over made me want to just run, but I made myself breathe deeply and keep walking. The car followed us and stopped when we turned left.

"Okay, let's cross the street. Stay in character, Tare. Old women don't do anything quickly."

The car turned out of the alley and pulled up right behind us as we stepped up to the sidewalk.

"He knows it's us, Sophie."

"He's trying to intimidate us."

"What are we going to do?"

"We'll get to my house, go inside, and lock the front door."

"No! He'll know it's us then, for sure."

"I know! But where else are we going to go?"

"Let's go to the next block. Connie Davis lives there. She'll let us in."

His car pulled up right beside us, but neither of us looked over at him as he kept pace with us. I dipped the umbrella lower so he couldn't see our faces. At one point, he gunned his car, but we didn't react.

"Intimidation, Soph," Terri whispered.

"More like incarceration."

It seemed as if it took forever to reach Connie's house. I rang the doorbell. Connie answered with, "Yes? May I help you?"

"Connie, it's me, Sophie O'Brion, with Terri Smaller. Can we come in for just a few minutes?"

"Well, of course, you can! Come in, come in!" She opened the screen door. I took one step inside.

"Sophie."

I froze at the sound of Burke's voice. My stomach did a topsy-turvy when I turned around to face him.

Should I pretend to be Mrs. Whoozit from Kalamazoo with a British accent? *Ah you speaking to me, Officah?* One of the last plays I was cast in had the setting in Yorkshire, and my Brit accent turned out to be pretty good.

He was leaning against the passenger door of his car, arms crossed, his cowboy hat shadowing his eyes. But even shaded, I could see he was serious and not in the mood for humor.

I could also see in his eyes that I'd disappointed him. I turned back to Connie and whispered, "We'll visit another time, Connie. Talk to you soon." Calmly, I walked to him and said, "Burke. Listen. I'm so sorry. I just had to find out what I could about Farnsberry."

"Both of you, get in my car." He didn't say another word until he drove up my driveway and stopped. "I didn't witness a crime today, but I can use my imagination for what you two were doing." To Terri, he said, "You're free to go home if you'd like. Sophie, I'll be back in about fifteen minutes to talk to you."

Terri and I got out, walked inside my home. When I turned around and looked outside, Burke's car was no longer there.

Terri washed off her make-up, dressed quickly, and touched my arm before opening the front door. "I hope everything is okay."

I nodded, my mouth tight with worry. "I'll let you know." When the door shut, I stood there for a few moments and realized I didn't want Burke to see me in this hideous old-woman make-up again. I ran upstairs, stripped, and showered off the gray in my hair and the make-up caking my face. I dressed quickly and made it downstairs a few minutes before the doorbell rang.

"Come in." I stayed by the window as I heard him open the door, step inside, and stand in the foyer.

It seemed like slow motion when I turned from the window, and our gazes connected. In silence, he studied my face and then looked into my eyes. After a few more seconds, he glanced around the room and blew out a breath.

Oh, how I hated those sighs. They brought back memories of my strait-laced mother's sighs of disapproval. My mother hadn't deserved a rambunctious child like me who led with her imagination instead of good sense. She'd deserved a little girl who played with dolls, not fought the neighborhood bully; who put on make-up, not turned her hair into spikes and wore a patch over her eye; who loved to play dress-up, not grab clothes that didn't match so she could hurry outside and climb the nearest tree to scout for pirates. She hadn't deserved such a child, and she let me know it at every turn.

"Sophie." Burke's gaze was fierce. "We need to get something clear right now. I'm law enforcement, and you're not. I'm the investigator; you're the writer. I can't do your job, and I sure don't want you doing mine."

"Okay." I nodded for emphasis, tried for a smile but it wobbled and fell flat. In keeping with how I handled most stressful situations, I chose to duck and roll. "How did you figure out we'd gone to

Farnsberry's?"

He stared at me for five heartbeats. "The luggage filled with costumes on your bed."

"Isn't that the technical definition of 'breaking and entering'?"

He grunted. "I didn't break in. Your front door was open, and my intent was not to steal but to find you."

"That's what I did. I'm trying to find Farnsberry. Why is it different when you do it?"

"It's my job, not yours."

We looked at each other. When I couldn't come up with a response, my stomach grumbled right on cue. "I'm starving. Glen's closes in an hour. How about I call in an order, pick it up, and we'll eat out on my front porch where you can't yell at me because my neighbors will be listening?"

I noticed a pattern here: both of us used Glen's as a deflection from discussing anything personal. We were both members of the chicken family.

The rooster nodded. "Sounds good. I'll get out of these duds, get my truck, be back in a few."

On my way out, I stopped in front of him. "Are you going to arrest me?"

"Not tonight. It's coming, though, when the paint report comes back."

I grabbed the doorknob. "Then what's our next step?"

"I keep digging."

"All right. I'll go get the food. You'll get back here first, so make some coffee for us."

"Coffee sounds good."

In fifteen minutes, I had returned with our orders. We sat quietly and ate. Burke didn't ask any questions. I didn't ask any questions. We looked at each other occasionally as we took our time eating. It was somehow understood that this meal was a reprieve not only from the investigation but from any discussions about personal issues. When we finished eating, we enjoyed a couple of cups of coffee, then both of us gathered up the trash and cleaned off the little wicker table.

"I enjoyed that," Burke said as he stood and turned toward his truck.

"I did, too."

"See you soon?"

"Probably."

He left then and walked slowly to his truck. As I watched him drive away, I realized that those thirty minutes of quiet were the most peaceful I'd had in a long time.

♦

With so much news circling my camp, I expected to hear from our nosy newspaper editor, Bertie, and she came the next afternoon just as I finished icing my cinnamon rolls.

Unless we're forced to speak to one another, we don't. We both entered a prestigious essay contest years ago in college, and I won first place, and she won nothing. My win, and probably my success as a mystery writer, had been a burr in her saddle ever since.

Although she'd never forgiven me for winning, I offered her a cinnamon roll with a smile and a wink. I couldn't help myself.

She looked at the roll with disdain. "This is official business, O'Brion. Did you have anything to do with Herman Farnsberry's accident out on Highway 22?"

"You seem to think I did."

"Your car was involved."

"That hasn't been proven."

"Did your car run him off the road?"

"If it did, then it was without any help from me." I scooped up a wad of icing and stuck it in my mouth.

My long-time rival pinched her lips tightly as if she'd just taken a bite of raw rhubarb. "As usual, you're being difficult."

57

I lifted my brows. "I honestly don't know, Bertie."

"I'll write the story with or without your help."

"You always do. Here, now. Let me help you find the front porch." I opened the screen door, and she huffed her way through it toward the van parked in my driveway. Despite the extra thirty she was carrying on her small frame, she stomped down the stairs with vim and vigor. I did notice, though, that she was breathing heavily when she reached the news van. "I have a gym membership in Crockett, Bertie. You're welcome to—"

The van door slammed on her glare. I waved cheerfully just as the driver took my picture. At least I hadn't brought the cinnamon roll knife with me. Now, wouldn't that have made a great picture?

I could hear my cell phone ringing. My screen door slammed behind me as I hurried to the kitchen and answered the call.

It was Burke. "The station received a card today wishing Sharon Farnsberry a happy fifty-seventh birthday, with the initials 'HF' on it."

"That's it? Just 'HF'?"

"Apparently, someone has sent a card to the police station every year since her death."

"Where was it mailed from?"

"Forman Falls."

"Any of her family live here?"

"Not that I know of."

Hmmm. "Maybe the sender thinks Herman Farnsberry killed Sharon, and this is his way of reminding law enforcement that Farnsberry was a suspect, and he doesn't want him to get away."

"Could be. I have a theory on what happened with your car. It was no hit-and-run accident. It was planned. Farnsberry wanted everyone to think you ran him off the road, so he and his accomplice picked up your car, pushed it down the street, started it, and left. They rammed his parked car and drove back here, quietly pushed your car back to its original position, and hustled to their stashed getaway car."

"But why?"

"To implicate you."

"But why?"

"I have no clue. You left your car in your driveway until two this morning?"

"Yes. Maybe a neighbor saw it and can verify it wasn't dented then."

"You still could have driven it."

"Okay. Maybe someone saw the car leave, thinking it was me. That would give us a time frame. What about prints on the wheel, evidence left in my car?"

"We're checking it out. Maybe Miss Ingrid's heard from her brother by now."

"Oh, uh, Burke." I prepared myself to be yelled at. "When Terri and I were in his house yesterday, we found Miss Ingrid's cell phone. There was a call from Mr. Farnsberry yesterday morning. He's alive and well and hasn't come home since the accident. I think you're right: Farnsberry is involved in whatever is going on, and his sister, Ingrid, is his accomplice."

"What's his cell phone number?"

I gave it to him.

"Also, Terri found a calendar with a notation on it, and I quote: 'Ingrid here for a few days'. She was to arrive yesterday. Her visit was planned."

"Then I need to ask Miss Ingrid some questions. Do you want to meet me at Farnsberry's house?"

Five minutes later, Burke pulled into Farnsberry's driveway. I walked outside and started across the street to where he stood and met Mrs. LeGraff mid-street.

"A taxi came by and picked her up," Mrs. LeGraff offered, huffing and puffing after rushing to tell Officer Maguire and me the very latest news. "Not ten minutes ago. She said she was going home, that Herman knew where she lived if he wanted to see her."

"She just left, with her brother missing? Why would she do that?"

I glanced at Burke.

"Seems out of character for the timid woman we met."

"I don't know about her character," Mrs. LeGraff added, "but I have dinner rolls in the oven that need to be taken out. If you have any questions, Officer, just come by my house. I'll be happy to answer them if I can."

Burke thanked her and turned toward Farnsberry's house, studying it as if it could give him some answers. "What happened to make her leave so suddenly?"

"Orders from Herman. They're meeting somewhere."

"Her house?"

"Maybe."

Our next stop was Miss Ingrid's home in Mapleton.

♦

"Haven't seen her in, oh, Mama, how long has that woman been gone now?" This, from an old man sitting in a rocking chair on a porch with the best vantage point for viewing Miss Ingrid's country house. He looked nine months pregnant in a white muscleman T-shirt and plaid shorts over skinny legs, his black socks struggling to reach mid-calf.

His wife—AKA "Mama"—placed a pitcher of lemonade on a well-used wooden table next to her husband's rocking chair and frowned as if in deep thought. Absently, she wiped her hands on her apron. "Well, now, Mason, didn't she leave the day you killed that snake in the washroom? What was that, Friday?"

"Yep, that's when she left. We heard her dog barkin' and carryin' on so, I went over there. She's just a pup, had plenty of food and water out, but she was missing her mama so much that I had to stay over there a good hour or so, tryin' to calm her down." The old man shut one eye and looked up at Burke without saying another word.

I lifted my ah-ha brows. "She owns a dog?"

When Burke glanced at me, I knew he remembered the shrinking violet who had clutched her shawl and whimpered at the sound of Samson's barking.

"Yes, ma'am, she does. Don't know why she left her Great Dane like that. She could've at least told us about leaving so we could check up on her dog."

Burke held out a business card to the man and asked him if he saw her, would he give him a call?

"If I see who? The dog?" He grinned like a stuffed possum.

His wife slapped his shoulder. "Oh, Mason. Shut. Up. I'll call you, Officer, if I see Ingrid."

"'Preciate it, ma'am, sir." Burke walked down the steps, then stopped and turned back to the woman. "Seen any taxis on this road today, ma'am?"

"Not a one. There's no taxi service in Mapleton, Officer."

"Have you seen her brother?"

"Herman?" The woman scrunched up her nose at Burke. "No, we haven't seen him either. Are they all right?"

"Thank you for your time, ma'am, sir," Burke said as we left.

I had a sinking feeling that we had now, officially, reached a dead end. "Ingrid doesn't like dogs, but she owns one? And how did she get to Farnsberry's house? No taxi service. She didn't drive herself—there was no car parked at Farnsberry's. Burke, I think her brother drove her to his house early that morning, so no one would see him. Do you know if she has family around here who might have helped her besides Farnsberry?"

"Their mother died recently in a nursing home in Minnesota. She was ninety-six and had Alzheimer's. There's a half-brother, but he died several years ago." He started the car. "Let's head back and visit with Mrs. LeGraff. Maybe Ingrid got a phone call just before she hailed that cab. If so, I can get into her phone records and find the number." He started the patrol car.

"It'll come back a match to my car, Burke."

61

"I know. Doesn't leave us much time."

We drove back to Forman Falls. Back to my dark house. And back to an envelope pinned to one of my porch posts.

Burke flicked on his police flashlight, shined it on the envelope, around the steps, the porch, the yard. I crept up behind him and looked around his shoulder. It was only an envelope, after all, and not even a bulky one.

He slipped on gloves, lifted the loose flap, and tugged out a faded, black-and-white photograph of a man and a woman smiling at the camera. "Do you know these people?"

I leaned closer. "No."

He turned the picture over. The words *Laura and Clarke* were written on back, with no date.

"Laura and Clarke? Who are Laura and Clarke?"

Burke put the picture back inside the envelope. "I'll take this to the station, check for prints. I'd bet the farm the same person who gave you this picture also sent cards every year on Sharon's birthday."

I nodded. "The only person on this planet who cares that she was murdered."

6

The next morning, I dreaded opening the screen door and seeing what Bertie had written about me in the newspaper. More, I dreaded seeing my picture on the front page. I glanced over at Jennie's door, but no hand or body appeared. Her paper sat under her door, waiting for Samson's snarl of retrieval.

Somewhere behind me, he barked. I spotted him dashing around Mrs. LeGraff's petunias, darting across Jonas' yard and my yard, and running straight for Jennie's porch. I shouted at him to stop, but he sailed up the steps, bit into the paper, raced off the porch as if he were being chased by a bear, and ran across the street toward the vacant house.

Jennie's screen door opened, and she appeared, screeching at Samson with a pointed finger. She glared at me as if this were my fault and let the door slam behind her.

Well.

I glanced around and basked in the cooler weather. Clouds covered Forman Falls, and rain was promised. It was a perfect day for writing, for escaping all the nonsense thrown at me this past week. I glanced at Farnsberry's house, and my eyes widened.

His front curtain moved! Someone was in his house!

As nonchalantly as possible—although my heart laughed in the face of nonchalance—I opened my newspaper. Of course, an oversized picture of me with my eyes half-closed, my mouth gaping as if I were drunk, and my hand in a downward wave was on the front page. There was no mistaking it was me with the blaring headline, "O'Brion's Car Involved in Crash".

No way was I going to read the article. It would only raise my blood pressure, and it was high enough these days.

I casually walked inside my house, tossed the paper, rushed to my cell phone, and called Burke to tell him about the person inside Farnsberry's house. "He's been hiding right under our noses, Burke. Wouldn't surprise me if Miss Ingrid was in there, too."

"Be right over."

I didn't have time to shower and dress, but I didn't intend to see anyone this morning, Burke included.

Three minutes later, he pulled into Farnsberry's driveway, walked to the front door, and knocked. No one answered. He knocked again, glanced around the yard, the neighborhood, and then cocked his ear toward the door. When no one came to the door, he headed down the steps and through Farnsberry's side gate.

Samson, ever the opportunist, raced across the street and followed Burke into the back yard. I expected to see Burke come back out with Farnsberry, but he didn't. Samson started barking. He barked and barked and then yapped several times.

It wasn't a friendly sound. He was frightened—which meant something was wrong.

Why wasn't Burke coming back out?

I ran—well, "moved"—as fast as my legs would go and cautiously walked through Farnsberry's gate. Samson was still yelping. I crept around the corner of the house and gasped. Burke lay face down on the ground with Samson standing protectively over him. I ran toward them, so horribly afraid that Burke was dead.

He roused and moaned. I helped him roll over, so relieved when he grunted into a sitting position. "What happened?"

"Three guesses." He rubbed his temples with one hand. When Samson licked his face, Burke patted his head without opening his eyes.

"Oh, don't be smart! Who hit you?"

He touched the back of his head. "Didn't see him. Waylaid me." His fingers were red with his own blood.

"Did he come out of the house?"

"He was in the yard when I got back here."

"One in the house, one outside?"

When Burke tried to stand, he wobbled and slipped an arm around my shoulders. I grabbed his waist and said, "Here, sit on the steps. Wait until the dizziness clears."

"I need to call this in."

"Then do it right here on the steps."

Burke sank onto the concrete steps and called in the disturbance while rubbing the back of his head. I had the feeling he had forgotten I was there. Then I noticed I was still in my ratty bathrobe.

He probably thinks I've forgotten how to dress myself.

I heard a car pull up to the house. Sheenen rushed through the gate, helped Burke to Sheenen's patrol car, and they drove off while I walked home.

♦

I opened my door and saw the newspaper scattered across my living room floor. My drunken-looking picture stared up at me under the large-lettered headline. The longer I scanned the article, the angrier I became. Bertie had accused me, at the very least, of running Herman Farnsberry off the road.

How in the world had I gotten to this place, in a little over a week, where my neighbors shunned me, my name lay in tatters, and my reputation in ruins among people who had known me my entire life? I had heard from my agent and my editor, both concerned about my status as a writer. I tried to make a joke: "Hey, I'll write a book about it." Heh, heh, heh.

My editor shot back: "They have computers in prison?"

I shuffled into the kitchen and poured myself a cup of coffee. I could call Terri. She'd cheer me up. But as I grabbed my phone, the hairs on my arm lifted. I spun around and faced a man standing in my kitchen! I stepped back, my heart racing. I thought I could take him. He was a little shorter than me, graying and thin, and didn't seem threatening at all as he held up his hands. "What are you doing in my house?"

"Sharon Farnsberry was killed by her husband," Skinny Man said. "Herman buried her somewhere in the national forest. Please don't forget her."

"Who are you?"

"Garrett Flint. Sharon's friend."

"Sharon's friend?"

"Her lover."

"Her lover?" Sheesh. I sounded like a wound-up parrot.

When he took a step toward me, I took another step back and positioned myself closer to my knife stand on the counter.

"Herman didn't love her. There was another woman, but Farnsberry killed Sharon before she could find out her name."

"Why didn't he just divorce her?"

"You'll have to ask him. I don't know."

"How did you get in my house?"

"The back door was open."

"Well." I slammed my phone on the counter. "Here in Forman Falls, we don't expect people to invade our privacy or hit our law enforcement officials over the head."

"I didn't hit anyone. I came here to visit with you."

"Why?"

"The police put out a warrant for my arrest years ago. They think I killed Sharon, but I didn't. I couldn't. I loved her. I've been looking over my shoulder every day for the last nineteen years. When I saw your story in the paper today, I came out of hiding to make my way into town to talk to you. They're trying to frame you, just like they framed me." The man seemed desperate, or he was a very good actor. "I know you didn't kill Farnsberry, Miss O'Brion. I talked to him just yesterday."

"After the accident?"

"Yes. He threatened to turn me in if I told anyone about Sharon."

66

"Farnsberry admitted to killing her?"

"No, but he knows she's buried in the national forest."

"How does he know that?"

"He didn't say."

"You and Farnsberry have been in touch the last nineteen years?"

"Not like you mean. He's no friend of mine. I don't know how he got my cell phone number."

Interesting but hard to believe. "If he killed Sharon, why hasn't he killed you? You know too much."

"His threats are enough to keep me in line."

"Apparently not, Mr. Flint. You're here, telling me your story."

He shrugged. "I'm not telling the police. I'm talking to someone who might be able to do something outside the law."

"What about a private investigator?"

"Can't afford one. You're a writer. Maybe you can find out what I can't."

I had to admit, I relished the challenge. And wouldn't that just thrill Burke? "Have you been sending birthday cards for Sharon to the police department every year since her death?"

"Yes. I don't want anyone to forget her."

"And the picture on my porch last night?"

"It's Farnsberry's first wife, Laura. He killed her, too."

He murdered *two* wives?

"I have to go. I'll be in touch." Flint walked past me, out my back door toward the hidden gate.

"Wait." I rushed after him. "Did you put a box on my back porch?"

He tossed the word, "No," over his shoulder and left through the gate, which was unsettling. He knew exactly how to open it from this side, which meant he'd been in my back yard before today.

Behind me, my screen door opened.

"What are you doing out here?"

Well, shoot. Burke had caught me in my ratty robe again. "How's

67

your head, Officer?"

"Not too bad now. Just a slight concussion. What are you doing?"

I sniffed the air with my eyes closed. I didn't want to turn around and give him the opportunity to see my still-unwashed face, my still-unbrushed hair, and wearing my tacky robe. "Smell that? That's a honeysuckle breeze. I love the smell of them, don't you?"

He chuckled. "A honeysuckle breeze?"

"Beautiful, isn't it?"

Four heartbeats later, Burke walked around me. "Sophie, what's going on?"

Uh-oh. You flunked acting in college, remember? "Just enjoying my back yard."

"Something's up. You're acting strange."

"I flunked it in college."

"Flunked what?"

"Acting. So, any attempt at acting would, of course, be strange."

"Are you on something?"

"Honeysuckle."

He took a moment to search my face. "You're hiding something."

Oh, all right. "Have you ever heard of Garrett Flint?"

"He was a suspect in Sharon Farnsberry's disappearance."

"He was also Sharon's lover. Farnsberry didn't love her. There was another woman, and he wanted Sharon out of his life, so he killed her."

"Maybe, but if she was Garrett Flint's lover, Flint could have killed her in anger because she wouldn't leave her husband."

Hmmm. I hadn't thought of that angle. He'd sounded so sincere.

"How do you know this?"

I turned my head and looked up into the giant oak in my yard. "A little bird told me."

"The little bird's name?"

"Garrett Flint."

"When did you hear from Garrett Flint?"

The suspicion in his voice almost checked my next words, but Burke needed to know Garrett was here. "Five minutes ago. He just left my house."

"Where?"

"Through the back gate. He must have watched Terri hide the key."

He ran across my yard...

"You won't find him!"

... to the gate...

"He's been on the run for nineteen years!"

... and through it.

Hmmph. "Fine. Then, go." I needed a shower. It had been a long day already, and it wasn't even nine o'clock in the morning.

◆

I didn't hear from Burke for two days. It was a relief, actually. I could pretend that the outside world didn't exist while I spent time cleaning my house, making cinnamon rolls and donuts, and writing my next book.

Late Wednesday afternoon, he called to ask me to meet him at the lake, at our favorite place in high school. "Do you remember it, Sophie?" Of course, I did. I told him I'd meet him at the picnic table at seven o'clock.

I drove to the lake early with Tchaikovsky filling my soul. Fresh air from the open windows whipped around me and eased some of the tension gripping my shoulders and neck. I didn't see any cars at the lake when I parked and got out. Beautiful fall weather wrapped around me as I walked barefoot along the shoreline, easing out into the water until my ankles were covered. I stood still, enjoying the glistening water as the last rays of sunlight stroked the tree tops on the other side of the shore and colorful leaves moved in the breeze around me.

I sat on the picnic table and breathed in the scents of nature. This was just what I needed right now.

"Don't be frightened."

I gasped and spun around. Burke was walking toward me. "Oh! If you're out to scare the bejeminees out of me, Burke Allen Maguire, you succeeded." I released a long breath, closed my eyes, and coaxed my heart into letting go of my teeth. "I didn't hear you drive up."

"I was across the lake. Thought I'd give you some time by yourself before I joined you. I walked up here from the parking lot." He sat beside me and rested his elbows on his knees. A security light sputtered on about twenty feet from us while cicadas began a steady tune. Samson appeared along the water's edge. He barked in welcome and raced toward Burke.

"Yeah, I'm okay, big fellow. My head's pretty much healed."

Samson seemed elated at the news, until Jim Peters appeared and whistled for him. He bounded over to him and followed him into the dusky night.

"What is it about that man that gives me the creeps? He's so secretive."

Burke grunted. "I hear he keeps to himself, doesn't bother anyone. He walks Samson every day, and the dog looks healthy. If Samson hadn't barked the other day, I'd probably be dead right now."

"What do you mean?"

"The man in Farnsberry's backyard was startled by him. It gave me a chance to duck. Tell me about Garrett Flint."

I filled him in and added, "Farnsberry called him after the wreck, threatened to turn Garrett in if he told anyone that Sharon was buried in the national forest."

"Flint would say that, to try to deflect suspicion away from him."

"You think he murdered Sharon?"

"The only warrant issued was for Garrett Flint."

"He admitted to sending the birthday cards and the picture."

"Did he say who the man is in the picture?"

70

"I didn't have time to ask. Maybe Farnsberry's sister, Ingrid, can tell us about her brother's first wife, Laura."

Burke shook his head. "Ingrid thinks she has to protect Farnsberry from us." He opened his mouth to say something, then closed it.

"What?"

"Talked to a jewelry specialist. Says Sharon's necklace is worth about a half a million dollars today."

Whoa. "Well, it wasn't a motive for killing her because she was buried with it."

"You think."

"I don't have any other theories on how Samson had her necklace under the vacant house. Do you?"

He shook his head. "I'm thinking of giving Samson another shot at leading me to Sharon's grave."

"We're going on a hike?" I wanted to add, 'just like the good ol' days', but I didn't.

"Could you, uh, hike a long distance?"

Well! "I walk every day, Officer. It's the *running* over a trail—" Like the good ol' days. "—that I'd have trouble with."

He chuckled. "We may be jogging or running. Samson's still a pup, and he's fast."

At the words 'may be running', my whole body shivered. I offered the best excuse I had to get out of the hike. "I do have a deadline with this book. I'm not sure how finding Sharon's grave is going to help me when the paint report comes back a match."

"One step at a time, Soph. We have a couple weeks yet before it's in. Since Farnsberry and his sister have disappeared, finding Sharon's grave is all we have. Except, I was thinking we might contact Farnsberry's former secretary at the middle school. She was with him during his tenure as principal, and she might know something that could be helpful."

Ah, yes, the secretary who was First Responder every time I was hauled into the office for one of my master pranks. "Virginia Crane. Last I heard she lived about fifteen miles from here in Ed's Orchard. I haven't heard anything about her in years."

"She might be the other woman."

"Or knows something about her."

Burke nodded. "I'll see her when I get back." He slid off the picnic table and faced me. "If you're ready to go home, I'll walk you to your car. I'm hoping to leave in the morning with Samson. Keep your fingers crossed that we find the grave."

I'll do more than that, Burke Maguire. I'm going to get on my knees and pray like a mad woman—and maybe pay Virginia Crane a visit.

♦

"Well, if it isn't our famous author."

I hadn't expected such a gracious greeting from Virginia Crane. After all the trouble I'd given her in middle school, I'd expected a greeting more like, "Well, if it isn't the little troublemaker herself." The taunt was started by Bertie King—my nemesis, even in fifth grade—just after I'd gotten in trouble for exploding a volcano prematurely in science class. The other kids picked up the 'troublemaker' moniker, and I would retort with, "You wanna see what trouble I've got planned for *you?*" Like this little wimp was a tough girl. Right.

I also hadn't expected the woman who stood there, smiling at me and holding the door open. Virginia Crane looked nothing as I remembered her. She had short, gray, carefree hair and the prettiest complexion for a woman in her mid-fifties.

"In the flesh," I answered cheerfully.

"Come in, Sophie."

Mrs. Crane guided me into a grand sitting room, but instead of sitting, she walked straight toward the huge picture window

72

overlooking an expanse of trees reflected in a small lake. Her house perched on a rise at the end of a long uphill drive, and her view out the window was beautiful.

"If we have a good freeze in late October, all those trees will be different colors. It's lovely, isn't it?"

"Yes, it is," I muttered. I didn't know a soul who would use the word 'lovely'.

Had living so far out here cocooned Virginia Crane from the world's problems? Why would she live where there were no people, no other homes, no churches or stores? Everywhere I looked, every angle, every nook smacked of aloneness, isolation.

"You grew up and used that imagination of yours, Sophie. I'm very proud of you. I always hoped—" Here, she laughed as if she were the speaker at a political function, that laugh that says you don't mean exactly what you're saying but you hope you can fool everyone into thinking you do. "Yes, hoped that the spunk you used to fight Mr. Farnsberry would someday be put to good use."

"I was a mess, wasn't I, Mrs. Crane?"

"Oh, honey, call me Virginia. You're not a child anymore."

I felt like one in the presence of such a refined woman. Had she been a lady even at the middle school? I could well remember her stern face as she said, "Sophie MacIvey, you'll either end up in jail or you'll end up as president. I'm not sure which would be the most regrettable." So, yes, I suppose she was a lady back then. Anyone else would have said, "Listen up, you little brat! Shape up or you're on your way to juvie!"

Virginia wore a dress, low heels, earrings that matched the lavender swirls in her dress, and lipstick that matched both. Did she dress this way every day? "I'm sorry. Did I catch you on your way out, uh, Virginia?"

"Oh, no. I was reading a good book, hoping a friend might come by, and you did."

A friend? She considered me a friend after not seeing me for years?

With a sweep of her hand, she indicated I should sit in a Victorian chair next to its identical twin. Everything in her home reeked of money. I should have left my shoes at the front door when I walked over white carpet to the chair. I hoped I didn't carry any debris in the grooves of my tennis shoes.

When we sat, she rang a little bell. In less than ten seconds, a maid entered, several years older than me, wearing a gray dress uniform with a white frilly apron.

Virginia wasn't entirely alone.

The maid smiled gently at me as she pushed a cart toward us. On top sat a stunning silver tea set. The tall neck of the teapot stretched proudly as it waited for our use, while the other pieces squatted in a circle around it.

The maid placed a small plate of cookies on the coffee table and then stepped behind Virginia and stood quietly. I didn't know her and wondered how long she'd worked here. Her spiky, short blonde hair didn't match what I considered the look of a woman in the position of a maid.

"Thank you, Rita." Virginia proceeded to pour out. She held a spoon of sugar over a cup of tea. "Sugar?"

"Please."

I glanced at the maid, Rita. She sent me a scrunched-up grin as if something funny wanted to spew out her mouth.

Virginia lifted the cream pitcher and held it near the rim of my cup.

I nodded. "Please."

Rita lifted her shoulders and her eyebrows in a this-must-be-your-first-visit-to-the-queen's-chambers expression. I didn't quite know what to do with the entertainment behind my hostess. But when Virginia smiled and lifted her teacup to sip, a somber Rita stepped into her line of vision, dipped her head at her employer, and left. When she reached the door, she turned back and wiggled her fingers at me.

I wanted to return the gesture, but Virginia looked over at me right then, holding up a pinkie when she sipped.

I tried to mimic her and ended up juggling my cup.

"I've read your books, Sophie. You're very talented."

"Thank you." I'd hoped for a little gushing, but her compliment matched her style.

"You're here because of Herman Farnsberry, of course."

I set my cup on the saucer. "As I was accused of harming his cat and its owner, Officer Maguire thought you might have some information that could help the investigation. Were you aware Mr. Farnsberry was having an extramarital affair when he was married to Sharon?"

"A secretary finds out far more about her employer than she wants sometimes." She set her cup on the saucer and folded her hands in her lap. "I knew about his mistress. She called him at the school. I was told by Herman to put her through regardless of the hour or his activities."

"Did you know her?"

At this, Virginia looked at her hands. "Yes. Sharon's sister, Selma."

"Her sister?"

Virginia nodded. "Her younger sister. I don't believe Sharon ever found out." She looked up. "Did you know that Sharon Farnsberry and I were best friends in college?"

"I hadn't heard."

"It isn't widely known. Herman and his first wife, Laura, were two years older than Sharon and me. We all went to school together at UT Austin. Sharon and I were soul mates."

"You never told her about the affair?"

Virginia abruptly rose and stood at her wide picture window. "There's the dilemma that's haunted me since Sharon's death. Should I have told her and been the instrument of destroying all her dreams? Would she have resented me for telling her?" She turned toward me.

"Sharon loved Herman. She mentioned another woman, but I held my peace and never said a word."

I couldn't come up with a single word in response to that.

"Did you know that I was on the school board before Herman moved to town?"

I shook my head.

"A few months after Sharon married Herman, I told her about the position of principal opening up in Forman Falls. Herman liked the idea, applied, and was offered the job. Soon after, I became the school secretary and not two months later, Sharon went missing." Virginia touched the thick curtains gathered at the side of the large window. She sighed and stood there quietly for a few moments. Then she turned from the window. "Please, have another cookie, Sophie." She sat as I took one.

"Is Sharon's sister, Selma, still alive?"

"She died several years ago. Cancer."

"Was she capable of killing her?"

"Absolutely not. Selma loved Sharon. She was devastated by her disappearance and left the area two weeks later. I kept in contact with her for about a year."

"Did she suspect Mr. Farnsberry of killing Sharon?"

"Oh, yes." Virginia sniffed. It seemed like a disapproving sniff to me. *That* I remember clearly from middle school. She slowly poured more tea. "She resented the fact that the police wouldn't arrest Herman on just her suspicions. She might have loved Herman, but not enough to cover up for his murdering her sister. But she was happy, I believe, with her third husband's extensive properties and their grandchildren."

I picked up my purse and produced the photograph that had been left on my porch. "Do you know these people?"

She gasped—a little gasp, in line with her demeanor. "That's Laura Farnsberry, Herman's first wife. Sharon showed me this very picture of her years ago. Where did you get it?"

76

"It was left on my front porch. Who's the man beside Laura?"

"I don't know. Sharon said she found this picture hidden in one of Herman's hunting boots. Laura favors Sharon, don't you think?"

"I've never seen a picture of Sharon Farnsberry."

Virginia rose and walked to an ornate china cabinet resting against a flower-papered wall. She opened a drawer and tugged out a photo album. As she sat on a love seat, she motioned me over and opened the album. "There." She pointed to a picture. "That's Sharon. Just before she married Herman. Can you see the resemblance to Laura?"

I reached for the photo and put them side-by-side. "They could be sisters."

"You add Selma to the equation, and it's uncanny. Three women who looked alike involved with the same man and all of them dead."

"Virginia, do you think Herman killed Laura and Sharon?"

She looked out the windows. "I've always thought he was the logical choice, but I never saw him as a murderer."

"Do you know his sister, Ingrid?"

"Ah, Ingrid." She sniffed. "I'd forgotten about her."

"What do you mean?"

"When she was between husbands, she would come and stay with Herman and Sharon on the weekends. I've never met her, but Sharon didn't like her. Ingrid seemed very territorial, as if no one was good enough for her brother. Maybe Ingrid could help you more than I."

If only.

As I was leaving, Virginia suggested we keep in contact with each other. I regretted agreeing to it. I've never been good with staying in touch.

As I drove off, I looked in my rearview mirror. Rita stood on the side portico, waving at me until I could no longer see her in my rearview mirror.

7

It surprised me to see my next-door neighbor, Jonas Whitworth, standing on my front porch with Madge Simmons and Joanna Carpenter when I pulled into my driveway. "A Grump, a Gossip, and a Librarian" seemed like a good title for this scene. Since none of them were particularly good friends of mine and since all of them were staring at me with frowns instead of welcoming smiles, I cautiously opened the car door and wondered what kind of trouble I was in. I braced myself for battle.

Terri and Mrs. LeGraff walked across the street toward me, frowning as well. The whole scene reminded me of an old-west showdown, guns drawn, hats pulled low, squinting eyes shifting with each step. The porch Gang of Three looked as if they couldn't wait to hand me a guilty verdict. I thought of my mother, the day she found out about a particularly funny lie I'd told at school that had landed me in detention. "Gee, Mom, I was just goofin' around."

Humor wouldn't wash with this crowd either.

Terri and Mrs. LeGraff met me at the car and the three of us approached the three of them. "What's going on here?" I whispered to Terri.

"They're ridiculous. It's all ridiculous. Just stay close to me."

Well, that sounded ominous.

I hated the feelings of resentment that overcame me. I hadn't done anything wrong, but here were three people who looked as if they were about to lower the boom, and wouldn't my mother love to be here to witness that?

My next-door neighbor and Moocher's owner, Jonas, stepped forward, his wide girth literally blocking me from walking up my own steps. "Sophie, we'd like a word with you."

"That would be fine, Jonas, if you'd let me pass."

He stepped back.

Madge, with pursed lips and a condescending, half-asleep look in her eyes, eased away from me as well.

I smiled. "Please. Have a seat. All of you."

The three of them attempted to perch on the wicker sofa but only two fit. Joanna had to cross over to our side. Terri and Mrs. LeGraff sat in individual chairs. I stayed on my feet, in an it's-my-house-after-all stance. "What can I help you with today?"

Jonas cleared his throat. "The bookstore has decided that, in light of recent developments, we will not sponsor the Celebration of Sophie O'Brion as planned."

Madge lifted her chin, signaling it was her turn. "And the Ladies of Forman Falls are rescinding our invitation to have you speak at the Ladies Retreat for Well-Being this year."

Joanna looked down at her hands. "I'm sorry to say that the library doesn't want to sponsor a controversial author, so your book signing has been cancelled—against my wishes."

"No offense taken, Joanna. Although controversy sometimes drives sales." I smiled at her. She nodded and smiled back. I could see it pained her to hurt me. She stood and quickly left.

It all hurt. What was happening to my life? A few accusations and I become a dirty word? "I'm sure you two can find your way down my steps."

Terri took one of my arms, Mrs. LeGraff the other, and we marched sideways through my open front door.

"It's a heckuva day at sea, sailors!" Terri shouted at the top of her lungs. Mrs. LeGraff and I laughed as my cinnamon rolls called our names. Nothing like sugar to soothe an aching heart.

And my heart was aching, despite my cheerfulness. Why had the good people of Forman Falls, people I'd known my whole life, turned their backs on me at a time I needed friends the most?

Terri said, "Hoist the sails, mateys! Rough waters ahead!"

Mrs. LeGraff added, "And to blazes with all the pirates!"

79

Ah, friends. Sweet, sweet friends.

♦

That night, I sat on the wicker sofa that Jonas and Madge had shared that afternoon and thought about Burke. Where was he and why hadn't he called? Had he found Sharon's grave?

I envisioned him sliding down a ravine and breaking a leg or falling into a bog. I'm not exactly sure if bogs exist in Texas but in my imagined world, they were deadly and stinky and clutched at Burke's legs as he sank. Samson could only do so much with a man being swallowed up by a swamp—I could picture man's best friend sinking right along with him. The only thing left of the pair would be Burke's police cowboy hat, sitting on top.

Surely, Burke had taken his cell phone with him.

His cell phone.

I jumped up and raced inside and called him. After two rings, his deep voice said, "Hey, Sophie."

"So, the national forest won't give up its secrets, huh?"

"Something like that. We'll give it another day and come home tomorrow night. Anything else going on?"

"Virginia Crane looks healthy."

A long pause. I had no idea how to read it. "You went to see Farnsberry's secretary?"

Surprise was in his voice but not censure. Wow. Someone who appreciated my sense of adventure, my investigating skills, my enterprising nature. "I found out some information. I'll fill you in tomorrow night if you'll call me on your way home."

"I just might, if you'll answer. Anything else?"

"Just be careful. The four-legged creatures I'm sure you can handle, but the two-legged kind can be deadly."

"It's the good-looking two-legged kind that I'm watching out for."

He chuckled.

Did he mean me? Oh, boy. I'd set that up nicely for him. Time to duck and cover. "Well, I'll talk to you tomorrow night then."

◆

I awoke—which meant I slept—to another beautiful fall morning and Laura Farnsberry on my mind. I tugged the old picture out of its envelope and studied the young man with her. His arm lay across her shoulders, his hand hanging comfortably near her arm. No hand holding her shoulder or head tilted toward her as a lover might do. Maybe he was her brother.

I turned the picture over. *Laura and Clarke* was written in a beautiful script. A woman's writing—maybe Laura's? When Burke gave it back to me, he said no fingerprints were found on it. It had been wiped clean.

My cell phone rang. Burke! "You found the grave."

"Samson took his sweet time getting us here. I doubt this is the grave Muriel and her father spotted. It's hidden inside a cave. I called this in, and a forensics team will be up here soon. Are you up to Glen's tonight?"

"Sure. I'll meet you there. What time?"

"I'll call you, as promised, and pick you up at your house."

I had plenty of time to clean my house, something I do when I'm nervous. And I was nervous about meeting with Burke tonight. He was sending out all kinds of signals that he wanted to pick up where we'd left off in high school—before he dumped me—but I wasn't there. I didn't know how to personally trust him. I trusted him professionally, and maybe that was a good place to start, for now.

Terri popped over in the afternoon and made a beeline for my bread box. She opened it and found it full of donut holes. "Mama called me this morning."

I crossed my arms. Terri was the worst kind of gossip. She gave out tiny morsels of information and expected her audience to ask questions to get the rest of the news. I had tried to train her to just spill it, but she was a slow learner. "Yeah?"

"She knew Sharon Farnsberry."

"And?"

Terri bent her head back, tossed a donut hole in the air, and skillfully caught it between her teeth. "Sharon had a diary."

I must be losing my touch. Farnsberry's house had been vacant for several days, and I hadn't attempted even once to go inside and snoop around. I closed my eyes, cocked an ear. Yes, I could hear that diary calling my name.

Terri tilted her head at me. "He wouldn't have kept the diary. He probably burned it. Mama also told me that they'd never, uh, been intimate."

"What?"

Terri nodded slowly. "They were never intimate. At all. Nada. Zilch. Mama said Sharon told her she'd tried everything to get him interested, but he wasn't. Mama thinks Sharon ended up having an affair."

"Garrett Flint."

"No. He was a nut case who came into Sharon's life the last six months of her life. He was psycho about her. Stalked her. Called her. Took pictures of her. Wouldn't surprise anyone if he was the one who killed her. Where are your cinnamon rolls?"

I pointed to the oven. "He was here, in my house."

Terri's buggy eyes bugged even more. "Garrett Flint?"

I loved that look of surprise on her face. Sometimes, I'll say something outrageous just to get a rise out of her, so she'd do that thing with her eyes.

"Here? In this house?" She culled a cinnamon roll from the herd.

I nodded. "And Burke found the grave."

"Okay. That helps you how?"

"Evidence. The first step in nailing Farnsberry. Losing his credibility will take some of the spotlight off me, except for my car

82

hitting his car."

"Unless he took your car and hit his own car to make it look like you'd done it, then drove your car back here, his sister picked him up, and they disappeared." Terri shrugged. "If, of course, he's out to get you."

I just blinked at her. How did she do that? I hadn't mentioned a word of Burke's theory to her.

"It just popped into my head." Terri can also read minds. "He wants people to believe you're after him, that you wanted his cat dead. What better way to ensure they do than to stage that wreck, since his cat was found alive?"

I nodded thoughtfully. "No sex, huh? Ever?"

Terri shook her head solemnly. "Mama heard it from Sharon's own lips."

"You know what I think? Farnsberry's after me because he thinks I know something about him. It's scaring him. But what could I possibly know that could hurt him?" I gasped. "Was there incriminating evidence in his truck where we stuffed the frog remains? A necklace he'd hidden? A bone? A wife?"

Terri chuckled. "We didn't find anything, Soph."

"But he doesn't know that."

"Too deep for me, girlfriend." Terri grabbed a handful of donut holes. "Here, catch."

Yep. Right between my teeth. Practice does make perfect.

When Terri left, I checked the time. I had just enough to catch a quick nap before Burke picked me up. I sat in my padded recliner, turned off the lights, closed the curtains, turned on the mini-waterfall, and allowed Tchaikovsky to lift me toward heaven. And, great day in the morning! I thought about Burke.

When I was seventeen, I was so much in love with the boy I'd grown up with. In my seventeen-year-old heart, I'd idolized Burke. I was so young and stupid and horribly naïve.

Am I still?

Uh, yeah.

What in the world am I doing going out on a date with that heart bruiser?

I closed my eyes, but too many other thoughts bombarded me. Why did Farnsberry accuse me when Yoda was alive and well? Why did he bury the jawbone? Why did he run away? Why stage the wreck? Who was Garrett Flint and what part did he play in all this? Who was Sharon's lover? Did the lover kill her? Who killed Farnsberry's first wife, Laura? What was Virginia Crane's role in all this?

Oh, and what in the world am I doing going out on a date with Burke Maguire?

Sitting in the dark, I eased back, closed my eyes, and said a quick prayer for guidance about Burke.

Sometimes, I wonder if a person like me is pleasing to God. I have a wit that most people don't understand. "A quirky way of looking at things," my aunt told me once. She actually thought I was funny. My mother did not.

I know God looks on the heart, and He knows I love Him, but just how happy is He with the quirky ones? It wasn't that I tried to be quirky; it just came naturally for me. If I could ever catch my mouth before it opens and spills out some nonsense, I would be in a better place. I think.

I felt myself falling into a deep sleep.

Then something touched my leg. I screeched and clutched my Cowboys blanket as I frantically searched the dark room. The hall light was on and it cast a halo-like glow around Burke. He stood at the foot of my recliner with his hands raised as if I had a gun pointed right at his heart. "It's all right, Sophie. It's just me."

"What are you doing here?"

"We had a date, remember?"

Oh! Our date.

I sat up and glanced at the lighted Cowboys clock on the wall above the fireplace. Six-twenty-nine. "Oh, Burke. I'm sorry. I must have fallen asleep."

"You didn't answer your phone, so I came on over. We can cancel." He moved to the other side of my chair. I could see his face now and the disappointment on it. "Maybe go out another time."

He stood before me in crisp jeans and a tucked-in blue shirt that matched his eyes perfectly. He looked so nice.

I struggled out of the recliner and stood, still clinging to my blanket. "If you can wait a few minutes, I'll be right back."

♦

"So, what news on the grave?" I slid into the passenger seat and shut the door, but something or someone flashed past my window toward my street. "What was that?" At my tone of voice, his hand stilled near the ignition while I looked out the side mirror. "Someone's—"

He turned around. "Duck."

"No, it's human."

"Your head. Duck." He shoved me down as he started the car, backed out of my driveway, and shined his spotlights on Farnsberry's house.

I edged up enough to see. "It's Garrett Flint, Burke!" He darted up and over Farnsberry's fence like a flying ninja. Burke spun his tires as he zoomed to the sign that said STOP—which he didn't—and turned into the alley behind Farnsberry's house. When Burke slammed on his brakes, I ended up sprawled half-way under the dashboard. Can you say 'cramped', tall girl?

"Stay down!"

"I'm as down as these legs will allow, Officer."

I lifted my head enough to see Garrett Flint race across the open field that abutted the national forest. He soared into the dark woods and disappeared.

Burke mumbled something under his breath and then helped me up. "Ready for some supper?"

What? Ready for some *supper?* Was he kidding? My shivering heart was stuck in my throat on its way to my teeth again. No way did food sound enticing to me. "We're—" I cleared my throat. "We're letting him go?"

"Are you dressed for running? I'm not either. And I'm not letting that man spoil my plans tonight. He might have just been taking a shortcut."

"To where, for heaven's sake?"

"He'll resurface. He has before."

Okay, okay. I took a deep breath. "Can we just drive around a bit, catch up on some news? Allow my body time to calm down?"

"Sure. How 'bout the lake?"

We weren't two minutes into the trip to Rogan Lake before I regretted this move. I didn't feel comfortable with Burke tonight. I wanted to talk about all the evidence pointing ugly fingers at me, but the sidelong, thoughtful glances he sent me and the pounding quiet in the cab told me the past was our next stop.

I didn't want to ever go there.

"I'm sorry I hurt you, Soph."

Okay, maybe it wasn't such a bad place after all.

"I'm sorry for everything. More sorry than you can know."

Oh, no.

Not tears, Sophie. Not tears!

The problem with holding my problems and pain inside is that I never know what little thing will trigger tears. I've mastered the art of overcoming anything by simply ignoring it, and since Burke's return, I've ignored him, the past, the hurt, and the crushing abandonment I've felt since the night he left me.

Oh, God, I don't want to feel anything for Burke Maguire ever again.

Dread filled me as I remembered our last night together and how devastated I was when Burke left me standing on my parents' front porch. I could still feel all the emotions that had bombarded my heart and soul that night. He left me. Deserted me. Flung me aside as if I meant nothing to him.

I had been such a young fool.

I had loved Burke my whole life, and I thought he felt the same about me. On that last date, I thought he was going to ask me to marry him, but he dumped me instead.

Over the years, I learned to forgive myself for placing all my hopes and dreams in him. And I forgave him, mostly, for leaving me. So why was I crying over it?

Because whether I wanted to admit it or not, it still hurt.

I looked out the window and swallowed down the last of my tears, took a deep breath, and willed my voice to be steady when I managed a one-word response: "Okay."

Burke looked at me. "Just okay?" He stared a moment longer, glanced at the road, and turned back to me. "Can't we just forget the past, Soph, and start over?"

"The past is a part of who we are. It's impossible to forget."

"Or forgive?"

I shrugged. I honestly had no idea what to say to him. If I could pick us up and transport us back to high school, then, yeah, I had plenty to say: "Don't join the Marines. Stay here and join up after I graduate high school. We'll get married and serve our country together."

But he didn't stay. We didn't get married. And he left me and never looked backed.

How do I learn to trust him again? Realistically trust. Not just saying the words, "Yes, I forgive you. Yes, I trust you."

For the first three or so years after Burke left, I waited for him. I didn't date anyone. I hoped and prayed he'd come back to me. But when I graduated college and had heard nothing from him in five years, I made a decision: I would stop thinking about him. And I did. "I wouldn't be here tonight, Burke, without some measure of forgiveness, but I've moved on."

Oh, some, but not completely. I chose to live alone and re-make who I was, like a character in a book. Add this trait; remove this character flaw; make this mannerism weaker; enhance this one. I can't change my basic personality—which is 'irritating', according to Mother—but I've tried to develop the best that's in me.

I straightened my sagging spine. Visiting the past was too painful, and I was ready to leave it alone. "Right now, I just want to get some supper and discuss all the evidence we have."

"All right." He made a U-turn and pulled over to the side of the road. "I'd like your forgiveness, though. I was a kid, a stupid kid. I had a dream, and I went after it, but the way I left you was reprehensible. It's eaten at me through the years that I did that, that I never contacted you. I wanted to, but I thought too much time had gone by. I—" He tapped a thumb on the steering wheel. "I've changed, from the inside out." He chuckled. "I actually go to church now."

"Well, heavenly days."

We both chuckled, and then silence filled the cab. After a few moments, Burke put the truck in gear and drove slowly down the road. When we hit a bump, the keys on his key ring jingled, and then they settled down.

He looked at me. "We're older now and wiser. I like you; I always have. That was the hardest part of leaving: I didn't want to lose my best friend. I'd really like you back in my life."

The hum of the tires on the road filled the truck. I sighed and focused on the trees and brush outside as we drove by. "You were my best friend, too."

"Then." The word filled his truck. "Then, can we work on being friends again? I know friends trust each other, and you're having trouble trusting me again. Maybe we could work on being friends and building some trust along the way."

"Friends *and* trust? That's a tall order."

"I'm willing to try."

I couldn't help myself. I thought, "And after the trust is there, are

88

you going to stab me in the back again?" But I just couldn't say it. There was no way I could ever see us getting close to what we'd been to each other in high school. But friends? I could handle that. When I said, "Me, too," I was just glad that we were done with this subject.

He seemed satisfied with my answer and sat for a few moments with a little grin on his face. "All right. What news from Farnsberry's secretary, Virginia Crane?"

I filled him in on my visit with her. "I searched the internet and found out she comes from money; her family's in oil. I can't understand why she'd become a secretary or live out in the middle of nowhere when she has such resources."

"Family money doesn't mean it's *her* money."

"If you saw her house, you'd know she has some of it. She was a college graduate, and she settled for being a secretary."

"Maybe it was all she could find in such a small town. Maybe she loves children. We'll get to Glen's and talk about all of it. A lot of pieces to put together."

I nodded. "I have some ideas."

"I'd like to hear them."

8

I wasn't sure what being friends with Burke Maguire meant at one in the morning when I couldn't sleep, and my neighbor's dog Moocher was barking up a storm. Moocher voiced what I was feeling right now—sudden anger that wouldn't let me go. A quiet drive to the lake. Meaningful looks at me. Remorse. Church. Asking for forgiveness. All of it was too... personal. I liked it better when Burke was law enforcement and I was the falsely accused trying to clear my name, and the 'becoming friends again' was something we organically grew into, not something we agreed upon like a contract because he wanted it. I suppose, to some degree, that I wanted what we'd had in school before we started dating, but those days were over.

Standing in the dark, I opened the window in the upstairs bedroom and peered into Jonas Whitworth's backyard, ready to screech at Moocher to lighten up and get to sleep so I could, too.

Something—someone—was cornered by the little dog under Jonas' huge magnolia tree. Jonas' porch light flicked on, and the screen door squawked open. I moved to the other window, which gave me a better view of his back porch. When I carefully opened the window, I heard someone say, "Shut up, Moocher!"

And then, shock of all shocks, the ninja sprinter himself, Garrett Flint, stepped out from under the magnolia and into the hazy light, a hat in his hands as if he were about to beg for food. I couldn't see Jonas, but I could see his hand urgently motioning Garrett Flint over. "You fool! Get in here before somebody sees you!"

Flint scurried across the yard. With one good yank, Jonas had him up the stairs and inside the house. The screen door popped shut, and all was quiet.

Moocher walked to the bottom step, sat, and stared at the back door.

Then he turned and looked me straight in the eyes.

Whoa.

I would have to be nicer to that dog. He'd just provided me a piece of the puzzle that I wouldn't have if he hadn't barked. But what that piece meant, I had no earthly idea.

♦

The first morning of my friendship with Burke started off with a dash for my paper—with no Samson in sight—and stumbling back to my kitchen. After two cups of java, I could claim to be human again, just in time to receive a call from our Gossip Control Manager, Madge Simmons.

"Did you know that Burke Maguire was dishonorably discharged from the Marines and the cause? Two women."

Her words literally buzzed with the excitement of the kill. But, by golly, I don't listen to gossip about friends. "Madge, this isn't—"

"Bertie King was one of them."

Now she had my attention. "Bertie the editor?" Sometimes I forgot Bertie had a last name. Everyone referred to her only as Bertie the editor, as opposed to Bertie the druggist who owned the local pharmacy.

"The same, girlfriend."

I gritted my teeth. Girlfriend? If I hadn't been facing so many problems, I wouldn't have listened, but maybe this information would be helpful. "How did Bertie cause his dishonorable discharge?"

"Well, she was living in Chicago at the time, sniffing out a story on a well-known, wealthy, and very powerful businessman. Pictures were sent to him of a seventeen-year-old girl and Burke Maguire— compromising pictures, if you get my drift. At the time, Burke was dating said businessman's daughter. The father was livid. Bertie's story was printed in a Chicago paper. Since Burke was an MP in the Marines, he was investigated, found guilty, and dishonorably discharged. I thought you should know, considering you're spending a lot of time with him lately."

"But a dishonorable discharge is serious. How did he get a job as a police officer in Forman Falls?"

"Oh, well, I don't know anything about that."

Why didn't I know this? I've lived here almost my entire life except for about four trips to Europe. How had this slipped by me?

Gossips, as a rule, never check their sources, many times pass on information that's unreliable, and thrive on reaction. So, I gave Madge none. "I really must go. My cinnamon rolls are about done." Okay, so I had two in the microwave with butter melting on top.

The sugar hit, but it didn't soothe. So, Burke hadn't been faithful to his Marine code of honor. "Build some trust", I believe, were his exact words to me last night.

I tried hard, *really hard*, not to let Madge's words affect me. Burke had seemed so sincere last night when he said we should start over as friends. Is that how he'd approached the seventeen-year-old girl? With that kind of sincerity, blinking those baby blues at her as he'd contemplated an affair with a *child?*

Oh, I'm such a fool. What was he doing with me? And why?

I should have listened to good sense and told him where he could take his friendship and his *building trust* plans: straight to the toilet.

Okay, maybe not a toilet.

But some place really scary and meaningful to the dark side.

♦

It wasn't an hour later that he called. "Hello, friend."

Oh, I hated this. He sounded so genuine. A smile laced his words; hope, his tone. I wanted to believe in him, but I couldn't, considering Madge's news. "Hey. Anything new with the case?"

He didn't answer me right away. Why hadn't he told me about the charges against him, his discharge? And how had he gotten the job of a police officer with a dishonorable discharge on his resume?

"Having a bad day, Sophie?"

"Not particularly."

"Is something wrong?"

I wished I could trust him, but right now, he was the police, and he needed to know what had happened this morning with my neighbor, Jonas, and Garrett Flint. "Yes, I need to tell you about last night. No, this morning around one. I couldn't sleep."

"You rarely sleep."

"I know, but this morning, I heard Moocher barking next door, so I checked it out and guess, just guess who was in Jonas' backyard?"

"Jonas?"

"My next-door neighbor, Jonas Whitworth." My dramatic pause only lasted two seconds because I couldn't resist answering my own question. "Garrett Flint. Jonas called him a fool and ordered him inside his house. What do you make of it?"

"Jonas and Garrett Flint? They go back to Sharon's day. They're both around the same age, I think."

"It's another link, but I have no idea what it means. Oh. And, uh, Terri told me something that might interest you. She said Sharon and Farnsberry never, uh, they never, y'know, had sex." I rushed on to my next thought. "Maybe Sharon had an affair with Jonas. Maybe Farnsberry killed Sharon when he found out about Jonas."

"Why would Farnsberry care, if he wasn't meeting those obligations himself? I'll interview Jonas and get back to you on it. Still friends?"

So, okay. Talking about murder always cheered me, and I'd warmed up to him again. "Sure. Any news on Sharon's body?"

"Unofficially, she died of a gunshot to the head, but the ME is checking for drugs. Somehow, word's gotten out about Sharon's body part being found."

I wondered if Garrett Flint had made sure of it.

"Bertie the editor is supposed to interview the M.E. this

93

afternoon. It'll be all over the news on Wednesday. AP'll probably pick it up. Nothing juices up the news like scandal, affairs, and murder. Talk to you later, Soph."

Later came not ten minutes after his good-bye. I answered the phone and Burke said, "Your next-door neighbor, Jonas, was found a few minutes ago, floating face-down in Rogan Lake."

◆

Two policemen arrived at my door thirty minutes later. A very professional Burke Maguire said, "Miss O'Brion, we'd like to ask you some questions."

"Certainly," I mumbled as I pushed on the screen door. Officer Sheenen walked in first, which gave me the opportunity to send Burke an inquisitive look. He was law enforcement now and not a friend.

Officer Sheenen positioned himself in the middle of my living room, legs spread, hands clutching his duty belt. "We understand, Miss O'Brion, that you witnessed the decedent this morning around one. Can you tell us what happened?"

"Yes, I saw him out my upper north window. Well, I saw his arm and hand. He yelled at Garrett Flint, who was standing under Jonas' magnolia tree, called Flint a fool, and yanked him inside his house. That's all I saw."

Officer Sheenen nodded slowly, his eyes squinting and his gaze solidly on me. Today, he wasn't the blushing twenty-three-year-old young man who couldn't get out of my house fast enough the day Terri and I said we'd sunbathe in the buff. "You're sure it was Jonas, ma'am?"

Well. Was I? "I assumed it was him."

"But you're not positive?"

"Not until you mentioned it. He had a white T-shirt on." But did he have that massive paunch? Trees covered his porch, and I couldn't see all of Jonas from where I was standing.

"And the dog?"

"Moocher? Yes. He barked for a solid five minutes before I went upstairs to see what was going on."

"Was the dog injured?"

"He was perfectly healthy. Why?"

"We didn't find him at Jonas' house."

"He's missing?" All I could see were Moocher's little eyes looking up at me this morning. Why would anyone hurt him? "Garrett Flint was there. He probably killed Jonas and took Moocher."

Officer Sheenen glanced at Officer Maguire.

"Sophie, did you see or hear Moocher after one o'clock this morning?"

Burke spoke so softly. My first thought was: he thinks he's dead. But wouldn't Moocher have barked at Garrett Flint or bit him if he'd tried to hurt or grab him? I squeezed my eyes shut, trying to remember any sound that might have been Moocher after one. But, no. After he glanced at me, I didn't hear another yip from him. "No, I didn't."

"Were you and Jonas on good terms, Miss O'Brion?"

"Depends on your definition of good, Officer Sheenen. We were neighborly, polite. Not friends, by any stretch."

"How did you feel when Jonas Whitworth told you the bookstore had pulled its celebration of your books?"

Oh, please don't go there.

I glanced at Burke. He stood about a foot behind and to the side of Sheenen. He raised his eyebrows at me and then slowly winked. I felt he was saying, "Just answer the question, Sophie. Standard procedure. Standard questions." I banked the temper that rose up at Sheenen's stupid question and declared, "About how you would feel. Disappointed. Hurt. I'd looked forward to the celebration for three months. To pull it at the last minute because of untrue rumors and vicious lies seemed unfair."

"Unfair enough to…?"

95

Oh, come on. "Well, shoot, you caught me. I've been plotting for days now to pay Jonas back. I marched right over to his house in the dark of early morning and punched the old coot in the face and dragged his body to my car, all six-foot, three hundred pounds of him. I drove to the lake and with one hand—yes, I get superhuman strength when I think life has been *unfair*—I hurled him into the shallow end. Is that what you want to hear, Officer Sheenen?"

I tossed my smoldering gaze over to Burke and dared him to say a word. He didn't, but he did offer me a "Good grief, Sophie" look as he shook his head at me. I was astute enough to know that Burke couldn't come to my defense as an officer of the law, but it still niggled at me that he hadn't punched Sheenen for such a foolish question.

"Well, ma'am, it's what I want to hear if it's the truth." Officer Sheenen sheepishly glanced at Burke.

"I think we can safely say that it's nowhere near the truth."

"And you'd be right, Officer Maguire. Of course, I didn't hurt Jonas. My proclivities don't lean in that direction, and, besides, I never left my home." I crossed my arms. "Are you finished with your questions?"

Burke stepped forward. "Can you think of anything else you saw or heard, Sophie?"

His conciliatory tone helped stop my lips from pinching. I closed my eyes and thought of that night, the light shining from the back porch, Garrett Flint standing under the huge magnolia tree, Moocher barking at him, and I set the stage for the two deputies, as I would in a book.

"The skies were clear, a breeze cooling off the calm night. Moocher started barking, not a friendly sound but one announcing danger, and after five minutes of it, I walked to the window upstairs. In the darkness under the magnolia tree, I saw Moocher dancing and barking. There was movement under the tree, but I couldn't make out what it was. The screen door opened with a squawk, and someone yelled, "Shut up, Moocher!" This person walked to the edge of the screened-in porch wearing a white T-shirt, motioned for Flint to come to him, and yelled, "You fool! Get in here before anyone sees you." Since Jonas' yard has a six-foot privacy fence, Mrs. LeGraff and I are the only ones who would have seen him. Flint walked to the porch. With one hand, Jonas—or whoever it was—yanked him onto the porch, and they both went inside to the sound of the screen door slamming. Moocher was sitting by the steps, and he looked up at me. That's all I know."

Sheened nodded at me. "Thank you for your time, Miss O'Brion."

And lo and behold, out of my kitchen came Yoda. How in the world had he gotten in here? The cat's meow was pitifully weak when he nudged my leg. "And here's my first victim. How did you get in here, Yoda?"

I scooped him up, nuzzled his neck, and when the deputies reached my front door, Sheenen went outside first. When Burke turned around and looked at me, I put my back to him and walked toward my kitchen.

♦

My back door was open. I checked Yoda's claws and sure enough, they were long enough and strong enough to yank a four-inch nail from an oak board—or open a screen door. "How did you get out of your backyard and into mine, hmmm?"

I held his head and looked into beautiful green eyes. "Are you hungry? Did you smell my cinnamon rolls?" I grabbed a couple cans of tuna. "Wait, sweetie, wait. Let me get the lid off." Before I could place the bowl on the floor, Yoda lunged. And ate. And ate. And ate.

"What's this, girlfriend?"

I jumped and turned around.

Terri grinned at me from the hall and folded her arms. "Since when did you become a cat lover?"

97

I huffed. "I've always been a cat lover." I tossed the lid in the trash. "I just don't gush."

"Uh-huh." Terri didn't move. She just stared at me.

I lifted the bread box door, took out a cinnamon roll, placed it on a microwave plate. I turned my back to Terri to open my curtains. "Say something. What have you heard?"

"Jill called." Officer Sheenen's girlfriend. "You and Burke hit a bump in the friendship road."

Last night, I'd called Terri about our ride to Rogan Like and opening the past a little bit. She'd sighed wistfully and told me that friendship was a good place to start. But that's the problem with trying to put a severed relationship from the past back together again. Trust becomes an albatross around the neck. It dangles there, thumping against the heart, reminding it constantly that there isn't enough trust to make it work.

"It's not the bump you're thinking of." I knew she thought it was the interrogation that troubled me, but I didn't really care about that. The seventeen-year-old, the affair, the dishonorable discharge, his plans to build trust? Those bumps bothered me.

With a spatula, I retrieved the roll and handed it to Terri. After she took it, I tossed the spatula into the sink with a loud crash. It helped my hurting heart to imagine Burke's head at the end of that spatula. "Do you know anything about Burke's dishonorable discharge from the Marines?"

When Terri didn't answer, I turned around. Oh, no. She'd known and hadn't told me.

"I don't know anything about a dishonorable discharge. You were traveling France when the story came out. No one believed it here. How did you find out?"

"Madge Simmons."

"She has a big mouth. No one knows what happened, Sophie. The story hit, and then nothing. No follow-up."

"What's to know? He slept with a child." I blew out a tired breath

98

and then more gently said, "I just don't know what to do about it."

"Talk to him."

Yeah, like that was going to happen.

Yoda licked the bowl clean, walked around me, and rubbed my ankle. He wasn't wearing his collar, and blood smeared the fur on his neck. I reached for him, and he let me pick him up again.

"Have you been outside all this time, hmmm? Did some mean ol' dog attack you?"

Terri grinned and stroked his matted back. "He's taken to you. Isn't that just the sweetest thing?"

"No way. I'll feed him until Farnsberry gets back, but that's it."

At that moment, Yoda snuggled into my arms and made himself at home. He nudged my breast and worked his stinky way up to my shoulder and rested his head against my neck. I honestly felt him sigh deeply, and before I knew it, he was purring.

"He's yours now." Terri chuckled and when she stroked his head, he didn't move.

"First, he's going to the cat groomer. Then I'll keep him until Farnsberry shows up."

"And if he doesn't?"

"Well, then, maybe we'll talk about our relationship and where we want it to go."

In his sleep, Yoda rubbed my neck and settled down again.

Oh, brother. Just what I needed. A temperamental cat who could work me like a twenty-four-piece puzzle.

♦

When Terri left, I decided to ask Mrs. LeGraff about Burke and his discharge, but I had to wait until the cat groomer arrived before I could go to her house. She finally came, picked up the Little Dirt Bomb formerly known as Yoda, and said, "I'll have him ready for you this afternoon."

"Wow. That soon. I mean, he's really filthy."

"I'm a miracle worker," she muttered, waved, and left.

As I walked past Jonas's yellow-taped yard next door, several policemen moved about while some of my neighbors huddled at the outside perimeter of the crime scene, mumbling and frowning and shaking their heads with worry and who-could-do-this questions in their eyes.

Mrs. LeGraff was on her knees in her flower garden, stabbing the earth with a vengeance.

"Stupid weeds," she muttered and swiped a gloved hand across her forehead. "Are you here to help me, Sophie?"

"Not exactly." I chuckled, sank to my knees, and yanked away. "But I'm not above weeding."

"Then why are you here?"

"Burke Maguire's discharge from the Marines."

She sat back on her heels and winced. "These hips. If I could have one thing in this life, it would be hips without pain." She sank to her bottom and swiped her hat off, fanned herself, and squinted at me. "Jonas was murdered this morning, and you're asking me about Burke Maguire?"

"You know Jonas and I weren't close. I'm sorry he was killed. Did you hear or see anything?"

"They questioned me just like they questioned you and everybody else on this street. I'll tell you the same thing I told them: I know nothing about his murder." She plopped her hat on and viciously attacked a weed with her garden trowel. "As to the other, his mother and I go way back, some thirty-five years. His family moved here because of our friendship. I've known that boy since he was a baby. He didn't do what they said he did."

Before I could blink, a weed dangled from her hand, its long roots twitching as it sailed through the hot air and landed on a heap of other discards. She grunted and stabbed the earth and worked another long root out of its comfy home.

When she started on another plant, I glanced over at her. "You're not going to tell me what I want to know, are you?"

"I just did. Good day to you, Sophie O'Brion."

I felt as if I'd been thwacked on my hands with a ruler by a disapproving teacher. I fumbled to my feet and waited for the blood to return to my legs. When I could stand and walk without looking drunk, I headed toward home, past the yellow tape, and past pairs of eyes watching every step I took.

♦

Word got out that yet another neighbor of mine was gone. Of course, everyone knew I was the last person to see Jonas alive, other than the killer.

"And that poor dog," Madge Simmons lamented, standing on my front porch with its clear vantage point to the murder scene. "Who could hurt that poor dog?"

Who could hurt that poor man?

I considered myself a big person to even let Madge near my front porch after her performance the other day on this very spot. I even let her have a cinnamon roll. Then I excused myself and went inside, away from the flapping jaws and the circus-like frenzy surrounding Jonas' death.

I thought back to one o'clock this morning. I had assumed it was Jonas standing on that back porch, motioning to Garrett Flint. I squeezed my eyes closed and tried to recall every detail of the short exchange between the two men.

The porch man wore a T-shirt. The arm reaching out for Garrett Flint had no weighty flab falling out of the T-shirt's sleeve. And the guttural words, *"You fool! Get in here before somebody sees you!"* Was that Jonas' voice looping in my head?

No. I don't think it was.

Maybe the man standing on the porch had already killed Jonas.

Maybe Garrett Flint was tentative because he could see Jonas' body through the screen door. Maybe it was Herman Farnsberry who'd killed Jonas and then threatened Flint.

But what had Jonas known or done that would cause Farnsberry to kill him at this late date?

And the best question yet: where was Garrett Flint, who probably had all the answers to my questions?

♦

All day, Burke came and went from Jonas' house, but not once did he come to mine. I worked outside in my garden in my big hat and kept one eye on the activity next door and the other on my petunias. I never caught Burke glancing my way even once.

It was a long and stressful day.

I went inside and showered and tried to work on my book, but I couldn't keep my mind in it. I wanted to know what Burke had discovered next door. Had they found Moocher? Did they have a suspect for Jonas' murder?

I thought of the Condolences Committee at church. I'd be in the know right now if I hadn't quit it four years ago. In the event of a death, the ConComs were in on everything. They notified family members, prepared a potluck dinner, served at the bereavement dinner, and organized any family get-togethers—which meant a basketful of information about anyone and everyone, with the appropriate "Well, bless her heart" and "No, I didn't know, bless his heart" after each bit of gossip. I'd left my name in as an alternate in case someone couldn't help out, but I hadn't been called even once to pinch hit in the last four years.

It looked like I wouldn't find out anything today.

Terri called. She didn't know anything, either.

I walked around my house, thought about watching television, but I'm not much of a television fan.

Wandering the bookcases didn't help either. None of the books grabbed me as I strolled by.

My mind was simply too tired. I'd worked in my garden all day to keep my hands busy, and I was exhausted.

It was midnight, time to put all this frustration to bed. I put on my pajamas, slipped into bed, and wondered who in the world could have done this to Jonas Whitworth. I'd worn myself out with worry and fell right to sleep.

9

I woke up after a horribly restless night to air that smelled like burnt molasses.

I trudged my way to the kitchen and scowled at the smoke hovering a good four feet off my ceiling. I usually set the coffee timer for five. I should be facing a full pot of steaming hot java, but only a red light and a stinky black pot greeted me.

I'd made decaf coffee last night about eleven and left the pot on, but it obviously hadn't turned itself off.

Yoda appeared, his head poking through the cat's door. He stood still, as if he were sizing me up. "Long night, huh, boy?" He came on through and curled around my ankles as I opened the back door to let out the smoke and the awful smell. Yoda promptly went back outside.

When I passed a mirror on my way to open the front door, I recognized a psycho serial murderess I'd seen profiled on TV a month ago. Under my eyes were dark circles worthy of a corpse or a zombie. And my hair. Every blonde strand I owned pointed toward a wall or ceiling.

The newspaper hit my front screen door. Nothing could make me run this morning, not even the prospect of Samson grabbing it and racing with it to the vacant house netherworld.

I plodded to the screen door and opened it. Not two feet from my paper, Samson sat, his tail flapping, his tongue dripping, his brown eyes gazing up at me as if I were his long-lost jailer with a key dangling from my mouth.

"Samson, don't you even think about getting my paper."

Well, shock of all shocks, he just sat there. Then he dipped his head and whined.

Oh, no.

A whining dog is one thing I cannot abide.

I squatted, and my knees creaked. I rubbed behind his ears. "Whatsamatter, boy? Are you missing Moocher?"

He barked, and his tail wagged harder. He nudged my hand, licked my fingers, and crawled closer to me.

I wiped my hand on my robe. "Do you know where Moocher is, boy?"

He answered with a bark, a body wag, and a dance. I glanced over at Jim Peters' home and then opened my door. "Come on, Samson. Let's text Mr. Commitment and see if he can help us find Moocher. Have you ever met Yoda?"

A horrifying screech, an indignant bark, scrambling claws on hardwood floors, a swinging cat door, and Samson and I were alone in the house.

♦

Forty-five minutes later, I opened the front door.

Burke stood on my porch wearing a grim expression. "You wanted to see me?"

Samson barked behind me. I quickly opened the screen door for Burke before Jim Peters realized his dog was in my house. "Hurry."

"Hurry?" Burke glanced over his shoulder as he stepped inside. "What's going on?"

"Trust me."

He turned toward me, a terribly sad look on his face. "Like you trusted me?"

Oh, that hurt.

So, he knew I knew about his past.

I shut the door. "I, uh, I can't offer you coffee this morning because I was up most of the night and I left the coffee maker on and the shut-off is broken so this morning I came down to the kitchen and found the pot had burned up sometime during the night so I may be a little cranky since I haven't had my coffee and my house stinks

105

like burnt molasses and I don't have a clue how to get that smell out of my house and I'm sorry if I hurt you."

He stared at me with his mouth pinched, his brows drawn together. "You can read all about my *honorable* discharge. I'll give you the website and the password. There were never any charges. It was obviously a set-up, and my buddies vouched for me. The words 'dishonorable discharge' were never even considered. Madge Simmons is spreading lies."

"Gossips usually do." Mrs. LeGraff had been right. I should have listened to her. "I have tea." I led him to the kitchen and put the tea pot on.

Burke sat at my kitchen table. He took off his hat, set it on the table, sighed heavily, clasped his hands, and said, "I was at a local hangout for Marines. It was late. In prances this seventeen-year-old girl. She walks over to me, crawls all over me, tries to kiss me. My buddies went crazy, hooting and laughing. I set her off my lap and left."

I quietly pulled out a chair and sat across from him.

He didn't look at me but continued to stare at his hands. "At the time, I was dating the daughter of a wealthy businessman. He never liked me." Burke leaned back in the chair, still without a glance in my direction. "The seventeen-year-old was staged. Lots of pictures were taken. She literally attacked me, but I did nothing wrong. The businessman paid for the girl and the photographer, so his daughter would stop dating me. It worked." For just a moment, his angry eyes softened, but then he blinked several times and the anger was back. "All you had to do was ask me, Sophie."

"I—"

"Instead of your neighbor."

"How do you know about Mrs. LeGraff?"

"Sheenen was standing at the back of Jonas' house when you sat beside her. He heard everything. Next time you have any questions about me or my life, just ask me. I'm an open book to you."

"I'm sorry, Burke. Really, I am."

"I forgive you. Why am I here this morning?"

"Samson knows where Moocher is."

When he heard his name, Samson barked again and nuzzled Burke's leg. "You know, big boy?" He patted his head. "You know where Moocher is?"

Samson trotted out of the room, turned around, and barked wildly.

Burke pulled out his keys. "Do you want to go?"

"Yes. But first, I have fresh cinnamon rolls. Would you like one?"

He laughed. "Bringing out the big guns, Soph?"

"I really am sorry I didn't come to you."

"Me, too." He stared at me.

I stared at him. The moment stretched into five or six, and one of us needed to say something. "I'll just, uh, get those rolls now."

"I've always liked your rolls."

His words felt like a caress. I looked down at my hands, my heart thumping so hard, it was difficult to concentrate.

The problem with re-igniting a friendship with someone you were romantically involved with is that the way things in the past were handled don't cross over into the present. When I was angry with Burke in high school, we'd kiss and make up. Kissing and making up was fun, back then.

"Sophie." Burke placed his hands on my shoulders. His gaze bounced back and forth over my eyes, and then he glanced down at my mouth.

But we weren't in high school anymore! We're not even dating! We're just friends! Friends don't kiss!

He tilted his head and headed for gold.

What was he thinking? A man was murdered yesterday! A dog was missing! Farnsberry! Garrett Flint! Laura and Sharon—

His lips touched mine like a brush stroke, and my eyes drifted shut.

"Sophie?"

"Hmmm?" I opened the windows to my soul.

"You have the most luscious mouth I have ever kissed."

And they're off! The horses have left the starting gate!

But I had to turn those horses around. "I—" Easing out of his arms, my face felt so hot. "I'd better get—" What was it? I stood for a moment in the middle of my kitchen trying to remember.

"The cinnamon rolls?" Burke chuckled.

When I glanced at him, he looked completely pleased with himself. He knew good and well he'd flummoxed me in my own kitchen.

"Yes, the, uh—" I found them, placed two in a box, and handed them to him on my way to the front door. "Friends don't touch lips, Burke."

He nodded, grinning. "You're right. I stepped over the line."

"And I stepped right along with you." I opened the front door. Burke was still grinning. "You don't look very remorseful."

"Neither do you, Sophie."

Now I was grinning. Time to find Moocher and get off the race track.

Samson barked and danced at our feet. Burke opened his rear passenger door, and Samson darted inside. "Come on, boy. Show us where Moocher is."

Samson led us to a ramshackle dwelling on a road just outside city limits. As soon as Burke parked the patrol car where the rutted path ended, Samson jumped out of the car and bounded toward the old shed.

"Burke, I hear Moocher!"

We raced—Burke raced; I followed—to the shed and with little effort, he had the door open. Moocher jumped into Burke's arms, wetting all over Burke's uniform. Burke handed him to me, and I snuggled Moocher's little shaking body as best I could since he'd already relieved himself on Burke. Samson threw a barking fit, so I put

Moocher on the ground, and they did a my-best-friend's-back dance.

"How do they do that, Burke? How did Samson know where Moocher was?"

Burke touched my arm and dipped his head at something behind me. I turned around and made out a small cabin about four hundred yards away, hidden in the woods. Burke tugged on my arm, nodded toward his car, and we got in. It was understood that we were to be quiet now. He punched the microphone on his shoulder and called for backup.

"What do we do now?" I whispered.

"We wait."

Not for long. Officer Sheenen drove up, and both men drew their weapons and started off. "But—"

"Stay here, stay down, and stay quiet, Sophie."

Well!

I looked around, not sure I wanted to be out here by myself. I watched both men step through the tall grass and separate as they approached the cabin. Since Burke had left his car door open, Moocher hopped in and crawled onto my lap. Samson sprawled over Burke's seat and panted. "You have a huge tongue, Samson." Moocher yipped at me. "And you, too, Moocher. Of course, you do, too."

I looked up. Both men had disappeared.

I decided to inspect the falling-down shed. When I got out of the car, Moocher and Samson followed and then sat in the grass, panting. I stepped through the doorway and looked around at rusted junk, sagging window frames and walls, and something white under a board.

It was the edge of an envelope.

It protruded from between two boards, its whiteness bright against all the old gray. Carefully, I plucked it out and gasped. My name was on it, written in block print.

The flap was open, and I eased out the piece of paper and read: "I knew you would find Moocher and this note. I didn't kill Jonas

109

Whitworth. When I landed in your backyard, I heard the little dog. He was whining and scratching on Jonas' back screen door. I climbed your fence and saw a man lying on the kitchen floor. It was dark. I checked on him. He was dead. No one else was there, so I took the little dog to this safe place. The rest was none of my business. Your last book is my favorite."

My last book?

Was this from a fan? The man who bought me the gift certificates? I read again, "When I landed in your backyard—"

"What's that, Sophie?"

I yelped, which started Samson and Moocher barking and circling us. "Oh! I didn't hear you." I gulped a couple of times and tried to swallow. Glancing around, I wondered if the man who'd written this was out here, watching me. "I found this envelope between two boards. It has my name on it." I handed the paper to Burke. Officer Sheenen leaned over to read it with him.

Burke grunted. "What was your last book?"

"Flames."

"I read it. What do you make of this?"

"I think he may be an obsessed fan."

"In *Flames*, your main character was a firefighter who was a serial killer, a serial arsonist." Burke tapped the letter on his left hand. "We'll check out the writing and see if this person sent you the gift certificates."

He nodded at Sheenen, who got in his patrol car and left. "No one lives in that cabin. It's completely abandoned. Let's get back to town. We have to take Moocher to the animal shelter before six."

"Animal shelter?" I got into his car. "Moocher's been through too much trauma as it is."

Burke eased into the driver's seat, started the car, and backed up. "He's a dog, Sophie, not a little boy. He'll adjust."

"In my house. He'll adjust very well in my house where he'll be safe. Not in some concreted, cold place where dogs stay in cages

110

until—"

Burke chuckled and turned right toward Forman Falls. Moocher snuggled onto my lap again, looked up at me, and then rested his warm head on my arm.

Oh, sweet Gussie Malone.

What will Yoda think of our new family member?

♦

The next morning, the newspaper slid to a stop at my screen door. When I opened it, Samson jumped off the wicker chair and greeted me with a nudge to my crotch. "Listen here, buddy boy. You don't do that to me. That's disgusting. Greet me with a growl or a bark but not with a sniff. Comprende'?"

No one appeared at Jennie Baker's house. I had given up on seeing her frowning face this early ever again, so it surprised me when the screen door opened, and her husband, Rich, stepped out.

"'Morning, Sophie."

"'Morning, Rich. Y'all doing all right?"

"Pretty good. You?"

"Pretty good. How's Jennie?"

"She's pregnant again. Throwing up a lot. Sick as a dog."

Samson barked and wagged his tail at Rich. When he did, he leaned against me and almost knocked me over. "He doesn't mean you, Samson." I turned back to my neighbor. "Tell her I hope she gets better."

"Will do. Have a good one." His door shut.

And my cell phone rang. It was Burke. "The APB out on Farnsberry hasn't produced anything, so he's found a good hole to hide in. No news on his sister, either. The mother in Minnesota is dead. We couldn't find any of Laura Caldwell Farnsberry's family. Family of Sharon Farnsberry was no help at all. We've posted the picture of Laura and Clarke on our website, hoping someone can identify the man. The handwriting expert says there's a match for the envelope on your back porch and yesterday's note, but the writer's not in the system. Otherwise, we're stumped."

"Now I'm in serious trouble."

"You've been in serious trouble for over two weeks. Are you going to Jonas' memorial dinner tonight?"

I barely knew Jonas Whitworth, although we'd lived side-by-side for years. "I suppose."

"It's at Hope Community. Jonas was born and raised in Forman Falls, so the place will be packed."

"I wonder if anyone would miss little ol' me?"

"A lot of the people are coming tonight just to see little ol' you, Sophie. Nothing draws the curious like controversy."

"Well." I found I could smile. "That's certainly my middle name lately."

♦

When Terri and I walked into the fellowship hall that night, it was indeed filled to the gills. Young and old, some dressed in black, others in colors, some sniffling, some laughing.

"Such a nice man."

"He gave every Sunday to those missionaries in Africa. Oh, what were their names?"

"Jonas Whitworth was anything but sweet, but I'll not speak ill of the dead."

"Jonas was one of my best friends for over thirty years."

Now that comment caught my ear, and I turned toward the speaker, a woman sitting next to Edna across from a man I didn't know. He seemed somehow familiar. My writer's eye studied his mouth, the shape of his nose, his eyes, his cheekbones.

And I gasped.

The man in the picture with Laura!

I nudged Terri back a few feet. "Look! That man with the white hair sitting with Miss Edna. He's the man in the picture with Laura, Farnsberry's first wife!"

I searched through the crowd for a uniform, but I couldn't find Burke or Sheenen. Then a voice right beside my ear said, "Are you looking for me?"

I spun around and faced Burke. He was dressed in cowboy boots and a black suit, a white shirt and black bolo contrasting with his golden tan and blonde hair.

"I'll be back," Terri said as she walked toward a waving Mrs. LeGraff.

"Burke, look over there." I flicked my head in the direction of the man I thought was Clarke. "Sitting at the same table with Edna Conroy and a woman. Recognize him?"

He casually looked over his shoulder. "No. Should I?"

"Clarke of Laura and Clarke. The picture."

That got his attention. He turned and stared at the man. "You're right." He took my arm and guided me through the crowd to the table just as the woman who'd been sitting with Edna walked off. "Miss Edna, good to see you," Burke announced. "Jonas would have been pleased to know so many of his friends were here tonight."

Well, I'll say this: the man is sure smooth.

"You know Sophie, of course."

"Of course, honey," Edna said. "How are you, Sophie? This is my friend, Frank Zagorsky."

Frank Zagorsky? The man who'd lived in Europe? "Mr. Zagorsky." I smiled. "A pleasure."

He dipped his head without moving a single muscle in his face. No laugh lines graced his gray eyes. The man took 'austere' to a whole new level. He rarely blinked. I counted to twenty-five before the man blinked.

"Are you from around here, Mr. Zagorsky?" I sat across from him, next to Edna. Burke sat beside me.

113

The man's gaze focused on something at another table. A few seconds went by. "No," he finally said. He didn't look at me or move or follow that curt answer with any explanation.

I looked at Burke and crossed my eyes.

He took the hint. "Are you any relation to the Zagorskys who live in Marble Hill, sir?"

Edna flapped a hand at both of us. "Oh, just call him Frank. He's not answering you because he doesn't know you're talking to him!" She giggled at this, looked at Frank, and her smile wilted.

"Miss Edna, how did you two meet?"

She glanced at Frank and smiled, which solicited not one ounce of a response. "At this church. It was bowling night, and you know how I love to bowl."

No, I didn't know.

"We rode together to the bowling alley and just hit it off, didn't we, Frank?"

Frank's gaze slid to Edna, and he nodded once. That's it. Just that no-humor look with those unblinking, steely eyes.

"Did you know Laura Caldwell, Frank?"

Burke's leg nudged mine, but, hey, the man was virtually ignoring us, so I decided to stir the pot and see what bubbled out.

This time, I saw a flicker of a smile. But those cold gray eyes never showed a hint of warmth when he said, "Dated her in college. She married someone else."

Wow. A whole paragraph. "Herman Farnsberry."

Yikes. That cloudy gaze slid to me, and I thought he was considering how he could make *me* bubble up out of that hot pot.

He nodded.

And that was it. Not another word did he speak for the next ten minutes, no matter how many questions Burke and I asked him.

Burke stood, took my hand, and said our good-byes.

"What are you doing?" I whispered. "He's a link. Why are we leaving him?"

"He has too much to hide." Burke tugged me toward the buffet line and let go. "When we leave, I'll run a background check on him."

That appeased me. I stood in the long line, nowhere near the food, and glanced around the room. Madge Simmons and my next-door neighbor, Jennie, stood together, leaning in, probably gossiping if their furtive glances and their covered mouths were any indication. Bertie the editor was talking to a man I didn't know, but when he turned around and looked straight at me, his gaze fumbled, so I surmised they were talking about me.

When I saw Bertie the editor making a beeline toward me, I grabbed Burke's hand and tried to yank him toward the door. But he pulled back. "Talk to her. Find out what she knows."

"O'Brion."

The whole room hushed. Several hundred eyes seemed to weigh me down. Terri dragged Mrs. LeGraff through the crowd and stood beside me.

I turned and smiled at our illustrious editor. "Bertie."

"I understand you and Jonas fought before his death."

"You understand incorrectly."

"You didn't fight."

"We didn't fight."

"Madge Simmons testifies differently."

Testifies? "Then Madge Simmons—" I purposely slid my pleasant gaze to her, which caused her to twitch, gasp, clutch her hands, and turn her back to me and her mouth toward her friend. "—is mistaken. And you're mistaken, Bertie, if you think you can use the memorial of a wonderful man—" I almost gagged on the words. "—to push a private agenda with me. Let's not forget why we're here: to honor a man's life."

It was a beautiful moment in my life.

Bertie huffed off, and I turned to Burke.

"You'll pay for that."

"I know. But at least—" I couldn't grab my thought. Virginia

115

Crane had just walked into the room, and everyone hushed again. She looked elegant in a dark gray, mid-calf dress with black high-heeled, knee-high boots and a black hat covering her beautiful white hair. Standing there, she looked like a model for a senior citizen's magazine.

When she saw me, she walked—floated—through the people and reached for me with black-gloved hands, hugging me as if she was thrilled to have someone to hold onto.

"Virginia, how are you?"

When she pulled back, her gaze rested on Frank Zagorsky and I physically felt her jerk. Her eyes widened. Her mouth dropped open but only a tiny bit. I checked out Frank's response to seeing her, and it was pretty much the same. Absolute shock.

I leaned toward her. "You know him, Virginia?"

She flushed. Fumbled with her purse. Looked down at her hands. "I-I thought I saw someone I once knew."

And I was born yesterday. "You know Frank Zagorsky?"

"Frank?" She smiled weakly and touched her washed-out face with the back of her gloved fingers. "No. I-I really thought he was someone I once knew."

"Was his name Clarke?"

She gasped. "How did you—? I'm sorry. This wasn't a good idea. I must go." Then she turned and walked toward the exit, floating again but in passing gear.

The room buzzed like swarming honeybees. Everyone turned toward me as if I were about to burst into a song and dance.

"What just happened, Burke? What just happened?"

"I'm not sure, but everyone thinks it's your fault that she left." He glanced at Frank. "He and Virginia obviously have a history, but Frank has more to hide than his relationship with her. Be right back."

Just as he walked off, I saw Virginia's maid, Rita, standing alone in the corner of the room. She held a plate of food in one hand. Two fingers of her other hand pinched a bite of food that lay frozen in mid-air near her mouth as she stared at her employer. An expression of surprise with a twist of fear clothed her face. For Virginia?

And what was Rita doing here? Had she known Jonas?

As if she sensed me watching her, she turned her head and took the bite she'd held enticingly at her mouth. Her gaze met mine, and her face instantly lit up with a dazzling smile. She waved, set her plate on a table, and walked toward me. Her extended hand reached me first. "You're the writer, aren't you? The famous resident of Forman Falls?"

"Well." I laughed. I never knew how to respond to those kinds of questions, so I did what I usually did: I moved on to another subject. "Good to see you again, Rita."

She glanced toward the door where Virginia had exited. "She's really sad over her friend's death. Did you know Jonas?"

That was my question for *her*. I assumed Rita was here because of Virginia, but I wondered if there was something else. "Yes. He was my neighbor. Did you know him?"

She shrugged and waved at someone. I followed her gaze and found a woman from my church—I'd forgotten her name—at the end of it. Her response to Rita was a weak smile and a turn of her body to speak to someone else.

"Maybe you and I can get together sometime over coffee or something."

I usually said no to invitations from people I didn't know, but she might have information that could be helpful. "Sure. That sounds like fun. Did you know Jonas?"

"Some." She shrugged again, much as a little girl might who stood among shards of glass after her mother asked her if she'd broken the prized vase.

"How long have you been working for Virginia?"

"A long time. Almost six months. She's a wonderful lady." Rita placed a hand on mine and said, "I have to run now. We'll get together soon, all right?" And she left, weaving her way through groups of people toward the same exit Virginia had used. Just as she reached the door, she turned around and smiled at someone.

I tried to follow her gaze but couldn't see anyone responding to the twinkle in her eye.

"Who was that?" Burke stood beside me again.

"Virginia's maid, Rita. I'm not sure why she was here, other than to support Virginia, of course."

10

When Virginia opened her front door, I blurted out, "You knew I would come, that I would ask about Frank."

Virginia seemed resigned to my being there and stepped back to usher me into her beautiful home. But this time, I'd brought Officer Maguire with me.

She attempted a smile. "Burke Maguire. I remember you from middle school. Welcome back to Forman Falls."

"Thank you, Mrs. Crane."

"Call me Virginia. I believe this day calls for informalities."

The large picture window drew Burke as it had me my first visit to this place. But Virginia didn't tell him about the leaves turning colors or the coming of the first frost in late October. She stood quietly behind us. What in life had taught her to have such reserves of serenity and poise just before she knew the boom would drop?

"It's beautiful." Burke turned to look at her.

Her half-attempt at a smile revealed the tension in the room rather than eased it. "Please have a seat." This time she rang no bell for a maid. She primly sat, crossed her ankles, put her hands in her lap, and leveled her gaze on Burke.

"What was or is your relationship with Frank Zagorsky, ma'am?"

"I haven't admitted to knowing him."

"Do you?"

"No. He looks remarkably like a man I once knew."

"Laura Caldwell's first husband?"

"No. My first husband. Clarke Zalensky."

Virginia was married to the Clarke of 'Laura and Clarke'?

Burke wrote down the name. "A relative of Frank's?"

"I'm not sure. The resemblance between him and Frank is extreme. They could be the same person except for the nose, the chin.

It was certainly a shock to see him tonight. My Clarke died years ago."

"Are you sure he's dead?" Oh! I wanted to slap myself. Where had that question come from? I could just imagine my mother sighing at me, rolling her eyes, and signaling me to keep my big mouth shut.

"The car exploded, Sophie. There was a body. Is that dead enough for you?"

"I'm sorry, Virginia. I didn't mean—"

"Yes, she did." Burke scooted to the edge of the sofa, his firm gaze aimed at Virginia. "Sophie is under investigation right now, and she's desperate to know the truth about some people connected to Herman Farnsberry. You're one of them. You lied to her about Clarke Zalensky. You told her you didn't know the man in the picture."

"I didn't want any of this to get out." She sighed and seemed to search for a good way to start her story. "Laura met Herman Farnsberry on a double date with me and Clarke in Austin at the university. Clarke was immediately smitten with Laura, but she was never that interested in him. He was older than the rest of us, by about five years. After leaving the university, Laura and Herman met again in Chicago and married after a couple years of dating. Clarke and I eventually married, too. He was killed three months after our wedding. A car explosion. I was heartbroken."

"But you didn't mention to me that you even knew Clarke."

"It was too complicated, Sophie. Laura and I were friends. Sharon and I were friends. Herman and I were friends. We all went to school together and went our separate ways, only to be re-connected when Sharon and Herman married and moved here. First, there was Clarke and Laura. Then, Clarke and I. Laura and Herman. Then, Sharon and Herman and, illicitly, Selma and Herman. I always seemed to be stuck in the middle of all those relationships."

I saw a different take on it. "You received the leftovers."

Her gaze sliced to me.

"Did it bother you to be Clarke's second choice?"

Virginia plucked a tissue from a glass box and dabbed under her left eye. "At first, but I think Clarke grew to love me."

"Where does Crane come in?"

"It was my maiden name."

"You didn't marry again after Clarke's death?"

"No." The tissue disappeared into her fist.

What was I missing? There was more, but I couldn't see it. "You haven't mentioned Edna Conroy. She was sitting with Frank Zagorsky at the memorial for Jonas. Didn't she go to the same school?"

"Yes, we were both chemistry majors, but she wasn't coupled with any of the parties we've talked about. She didn't date much, so I didn't mention her."

Burke had sat quietly while I questioned Virginia, then he leaned toward her and asked, "Did you love Herman Farnsberry, Ms. Crane?"

Tears filled her eyes, and I instantly felt sorry for her. The answer was yes. Yes, she had loved Herman Farnsberry, desperately. She'd received the leftovers but not all of them. Not the one she wanted the most.

"I think it's time you both left. I'm tired. I need to rest."

Burke stood. "One more question. Where were you on the day Laura went missing?"

"I don't know. I don't know when she went missing."

"Thank you for your time." Burke put out his hand to stop Virginia from rising. "We'll see ourselves out, ma'am."

We walked in silence to his patrol car. I stared at the late-model Cadillac that we had parked behind. It was a beautiful frosty gold color. I reached for the door handle of the patrol car and got in.

"Are you thinking she loved Herman enough to kill both his wives, so she could have him for herself?"

Burke actually chuckled, but it was smirky, not funny. "Come on, Sophie. You can't possibly think she killed Laura and Sharon."

"Love's a powerful motive."

"And opportunity? Herman and Laura didn't live in Forman Falls.

I don't even know where Virginia lived at the time of Laura's disappearance. You're saying she flew to wherever they lived and killed Laura? Then killed Sharon? At the supermarket? Over the cantaloupes?"

"If not Virginia, who then?"

"Garrett Flint. Herman Farnsberry. It's a stretch to think that someone would follow him and kill both his wives. I think Farnsberry's our man."

I nodded. "Let's go to my neighborhood and take a long walk. I'm all tensed up."

"You're ready for people to see us together?"

I wanted to laugh at the naiveté of my newest friend. "Any one person on my street can tell you how many times you've been to my house in the last few weeks, when you arrived, when you departed, and your mode of transportation."

A nudge to my arm produced a stick of gum. The man made me smile.

"How about some ice cream with that walk, Soph? It'll do us both some good."

◆

"Szzzzttt! Szzzzttt!"

The last of my ice cream dripped down my fingers, and I needed a napkin in a serious, for-heaven's-sake-wipe-that-baby's-drooling-mouth way. I nudged Burke. "That's our resident Hobbit signaling us, Vivian Blake."

"Hobbit?" Burke offered me his wadded napkin, and I gladly took it.

"Well, if not a Hobbit, then our resident good witch. Do you remember her from when we were kids?"

"Not at all."

"Szzzzttt! Szzzzttt!"

I called out, "Hey, Vivian! How are you? It's a beautiful day, isn't it?" To Burke, I said, "She's a recluse and, uh." I lifted a shoulder. "She's, uh, well, just be prepared."

"For what?"

"You'll see."

It wasn't uncommon for my friend Vivian to ignore people offering her a friendly wave or two as they passed by. Most people didn't know she was standing there. But if the light from her open back door was just right, a person could make out her silhouette in the black metal screen door. When she disregarded my friendly greeting, I continued walking with Burke, assuming she was in her usual get-out-of-my-sight-and-leave-me-be mode.

When she szzzzttt'ed me again, her screen door opened with the help of a broom handle.

"And there's the broom she uses." I sent Burke a see-I-told-you-so smile. "We've been invited inside, Burke. A rare treat."

We walked up the path to her house. No flowers graced any of the old plant boxes flanking her front porch. No bushes hugged her walls. No rocking chairs or any chairs sat on her wide porch welcoming neighbors or friends to stop by and enjoy the evening with her.

And the statue of a snarling dog at the top of the stairs? A reminder to anyone *thinking* of approaching her house that she could probably turn that statue into the real thing.

We walked up the steps. "I got it, ma'am", Burke said as he grabbed the door and held it open for me. The broom and Vivian disappeared.

We stepped inside.

The windows were covered with black curtains. Two candles were placed on either side of a large ornate mirror hanging on a wall. Under the mirror, a thin woman wearing a spaghetti-strap gown more appropriate for a Hollywood starlet than a forty-eight-year-old bony woman sat on a black sofa.

And, of course, she was barefoot.

123

"Please, have a seat." Vivian squinted one dark-brown eye up at Burke and then shifted her attention to me.

I watched for Burke's reaction.

Yep, I saw his eyes widen a fraction when his gaze slid to me. He was polite and didn't gawk. I appreciated that he was a gentleman to my friend.

I'd felt so sorry for Vivian through the years. Too many of the area children had taunted and teased her about her nose. The whispers of her neighbors had hurt her. No man had ever asked her out, because they couldn't get past her hook nose.

I promised myself a long time ago that I would write a strong heroine just like her in one of my books, but I'd never followed through for fear of hurting her. I wanted to be her friend. She was intelligent and nosy, pun intended—a combination I couldn't help but admire.

"It might interest you to know, Officer," she spoke quietly, "that Sophie's next-door neighbor, Jonas Whitworth, and Miss Edna were married briefly years ago."

"I didn't know that." I turned to Burke. "You remember Miss Edna was at the memorial for Jonas, sitting with Frank Zagorsky."

Vivian nodded. "Bad blood between Jonas and Edna. I well remember the nasty divorce, the fight over their possessions, their dogs. No children, thank the good Lord. Seemed to take forever for them to stop clashing. But they did, finally, and moved to opposite corners, never to speak to each other again—until they met two days before Jonas' death."

"Did you see them, ma'am?"

"Yes. They were in his back yard, under Jonas' magnolia tree."

Burke tugged out a little black book from his shirt pocket, flipped a few pages, and started writing. "What time?"

"Around midnight."

Burke lifted his head and his brows. "Where were you?"

Here we go.

"In the magnolia. I have a favorite perch."

Burke glanced at me.

I imagined few things could surprise Burke, but Vivian had just done it. I laughed out loud. "The only time she goes out is at night to climb trees. She's part owl and part Hobbit." I glanced down at her thin, bony feet. Her long toenails looked as if they could slice the bark right off a tree.

Burke opened his mouth to speak, but Vivian beat him to it. "I was in your yard the night someone placed that box on your porch, Sophie."

Now I couldn't stop *my* mouth from gaping. "You *saw* him?"

She chuckled. This woman had always amused me. She stayed in her house during the day for months at a time, with no contact with anyone but the grocer who delivered her food once a week.

"Were you there the night Jonas was killed?"

"No, I wasn't."

Burke scooted to the edge of the sofa. "Can you identify this person in Sophie's yard?"

"He was all covered up. Hoodie. Gloves. Black clothes. That's all I have."

Burke wrote quickly. "What was the meeting between Edna and Jonas about?"

"They were yelling—"

I didn't hear the rest of her sentence. A casual glance through her kitchen and out her open back door revealed Garrett Flint looking between her privacy fence and the barbed wire above it. "Excuse me, Vivian. May I have a glass of water?"

"He's there, is he? He's late today. Usually comes in the morning to see me." She rose to her feet like a double-jointed toad stretching to its full height and walked through the kitchen to her back porch just as Flint tried to sail over her tall fence, but his pants leg caught on the barbed wire. She cried, "Oh, no!" and covered her smile. Her gaze darted to me as if she was a little girl giggling too loud in church and the preacher was calling her out for it.

I spewed out a laugh as Burke scooted past us and did a little sailing himself out the door and down the back steps.

But Garrett Flint wasn't going anywhere.

His short skinny body hung from the fence as if someone was planning to build a smokehouse around him.

Vivian and I caught up with Burke in time to hear him say, "Need a little help there, buddy?"

A bold shade of red tinted Flint's face as he gritted his teeth and twisted and jerked his leg several times, but the barbed wire wouldn't let go.

Burke, the giant, grabbed Flint's ankles and lifted him as if he were a toddler instead of a grown man. "There ya go, sir."

The red turned to white as Flint, the wanted man, stood in front of Morgan County's newest police officer.

And then the strangest thing happened: Vivian turned a couple shades of red herself. Her gaze never left the feet of Garrett Flint. She was blushing. Vivian has a crush on Garrett Flint.

But in the split second that Burke turned to her, Flint did the flying ninja thing and sailed right back over the fence.

I gasped. Vivian giggled. Burke glared as he said, "No way am I going after him."

Vivian looked relieved.

I took her elbow and walked companionably with her back into her house. We stopped in the kitchen and sat at her small table. "Did you know Sharon Farnsberry?"

"I did. The rumors weren't true about her having an affair, just to let you know. Garrett Flint started those stories hoping Farnsberry would divorce her, but he killed her instead. Flint didn't expect that, of course."

Burke glanced at me and his look said, "Do you believe her?"

I nodded. She'd always been honest with me. But I'd have to ask Terri to talk to her mother again and get details. "Vivian, how do you know Sharon wasn't having an affair?"

"I'm too nosy for my own good, that's how I know."

"You have the right equipment."

She playfully smacked my arm and added, "God-given, girl." She smiled at Burke. "A person can learn a lot sneaking around at night, Officer."

I sent Burke an isn't-she-great lift of my eyebrows. I'm sure he thought we were both a little on the kooky side, but of all my friends in Forman Falls, I knew I could be myself with two people, Vivian and Terri. "Who was Farnsberry's lover?"

"I don't know. He never had a woman in his home."

And that was Vivian's limitation: she only saw what happened in the neighborhood at night. "How can you be so positive about Sharon?"

"She stayed home nights, and she was my friend. I saw her in the middle of the night, when she felt the loneliness the most." She looked at Burke. "I want to help with your investigation. Time is short before that car report comes back."

"Is there anything you don't know, Miss Vivian?"

"I keep my eyes and ears open, Officer. However, the one night that mattered, I was sick in bed. Sharon was killed, and I wasn't there to help her. Maybe I can help clear Sophie's name." She fiddled with a fold in her gown and looked at Burke. "She talks to me and notices me."

Burke nodded. "Who wouldn't notice your beautiful eyes?"

Vivian blushed deeply.

We left shortly after that. It was good seeing my friend again. This was the longest visit we'd ever had. I felt closer to her and really wanted to get to know her better—and I wanted to find out what other secrets she was holding onto.

As we continued our walk, I glanced at Burke. "Thank you."

"For what?"

"For being so kind to Vivian."

"It was the truth."

Dark clouds were moving in. "We'd better turn around. It looks like it's about to rain."

◆

The early evening shower hinted of a cooler night, but it didn't materialize. The air was sticky, warm, and soft on my skin. The light rain lasted two minutes, enough for the ground to slurp up the moisture and completely dry out fifteen minutes later.

Humid air enveloped me as I sat on a blanket in my backyard and gazed up at the starry night streaked by lines of thin clouds. I couldn't think about stars when zillions of bugs surrounded me. I hated bugs. Even though I was reeking of bug spray and dressed in long sleeves, jeans, long socks, a scarf around my head and neck, and a cap on my head, I hated sitting this close to that creepy-crawly world, knowing it would take a spider just three seconds to reach me once it discovered I was here.

I needed to find out from Vivian what Edna and Jonas had quarreled about. I get restless when I can't figure something out. It's a major character flaw at times, and at other times, this 'need to know' propels me into writing, to find out what mischief the characters in my head are up to.

Tonight, it was worth the risk of a few bug bites to talk to Vivian. I hadn't been able to reach Burke since our meeting earlier with her. I hoped she'd come here tonight.

I sat on my blanket for a while. Then I rested on my elbow and tried to read a good book on my phone, but after a few minutes, I gave up and lay on my back. I imagined spiders making their way toward me, but I was pretty much armored up from head to toe. After reading for a few more minutes, I looked around, but Vivian wasn't in the trees. I lay back down, couldn't keep my eyes open, and slept, because a rustling noise woke me.

She was here.

In the tree near my hidden back gate.

The moon shed just enough light for me to see her and, I was sure, for her to see me. "Hey. Are you up there?"

The rustling stopped. Would she even acknowledge me? This was her world, and I didn't know if she felt I was intruding on it. Maybe she'd grunt in answer to me or sit still and enjoy the night with me without talking.

She apparently chose the latter.

But I couldn't. "Do you want to come down and join me on my blanket?"

"No, thanks. I'm pretty comfortable up here."

"What were Edna and Jonas arguing about?"

"Jonas thought she was making a mistake by hanging out with Frank Zagorsky. I think he was jealous because he'd never stopped loving her."

"Do you know Edna, Vivian?"

"Yes and no. I spent time at her house when I was a kid. Her mother and my mother were good friends. After Edna left for college, I saw her occasionally when she returned. She traveled Europe for several months after graduation. When she came back here, we'd speak when we passed each other, but that's about it."

"Except at night, when you visited her home?"

"Not much going on at that time either."

"What about her and Frank Zagorsky, the man from Europe? Are they still seeing each other?"

"Yes, almost every day. He doesn't seem that interested, but he doesn't seem that interested in anything."

"Do you think Edna had anything to do with Jonas' death?"

"Not at all."

A dog barked at my gate—probably Samson. That dog could sniff out two cockroaches having lunch in a barrel. "Any idea who *did* kill Jonas?"

"None."

"You don't think Garrett Flint offed him?"

"Garrett's too idealistic. He believes justice will prevail, but not by his hand."

We didn't speak for a few moments, then I thought of Sharon. "Do you really believe Farnsberry killed Sharon?"

"He's the only one I can come up with, but I don't know that he did."

"Who would be your second choice?"

"I don't have a second choice. A drifting serial, maybe. Ted Bundy."

We fell into silence. I'd asked every question I could think of, and she seemed content to let the conversation die. The quiet of night covered us, and I lay on the blanket with my head on my hand, and a cramp started on the left side of my neck.

The next thing I knew, I startled awake and found myself alone. It felt eerie being outside in my own back yard in the dark, listening to absolute silence. I wondered where Moocher and Samson were. I quickly gathered up my blanket and searched the trees for Vivian before I went in.

Just as I reached the back door and opened it to turn on the kitchen light, I looked over my shoulder and gasped.

A man was standing in my backyard!

Our gazes locked. It was Herman Farnsberry.

White lights burst through crushing pain, and my world swirled into blackness.

◆

I was in a fog, spiraling, thick, and cold. I had no clue where I was or what had happened to me. I became aware of a sputtering hum. I recognized the noises of my refrigerator just before ice tumbles into the freezer bucket. I mentally clung to the sound. Ice fell. Then the fridge's purr softened until I could barely hear it.

I tried to move my body, but pain—stabbing, blinding *hurt*—shot through my head. I couldn't open my eyes or pull myself up or over. Nothing on my body seemed to work.

I kept thinking, "What happened? Why is my head on fire? Why can't I move?" My skull pounded as if someone had his hands around it and was slamming it into concrete, again and again.

I must have passed out again, because I opened my eyes in a sleepy stupor and focused on my back door. It was wide open, and it was night and I was looking at the door from my floor.

I needed to clean under the cabinets.

Crumbs, lint, and flaxseeds hugged the back boards. Was that a cranberry? I studied the dried-up blob. It seemed really important that I figure out if it was a raisin or a cranberry. Yes, it was a raisin. Tuna salad with raisins and apples. My mother's recipe. And there was the backing to my earring that had escaped me last week.

I groaned and lifted my numb hand—it felt like a dead fish. It started to come back to life, and I gritted my teeth against the pain and shook my hand but that made my head hurt worse and I thought I might be dying so I turned my head. OH! BIG MISTAKE!

For a moment, I saw pieces of glass behind me.

I simply couldn't put this puzzle back together and needed to close my eyes. I was out again.

◆

I managed to drag myself into a sitting position against my dishwasher. I thought the blazing firestorm in my head would be put out if I could just get my head above my heart. Funny, the things we think of in a crisis. Somehow, in all that haze and pain, I knew I was in real trouble.

I heard Samson whine, and then he began to lick my face. When I slipped toward the floor, he positioned himself between me and it, and he caught me. I landed in coarse hair. My face lay against his belly, and my head bobbed up and down with his quick breaths.

Good ol' Samson.

I passed out again.

◆

Moocher barked. Samson joined him. I waited for a meow, but it didn't come. Seemed Yoda hadn't bonded yet with the boys.

They barked several more times, and I mumbled, "I'm awake already." I just didn't want to open my eyes. Both dogs licked my face, and I growled at them. They backed off and yelped again.

"Okay, guys, okay. I'm awake. You're worse than my alarm snooze." I dragged myself to a sitting position again. All my appendages seemed to be working now but standing seemed out of the question, and I sat against the cabinet door.

I reached for Samson, and he licked my hand. "No more licking, guys. Really. No telling where your tongues have been." I wrinkled my nose at Samson. "I know where yours has been, you four-legged klepto."

That brought another round of barks and growls, ecstatic jumping, tail wagging, and drive-by slobbery kisses. Just the motivation I needed to move to my knees. "Both of you, your breaths stink." Shards of glass lay strewn across my floor.

Someone had hit me over the head.

But why? And who? What did he think I had in my house?

He?

She?

I patted my head and found a huge lump in back. I stuck my hand in front of my face and blinked furiously. Five digits. My vision seemed okay. I wasn't dizzy, but my head ached. I glanced outside; the back gate was wide open.

I grabbed the broom by the back door and shoved the dogs out of the glass. How do they do that? Dance and prance in glass without getting cut, without looking down at their paws?

I glanced at the clock. Only 4:12. It felt as if I'd been hugging the floor for days.

And another thing: how do dogs know when a person's in trouble?

Samson nudged my rear as if he knew what I was wondering.

"Hey. No nudging, remember? We don't bend that rule one iota, buddy boy."

He barked at me, which reminded me of the day he barked and saved Burke from the man in Farnsberry's back yard. Which reminded me that I should be calling 9-1-1, but I didn't know, I couldn't remember, where I'd put my phone. Which made me think that Burke would be the one to respond to the call. I needed to let him in on the latest news: that I was the victim of a crime. Sheesh. Was I a magnet for this stuff or what?

Someone was after me.

I had no idea who he was or what he wanted.

I stood, and the room tilted. Okay, so maybe I was a little dizzy. I made my way to a guest bedroom and sat on the bed. A terrifying screech came from the kitchen, followed by scuttling feet, falling things, several growls, and more barking.

My blended family had lumps to work out but tonight—this morning—wasn't the time to get out the mixer. I lay back, closed my eyes, and fell into a deep sleep.

I dreamed I was sinking in a stinky bog with prickly things gouging my ribs. I awoke to find Samson sprawled against me on my right, Moocher taking up most of my pillow, and Yoda settled comfortably in a knot at my feet. I smiled. The boogeyman didn't stand a chance against this threesome.

11

Vivian crouched on my ceiling, cackling. Frank Zagorsky slithered down my wall to my bed with a foot-long needle in his gnarled hands, screeching like a deranged monkey. Edna and Joanna Carpenter sat on my floor playing jacks with Missy the cat perched on Edna's head.

I knew I was dreaming, but I couldn't pull myself out of it.

My front door slammed, doing the trick. Wild barking and someone's footsteps pounding my wood floors in the hall made my eyes open. Burke raced into my guest bedroom with an excited Samson beside him.

"Sophie, what's wrong?"

"I'm not sure. Someone hit me over the head. I woke up on my kitchen floor."

"Are you okay?" Frowning, he took a step toward my bed. "When?"

"I'm okay, I think. I don't know the time, but Vivian and I talked in my backyard until midnight, I think. Then I don't remember a thing."

"Did you see someone inside or outside?"

"No. Nothing." Or, wait a minute. Something hazy in my back yard. Something—*someone*—standing on… I shook my head. "I don't remember."

Burke held up a hand. "Stay here, Sophie. I'll check it out."

Stay? I don't think so. I flipped the covers off, and my entourage and I made our way to the kitchen just as Burke walked outside. Broken glass lay scattered near the back door. It looked like the old wine bottle I'd found at a flea market several years ago. The colorful picture on the bottle lay on the floor. I looked outside. My back gate stood wide open.

Who was in my house, and why had he struck me?

Burke appeared in my kitchen doorway. "This is a crime scene now. Call Terri. Have her come and get you." After my eyes rolled upward, Burke added, "You're doing what I say, Sophie." I could see temper building in his demeanor. "What about your head?"

"I—"

He walked over to me, placed one large hand on my shoulder, the other on the back of my head and felt for a lump—tenderly, which surprised me, given his anger. "That's huge. How long were you out?"

"A few hours. And no, I don't need to go to the hospital. I'm fine."

"Yes, you're going to the hospital. I'll call Terri and have her take you. You're officially barred from this house."

"Okay, okay. Pushy, pushy. Would you mind shutting my back gate?"

I called Vivian. No, she hadn't seen anything in my yard, but wasn't it interesting, she said, that she'd seen Herman Farnsberry's sister, Ingrid, skulking around Jonas Whitworth's house around two this morning?

"Was anyone with her?"

"Not that I could see. I was in my favorite perch, the backyard magnolia. She fiddled with the back lock, and the door finally gave. She didn't turn on any lights, but I saw the light of her flashlight moving around at times."

"When did she come out?"

"I don't know. She must have gone out the front door."

Hmmm. "Farnsberry's behind this, I'm sure of it. What could he be afraid of, in my next-door neighbor's house?"

"Ask Ingrid. This was her second visit over there. Come with me tonight. We could hide in Jonas' tree or his house and catch her red-handed."

And wouldn't Burke just love that?

I made the date with Vivian and hung up. When I turned around, Burke had that good-gracious-woman-can't-you-control-yourself look on his face. He grunted and opened his mouth to speak but I beat him to the draw.

"Vivian and I are tree-hopping tonight. Care to join us?"

"And if I say no?"

"I'd say you'll be less sore than I'll be in the morning."

"What about your head? You'll probably fall out of the tree."

"I won't be in a tree. That was for dramatic effect."

"Well, Terri just pulled up. I'll help you to her car."

"I don't need help, and I don't need to go to the hospital."

"Yes, you do. C'mon, Sophie." He tugged on my arm. "You need to get your head checked out." I twisted out of his hold. He sighed. "All right, I won't help you to Terri's car, but I'll walk with you. How's that?"

♦

Terri and I left the hospital. She opened the car door for me and huffed, "Don't tell me again to forget it, Soph. You were assaulted. The doctor said you had to keep quiet, so you're staying with me until the police find the jerk who did this." She slammed the door, walked around to the driver's side, and slipped into the driver's seat.

"That could take months. I'll go back home when Burke clears my house."

A knuckle hit Terri's window, startling both of us. Burke motioned Terri to lower her window, and she did. "What are you doing here at the hospital, Burke?"

"Edna Conroy was taken in by ambulance," he said as he leaned over enough to see my face. "She's in a coma. She was beaten within an inch of her life."

Dear God. Miss Edna? "When did this happen?"

"I don't have the details. Sheenen is on his way to pick up Frank Zagorsky, see if he has any information."

I couldn't focus. Edna Conroy? Who would want to hurt sweet

Miss Edna? Her poor cat, Missy, won't know what to do without her.

Oh, no. Get that thought right out of your head, Sophie O'Brion. Yoda jumped Missy, remember? "Who found her? Where did it happen?"

"The librarian, Joanna Carpenter, found her. She couldn't tell us anything, only that Edna was unresponsive, lying on her bathroom floor, and had been very badly beaten."

Oh, dear God. I closed my eyes and rubbed my temples. "Her ex-husband, Jonas, was just murdered. Are these crimes related somehow?"

"I don't know. I'm on my way to the hospital to see if she can answer some questions. Even one word, a name, would help."

I perked up. "Then I don't have to leave my house?"

"It's even more important now that you leave. Stay at Terri's tonight at least. Lock your doors. I'll talk to you soon." He marched to his patrol car and drove off.

I stared ahead at nothing and thought of Miss Edna. "Terri, why would anyone in their right mind ever want to hurt such a sweet woman? And more importantly, *who*, in this close-knit town, would do such a thing?"

And who would hit me over the head? Did Miss Edna's beating have anything to do with me? Or Jonas?

"I don't know. Come on, Sophie," Terri said as she started her car. "Let's get you to my house and into bed. You look like crap."

♦

I slept deeply in Terri's spare bedroom. Racing pictures flew before my eyes: a white T-shirted arm reaching out, a man standing in the shadows of my back yard, glass flying around my head, bones rising out of the ground and chasing me. I cried out.

"Sophie, wake up." Terri's voice made the pictures slow down. "Come on, sweetie. You're having a bad dream. It's Terri. Now, wake up."

I opened my eyes. "It's all connected, Tare. All of it's somehow connected." I closed my eyes. "I have to find the missing pieces. It's all connected."

"When you're better. Do you feel like eating something?"

"No. How's Miss Edna?" I mumbled and drifted back to sleep.

♦

The next time I awoke, I knew I'd turned a corner. I felt better and made my way toward the wonderful smell of lasagna.

"Hey." I stood in the doorway to Terri's kitchen and sniffed. She wasn't the greatest cook in the world, but she had specialties that could make my mouth water, and lasagna was one of them. "Hmmm. Smells scrumptious."

Terri's kitchen was dressed in bright and bold greens, yellows, and cobalt blues. Terri has an eye for patching absurd things together and making a beautiful quilt, like the shiny yellow frog with the buggy, cobalt blue eyes. It's ridiculous by itself. I would never think to buy such a thing but put it on top of a blue mushroom in tall green grass, and it becomes a 'setting', as she calls it, a scene in her frog-inspired kitchen.

Terri wiped her hands on an apron with green, yellow, and blue circles. "Are you still nauseous? Can you eat?"

"The growls woke me up. I think I need to eat. Is it time for me to take a couple more pain killers?"

Terri glanced at the bright green clock. "Two more coming right up. Sit. You look like you'd fall over if I tossed a donut hole at you. But I don't have any here." She lifted her brows in a friends-don't-leave-friends-without-donuts accusation, pulled out a chair, and helped me sit.

"I'll get you some soon if Burke doesn't eat all of them at the crime scene." I closed my eyes as I placed my forehead on the cool plastic table cover. Oh, my head hurt, but it was a little better.

I opened my eyes. I was surrounded by ceramic frogs in motion—jumping, sitting, soaring after a fly—and my eyes wilted shut against the chaos. "At least you didn't say I look like crap."

"Well, you do. Burke called to check on you and to let us know that Miss Edna is still alive."

"Thank God. Did he get a name out of her?"

"No. He said she's in a deep coma, fighting for her life."

"Will she make it?"

"The doctor doesn't know. The brain injury is what they're focusing on. Apparently, the assailant—I don't believe I have ever used that word in my life, but that's what Burke called him—kicked her several times. It's rage, he said, and it's personal."

I tried to lift my head, but it hurt too much. "Someone she knew then, which means we probably know him, too. Jim Peters—does he know her? He's strong enough."

"And Farnsberry."

"Garrett Flint, too. We know nothing about him. Could be a woman. Maybe Joanna Carpenter has that much anger in her—"

"Working in a *library*?"

"Or Madge Simmons—but I'd think she'd get rid of her aggression through gossip. It makes sense that whoever killed Jonas also hurt Miss Edna, since they were once married."

"Maybe."

"Or maybe not. I have no clue about anything."

"Burke said it doesn't look good that you're injured, too."

That got my attention. "What do you mean?"

"He says you'll be accused of knocking Edna around, that she tried to stop you by hitting you over the head. And you didn't feel the effects until you got to your own kitchen and passed out."

"That's just absurd." But, of course, no one could verify my story, except the broken glass on my kitchen floor. 'You staged it'—I could just imagine Burke saying that when I mentioned the glass. Oh, my

139

head pounded wickedly. I just couldn't think about this right now. "One more thing to deal with."

"Here, Soph." A luscious-looking pile of lasagna blocked my view of Terri's kitchen. "Stop talking and eat." Terri gets bossy in her mother mode. "You'll need your strength to tree-hop with Vivian tonight."

I glanced over at my sweet friend. "You might have to take my place. You're certainly dressed for it."

She placed a napkin by my plate. "I'm in my pajamas because you are. I'm pretending we're having a slumber party." She looked outside. I could see worry in her eyes.

My eyes watered.

Wait a minute. My eyes watered? I never cry. Not ever. I usually sit in a stupor and stare, if I have the emotions that evoke tears, and then I happily rip someone's head off, even if it's just imaginary and inside a book. "Wearing pajamas won't put a happy face on what's happened to Jonas, Miss Edna, and me." I grabbed her hand. "Thank you for this. You're my BFF always."

She nodded and tried to smile, but her mouth wobbled. "The second F means forever, silly."

"Forever always."

Then she teared up, I fought back tears, and we hugged and cried together and let our food get cold.

♦

I sat inside Jonas' four-foot by six-foot metal shed on an oily-smelling push mower covered with a plastic tarp, with Vivian's bony knees in my side. She sat on a small table, the only other place to sit, while Terri stood and looked out the slit in the door.

The tiny shed was crammed with machinery, yard tools, a moose head, old furniture, paint cans, rakes, and a mounted deer head. The smell from oily rags almost made me gag. Spider webs and accompanying spiders caused me to shiver and curl up in a tighter knot. Words like "sardines" and "peas" and "stuffed turkey" came to mind. And maybe "duh" and "dim-witted", too.

But here we all were.

Jonas didn't have a night light in his yard, but the light spilling over from Mrs. LeGraff's pole—and mine—was enough for us to see, a kind of Twilight Zone feature with just enough dark in it to thrill the fiercest lover of terror.

I could think of only one thing: monsters love this kind of setting. I hoped—and sent a prayer of protection to God—that no monsters would find us in our attempt to solve these mysteries. "I can't believe we're doing this," I whispered to my cohorts.

"It's better than sitting in a tree for hours." Terri turned to me. "How's your head? You shouldn't be here, you know."

"It's fine. I had three naps today. Besides, I can't let you and Vivian have all the fun."

Vivian grunted and sent one of her skinny legs airborne over the lawn mower. The other one followed. She looked out one of the many holes in the door that appeared to have been made by gunshot. "Szzzzttt."

I leaned over and placed one of my eyes in a hole in the wall. "What is it? Is she here?"

"No. Samson and Moocher are." Vivian opened the door to the metal shed and the two dogs, with wagging tails and slurping, oh-boy-it's-a-party tongues, joined us.

Both dogs found my face and lathered it, despite my protests. "All right, already, boys. Hey, hey. No sniffing. No licks. Now, behave. We have to be quiet."

Every creature stilled when something sniffed at the door, followed by a "Meow" and scratching.

"Yoda's here, boys." Terri leaned over and caught the cat as he stepped inside.

I took Yoda when he squirmed out of Terri's arms. "Well, the

141

gang's all here. I hope Ingrid plans on joining us."

Vivian moved to another hole. "If she does, wouldn't it be a hoot if she came back here, looking for a tool or something?" She snickered, I laughed, Terri giggled, and Samson barked, which caused the hair to rise on Yoda's back. Moocher nudged Yoda, and Yoda responded with an indignant screech.

"All right, boys. Enough." I tapped each on the head. Surprisingly, they quieted, but I could still hear giggles coming from Vivian and Terri. "Oh, stop it, you two. It's bad enough—"

"Szzzzttt."

Jonas' back screen door squawked. I moved to where I could see, but whoever it was had already entered the house.

A flashlight appeared again, sweeping each room that we could see. In breathless silence, we watched it head toward the back door again and click off.

"Szzzzttt."

"I know, I know. What's he doing in there?"

"No, what's he doing out here."

I looked through the slit again and out sauntered Burke onto the back porch. The light came on again as he swept the back yard with it. The light smacked me right in the eye. "Oh, no." I tried not to groan, but I knew what was coming. "Everybody be quiet," I pleaded. Maybe, just maybe, he won't—

"Here he comes."

"Hurry. Lock the door," I whispered.

"There's no lock on the inside," Terri whispered back.

We all held our breaths, even the animals.

Burke stopped just outside the metal shed.

Then the door opened.

I stifled a giggle. Terri spurted a laugh and quickly covered her mouth. I couldn't help myself: I laughed out loud, and beside me, Vivian giggled. The dogs jumped up, wagging their tails, and licked Burke's hand.

142

The flashlight landed on my face. "Sophie, what in God's green earth are you doing out here?"

It was uncanny how this man always caught me doing something wrong. I did a lot of good things, too, but was he ever around when I did? No. He must have an internal radar system aimed right at me when a law is being broken. "Uh, we, uh."

The light shined in Terri's eyes. "Terri? She pulled you into this? Why, hello, Vivian. You don't surprise me, but the rest of this hunting party does."

"Szzzzttt. Someone's here."

Burke turned off the light and gently shut the door. But before it closed, Samson's nose caught it. I whispered, "Samson, no!" and reached for him, but he was too quick. He shot out the door, barking and snarling.

Burke stood in the crack of the door, blocking my view. I nudged him aside, and he pushed me back. "This is now official business, Sophie."

"Official business, my eye. Move over." I bared my teeth for special effect. He hipped me back, clearly unimpressed with the threat of danger facing him.

Only Samson's whimper stopped my hand from shoving Burke. "What's wrong with Samson?"

"He opened the back door and went inside."

"Wow. That's great eye-paw coordination."

Burke chuckled and opened the metal shed door. Moocher zoomed past him, nosed Jonas' not-quite-closed screen door open and joined his friend inside. "Partners in crime," Burke said just as someone screamed from inside the house.

Out stumbled Virginia Crane. She was sucking her thumb like a two-year-old.

"Virginia Crane? What is *she* doing here?" I demanded of Burke, but his response was to step outside, shut the door—grrrrrr!—and call out to the woman.

143

"Mrs. Crane? I sure am surprised to see you here, ma'am."

"Give it up, Virginia," I murmured as I eased the door open a crack to see what she was wearing since all I could make out were her face and hands. Black tennis shoes, black pants, a black blouse, and a black knit cap.

Virginia tugged out her thumb and studied it. "That little dog bit me!"

Burke shifted his feet. I couldn't see his face, but I'm sure it wore a pleasant ah-that-mean-ol'-dog-bit-you-honey look. He shined the light on her thumb, bent over, and held the injured digit while his head and the light rotated around it. "He got you, Mrs. Crane. That's for sure."

She tugged her appendage out of his hold. "I need to get home and bandage this." She started around Burke, but he turned, stopped her by saying, "I'll be happy to take you, ma'am."

"I have my own car, Officer."

Now that he was facing the shed now, I could see the pleasant look on his face. "What are you doing here, ma'am, at this time of night?"

"I was... I was...." Virginia glanced over her shoulder as if she could feel me leaning toward her, trying to help pry the words out of her. "When Jonas and Edna were married, we were all good friends. Jonas took pictures of me and my late husband years ago. I was trying to find those pictures when I was interrupted by these two dogs."

"You don't have pictures of your husband, ma'am?" There was that sweet smile again.

"He took them. The day he died."

"He?"

"My husband."

"Took them?"

She fidgeted with her thumb. "The car burned, along with my pictures. I wanted one to compare it to—" She gasped and placed the sore-thumb hand over her mouth.

144

"Compare it to?"

"Frank Zagorsky, if you must know." Her voice wobbled. "I haven't slept since that night. I just need to know. Is he my husband, Officer? That's not too much to ask, is it?" From her pants pocket, she pulled out a hankie and dabbed at her eyes. She folded it and stuck it back in. "My thumb hurts, and I need a bandage. Are you arresting me?"

"Not tonight, ma'am." When she walked past him, he said, "Oh. Did you find any pictures?"

"No," she answered as her lips thinned into a firm line. "I checked Edna's house, too, if you must know. I couldn't find any there either. And, yes, I have a key to her house as well as Jonas'."

"Yes, ma'am." With those two little words, Burke had given his permission for her to leave, and she did.

After a few moments, I marched out of the metal shed. "Why are you letting her go? You could have asked her more questions. Like, 'Why would your husband come back here as Frank Zagorsky if there was even a remote chance he'd run into you?' Or, 'Why would your husband have all the pictures of himself in his car the day he had a wreck that burned him to death?' Wait. Wait just a minute." I touched Burke's arm. "He was leaving her. He took everything he owned, including the pictures, and drove off with them, not knowing he'd be leaving this earth, too."

Instead of responding to my theory, Burke went inside Jonas' house. I followed him. He didn't turn on any lights, and I was spooked. "What are you looking for?"

"I don't know, but the picture story doesn't wash. She took something or planted something in here, and I intend to find it."

"Planted? But why? Who would find it now that Jonas is gone?"

"Me. Or Garrett Flint."

I could not follow the man's logic an inch. "But you weren't expected here. And why not *hand* it to Garrett? Why stage a break-in and admit to entering Edna's house as well?"

"Go home, Sophie. You're beginning to make sense."

"I always make sense. Do you think Garrett could have killed Jonas?"

"And Sharon. Yes."

"Vivian said he's too idealistic to kill anyone."

"She would say that now that she and Flint are in a relationship."

A relationship? "Oh, that's wonderful. Unless, of course, he *is* the killer." I stepped out the back door, but my head hurt like the dickens, and I felt woozy.

"Here." Terri wrapped me in her arms and led me down the steps. "You and Vivian and I can have a cup of tea at your house."

Burke stood in the doorway.

"Is my house cleared now, Officer?"

He waved us on.

I didn't argue. But when I turned around to invite Vivian to our party, she was gone.

Terri said, "She's onto something."

"What do you mean?"

"I was watching her when she saw Virginia Crane. It's like she put two and two together. She knows something, and Virginia is the key."

"Then we'd better make sure Virginia got home tonight in one piece."

♦

But she wasn't home. I stood on her front porch and threw up my hands. "Now what?"

A breeze rustled the leaves of the trees surrounding Virginia's house while a soft moon hid behind them. Ghostly light filtered through the branches and made the night even creepier.

"We wait?" Terri stifled a yawn.

"We could be here all night. You're tired. I'm tired."

A hooded head popped out from behind a large tree.

146

I was totally freaked now. "Did you... did you see—?"

"Yeah." Terri grabbed my arm and tugged. "We're leaving."

I tugged back. "Did you see his face? We can't leave without knowing who he is."

"He might be the one who hit you over the head. We're out of here." Terri opened the car door and shoved me inside.

I jumped back out and clutched my aching head. "I need to see—"

"He's gone now, Soph."

"You don't know that."

"He ran the other way."

"Then it's safe to go over there."

"But he might be there!"

"Good!"

"Then let me get in the car and shine the lights so you can see."

"All right." I waited until the lights were on. I fast-walked to the nearest tree and did my own head-popping. At the corner of the lot was a small house—a guest house?

"Are you looking for me?" A head popped out and frightened a scream out of me.

"W-Who are you?"

Herman Farnsberry pushed off his hood. "Listen to me, Sophie. Stay away from Virginia. You'll only end up getting hurt." And with those words, he jogged toward the woods.

"Wait! Wait!" I ran after him. "Mr. Farnsberry, I deserve some answers from you. Stop!" Surprisingly, I caught up with him.

He started fast walking. "I can't tell you anything. After tonight, you'll never see me again." He pulled out a flashlight and turned it on when we entered a darker part of the woods.

"What do you know? Who killed Jonas? Who killed your two wives?" I grabbed his arm and made him stop. "Tell me. Please. You know I'm hip-deep in this mess. I need your help."

"That, I can't give you."

147

He tried to pull away from me, but I found myself surprisingly strong when I held him still. "Did you set me up?"

"No."

"But you know who did, don't you?"

The look he sent me said he did. But the sadness and pain I also saw there made me lower my voice. "Why can't you tell me?"

"Because you'll end up dead, too, if you know. I didn't find out until two months ago, but it's too late for me. I made a promise, and I have to keep running."

His words chilled me. "Who is it?"

He shook his head, and I let go of his arm.

Twin beams appeared out of nowhere, aimed right for us. Of course, his sister, Ingrid, was driving the SUV. Farnsberry looked at me. "I have to go. Leave Virginia alone, and you won't be targeted."

"Why are you here now?"

The SUV stopped beside Mr. Farnsberry. He opened the car door, glanced back at me, said, "I'm so sorry," and got in.

The wilting old woman I'd met on Farnsberry's front porch wasn't at the wheel. In the dashboard's glow, I saw a modern-looking, fashion-minded, face-made-up Ingrid frown at me, her lips firm. Seeing her like this, all dolled up—she reminded me of someone, but I couldn't think of whom.

Off they drove. The little light above the license plate gave me the number. I walked toward Terri's car, but every time I startled at the wind in the trees or a snapping twig, the numbers and letters flew across my brain like shuffling wood chips.

Terri hurried toward me. "Are you okay? Who was he?"

I shook my head and slid inside. "Herman Farnsberry."

"You're joking." Terri got in and started the car.

"I wish I was." What could he have possibly meant by telling me Virginia was a threat? No, no. He didn't say *Virginia* was a threat, just that being near her was a threat. Was someone targeting her?

"What did he say to you?"

"Not enough. I know nothing more than before I talked to him."
I rolled down the window and let the warm humid breeze buffet my
face. Terri knew me well enough to know I would talk when I was
ready. Thankfully, she drove me home in silence.

When she pulled into my driveway, she announced, "I'm staying
over." I opened my mouth to protest, but she said, "Don't argue with
me. We'll have a real slumber party this time. I can borrow a pair of
your pajamas."

"If they won't fall off your skinny bones. But first, call your
mother and see if she can dig up some dirt on Virginia Crane."

I opened my front door. My security lights were on, and
everything was in place. My phone rang. It was Vivian. She was in my
backyard tree.

It seemed a perfect ending to this bizarre day.

My time was short to get this mystery—several mysteries—solved
before the paint report came back. I heard Terri on the phone with
her mother as I opened the back door and stepped outside into
silence.

"Vivian?"

Leaves rustled. Since she didn't answer, I supposed that was all the
response I could expect. "Why don't you get down and come inside
for some tea?"

When she didn't respond, I went inside, let the screen door shut,
and closed the back door. I was in no mood to play games with her
tonight. But after a couple more minutes and she still hadn't come
inside, I opened the back door.

A note was between the door and the frame: *I think I know who
killed Farnsberry's wives and who hurt Jonas and Edna. I'll talk to you soon.
Your friend, Vivian.*

12

I paced. I fretted. I worried. Vivian wasn't at home, and I had no idea where to check for her. Surely, she wouldn't confront the killer by herself. Surely.

I now believed that Farnsberry wasn't involved in any of this. Really, I never thought deep-down that he was capable of murder. The man is a grouch and unfriendly and just plain grumpy, but I struggled with connecting any dots that seemed to point to him as the culprit, which meant the murderer was good at misdirection, and my friend, Vivian, might have fallen for it.

What did she see that I hadn't seen? What clues did she add up to figure this out? The only time she could gather clues was at night.

My sleepless nights might be put to good use now.

Right. Climbing trees. Good grief. What had my life come to?

And where should I look for Vivian? Virginia's house? No need to climb trees there. The woman was alone in a vast sea of trees and brush. It was the only logical place to start, since the other people involved in this were out of the picture—Edna, Farnsberry, Jonas, Clarke, Laura, Sharon and her sister Selma.

So, back to Virginia's house.

The headache that had been stomping around my brain the past two days was gone this morning, thanks to several hours of deep sleep. I dressed quickly and quietly so I wouldn't wake Terri. She'd been a trooper until about midnight, when I made her go to bed. Hopefully, she would sleep until ten or so. I tiptoed down the hall and reached—

"Where are you going?"

I spun around to face Terri's mussed hair, poofy eyes, and cranky glare. Her crossed arms said I could hang up any protest or any attempt to talk my way out of this one.

Okay. Plan B, the truth. "I'm worried about Vivian. I think the first place to look for her is at Virginia's house."

"Why there?"

"Because Farnsberry warned us to stay away from her, not because she was a threat, but because she was being targeted by someone. If Vivian went there, then—"

"All right. Got it."

I grabbed my purse off the hall table. "Are you going with me? Because if you're not, I need to go."

Terri sighed, looked at the ceiling, and then flapped a hand at me. "Give me five minutes to brush my teeth and hair and clothe my bod. It's a good thing I took off a couple days. I just didn't plan on spending them like *this*." She stepped into her room and then popped her head out. "Don't leave without me."

Thirty minutes later, under overcast skies, we drove up Virginia's long driveway. I expected to see something hooded pop out from behind every tree. I hadn't called Burke yet to tell him about seeing Farnsberry. It really made no difference in the investigation. So Farnsberry was hiding out. What else was new?

I gasped as we approached Virginia's house. Her front door was wide open, and leaves somersaulted their way into the foyer.

"Stop, Terri. The door."

"I see it."

"What should we do?"

"Call Burke."

"And get yelled at for being stupid again?"

"Are we being stupid, Soph?"

"Probably. But aren't you even a little curious why her front door is open, and leaves are blowing inside her perfectly meticulous home?"

"Not at all."

"Well, I am. Her car's not here."

"Maybe she parked it in the garage. If it's not there, maybe she forgot to shut the door when she left."

151

"That's not likely. Pull up to the garage and let me check through the window." She did, I looked inside, and the Cadillac wasn't there. But another car was. "I'm going inside the house."

"Here." Terri tugged her folded up, teeny-tiny umbrella from under her seat and handed it to me. "Use this, if you have to. But I'm only giving you one minute inside the house. If you're not back in one minute—" She pulled out her phone, punched some buttons, then showed me the stopwatch. "—I'm calling Burke."

I took the umbrella. On some level, I was sure it was better than absolutely nothing.

"Okay," Terri said and punched her phone. "Go!"

With the umbrella in front of me like a sword, I walked slowly into the house. I wanted to say, "Hey, Virginia. We were just passing by and thought, since your door was open, that we'd—" But the mess in her living room caused me to bite my tongue.

Quiet.

Hot.

Stuffy.

Nothing stirred in the house but the leaves at the front door. I was so afraid I'd find her body. I inched toward the sofa. On the coffee table sat a teacup on a saucer and a bagel on a plate.

I stopped. My heart raced. My breathing hitched.

I cocked my ear and listened for any sound, like maybe footsteps, heavy breathing, blood dripping. The air conditioning came on, and I just about jumped out of my skin.

I tiptoed farther into the room. "V-Virginia?" I could hardly breathe. Where was Rita? It was after eight in the morning. Surely, she showed up for work by eight o'clock. If so, she was late.

I rounded the sofa and screamed bloody murder!

Her high heel shoes were the first thing I saw, but they weren't attached to any feet. Shaking like a scaredy cat, I crept closer and spotted a small pool of blood on the floor beside her sofa. I captured another exiting scream with my trembling hands.

Terri appeared in the doorway, wide-eyed and breathless with her cell phone in her shaking hand.

"Call Burke!" I screamed. "Call Burke! Something's happened to Virginia Crane!"

♦

Virginia's maid, Rita—who usually arrives at nine—and Terri huddled with me in a tight circle on a concrete bench while police walked the area on the other side of the yellow tape. I was still shaking. When someone—I think it was Burke—placed a light blanket across my shoulders, I just about jumped off the bench. An overcast day in Texas in early October didn't necessarily translate into the use of a light wool blanket, but I suppose my hysterics when Burke arrived prompted him to give me one.

I let it slide off my shoulders and onto the bench. I imagined Virginia sitting on this bench on a cool evening, enjoying a cup of hot tea or coffee. But if Virginia was dead, where was her body? And if she got away from her killer, then where was the blood trail? Burke said with the amount of blood she'd lost that there should be a blood trail if she was able to get away. Maybe someone wrapped her head so there *wouldn't* be a blood trail and removed her body.

Who could have done this to her?

Rita sobbed beside me.

I glanced at her. She seemed genuinely upset that Virginia might have been hurt or killed.

"Are you okay now?" Burke whispered in my ear as he touched my shoulder.

For the life of me, I couldn't stop the chills running up and down my arms. It seemed inappropriate at a crime scene to have such reactions to a puff of air. I nodded quickly, rubbing my arms. "I am. Thanks." I hoped he wouldn't move his hand, but he did. Despite the warmth of the day, my shoulder felt cool where his hand had been.

"Tell me again what happened here, Soph."

"Okay."

This time, he didn't write anything down. He recorded it. I told him about Vivian's note, about my conclusion that Virginia's home was the reasonable place to look for her. I described how I crept into the house and found the pool of blood on the carpet.

"You didn't see anyone, hear anyone?"

"No. After I found the blood, I screamed. Terri came running, and I told her to call you. I had no idea Virginia was in trouble. I was just looking for Vivian—she said she knew who the killer was. I'm afraid Vivian is in danger."

"Did you try her house?"

"Yes."

"I'll need you and Terri to come down to the station and sign your reports of what happened here. Terri, you have your car, so we'll meet you there."

As he walked off, I hurried to catch up with him. He didn't think I had something to do with whatever happened to Virginia, did he?

He reached his car and opened the front passenger door for me. On the way over to the station, neither of us said a word. I'd told the truth as best I knew how. If he didn't believe me, then that's fine. I wondered if this was a good time to remind him of our friendship pact.

When he frowned at me, I decided it wasn't. But I'd remind him of it at the first sign of handcuffs heading my way.

◆

I signed the papers, but the police chief wanted to see me. He and my father had been friends since kindergarten. Linc Johnston was of medium build and height, in his mid-fifties, with the meanest eyes you've ever seen—pale steel, with a black ring around them. He would've made a good vampire in a horror movie.

"Young lady, you're in a heap of trouble."

154

Well, what did that mean? What kind of trouble? My editor and agent couldn't be happier. My last three books have soared in sales the past two weeks, so I'm not in trouble with them. I haven't broken any laws—well, illegal trespass, but no one pressed charges. I haven't seen my parents in about three years. Daddy called from time to time to check on me, but the chances of them coming here to see me were little to none. And my older twin brothers would just want to know details about the bloody crime scene, so I was okay with them.

Who was I in trouble with?

"I am?"

"You am." He smiled. No, it was more of a drunk smirk. I sniffed. I didn't smell alcohol. I wondered if I had any hope of getting out of this trouble because he and my dad had been friends for years. I looked into those mean eyes. Nope. No hope of that at all.

"You have a penchant for getting into trouble lately."

"It's a mess, for sure."

"Is that what you call it? Your neighbor's cat goes missing, and he accuses you."

"Yoda's alive."

"Then Jonas Whitworth's death. You were the last to see him alive."

I cleared my throat. "Not exactly, Chief. The killer saw Jonas last alive. Uh, alive last. Was the last to see Jonas alive." I smiled and blinked quickly—convincingly, I hoped, as an innocent would when accosted by a surly ol' pirate with evil intentions.

"Then there's Edna Conroy. You sat with her at Jonas' wake. Y'all pretty chummy, are you?"

"Not really. She goes to my church."

He raised his brows.

"Yes, I go to church. Edna and I have known *of* each other for many years, but no, we're not chummy. Close enough to talk from time to time but not close enough to spend time together like girlfriends do."

That seemed to amuse our police chief because he laughed, scanned my report, and then sobered. "And now Virginia Crane. What is your connection to her?"

Do you have all day?

I sighed, resigned. "She worked at the middle school I attended when Mr. Farnsberry was my principal. I visited her the other day for the first time since then and found her very interesting. I asked her questions about Mr. Farnsberry."

"Why?"

"He accused me of killing his cat, which wasn't true. I wondered why. They're old friends so I thought she might be able to help me figure out the why."

"And did she?"

"Not really."

"You saw her at the memorial dinner for Jonas Whitworth."

"I did."

"She left suddenly."

"She did."

"Why?"

"I couldn't say, Chief. She seemed rattled when she spotted Frank Zagorsky."

"Rattled?"

I lifted a shoulder, knowing this next statement would cause a smirk or a rolling of his eyes. "She thought he was her husband, the husband who was blown up in his car years before."

But he did neither. He calmly closed the file, laced his fingers, rested his hands on the file, and stared at me for at least five seconds. "And now Virginia Crane is missing. Sophie, I know your father very well. I don't think he'd appreciate the fact that you're somehow involved in these crimes. If he was here, what would you say to him?"

Oh, brother. I tried hard not to look angry or show how ridiculous I thought this question was. "I'd tell him I knew two of the murder victims just a little and that I was sorry they had died."

"I talked to your daddy yesterday. He's worried about you. Asked me to keep an eye out for you."

"I might need both your eyes on me, Chief." He chuckled, and I said, "Do you have any suspects? Any idea who might be behind all this?"

He nodded. "We do, but I can't say any more. Ongoing investigation and all that. But I can say this: be careful. You might want to stay with a friend until the suspect is apprehended."

Well, what did that mean? "Are you saying I'm a target, too?"

"I'm not trying to frighten you, Sophie, but you need to take this threat seriously. Simple things. Don't answer the door unless you know who's there. Lock your windows. Keep your doors locked at all times. Keep your cell phone handy. Do you have a gun?"

"No."

"Then get one." He stood, pushed in his chair. "Thanks for your time. You're free to go."

I was rattled by his words. I loved living alone, so staying with someone—it would be Terri, of course—until these crimes were solved was not an option. At least I had Moocher. He'd bark and warn me if someone tried to come into my home.

The sun had come out. Its brightness made my eyes water, and I rubbed them fiercely. I wondered how I was supposed to get home. Burke had driven me here, but he was nowhere in sight. Nor was Terri.

I walked to the sidewalk and looked right, then left, and spotted Madge Simmons coming out of the Pastry Shoppe. She carried a big box and smiled at someone hailing her from a passing car. She worked at City Hall as a utilities department collector. I was sure that's how she uncovered most of the secrets in Forman Falls: "I'm sorry; I can't pay my bill; my husband ran out on me last night with that bimbo from Crockett, and he didn't leave me a *dime*, I tell ya. Not a dime!"

Uh-hmmm. A veritable gold mine of gossip, working at the utilities department.

She spotted me and lifted her chin. "Hey, Sophie. You got a minute?"

I walked in her direction. She set the big box on her back seat, shut the door, and met me in the middle of the street. "Do you have time for a cup?" she asked and guided me away from her car toward the coffee shop.

"Sure," I said. I couldn't imagine what in the world she wanted to talk to me about. Maybe the ladies with the Well-Being Retreat had changed their minds about inviting me to speak at their event.

Madge ordered a latte. I ordered green tea. I hate it, but in my effort to become healthier, I've taken up green tea with lots of honey and half-and-half—a girl can change just so much all at once. I glared at Burke, wherever he was, for pushing me in this direction. *Could you hike a long distance?* Inferring, of course, that I couldn't make it on the hike with him to find Sharon's grave. Well, we'll just see about that, Mr. Fit and Firm. I glared at the green tea for good measure.

Madge and I sat by the window.

"Did you know—" Madge leaned in closer. "That—" She lowered her voice even more. "Edna had a baby in Europe while she was in college?"

Well, she'd shocked me. "No, I didn't know she had any children."

Madge nodded in wide arcs. "She gave it up for adoption somewhere."

Really? "Okay. I'll bite. Where is the child?"

"I have no idea. I was told Edna doesn't even know where he or she is."

"Who told you?"

"Someone whispered it at Jonas's memorial dinner when I was walking by, but I don't know who said it. They were standing behind a partition." Madge lifted her brows, dipped her chin, and blinked at me.

What did that look mean?

She innocently shrugged. "I'd never heard it until that night." She nodded slowly and didn't say anything else. Was she like Terri, that I have to pull every morsel of information out of her mouth?

"Does anyone else know this?"

Madge shrugged, pursed her lips, and shook her head. "I've only told you."

I didn't know that "only told you" was in Madge's vocabulary. "Do you know anything about the baby?"

"Given up for adoption. Nothing else."

I didn't want to hear any more, but then again, I did. *Let no one deceive you with empty words.* My mother's most cited scripture. 'Empty words' being what? Gossip? Lies? Truth that could kill, wrapped in a whisper? Or just plain having a conversation? "I really can't stay, Madge." I picked up my tea. "By the way, your information on Burke Maguire was wrong. He didn't have a dishonorable discharge. It was honorable. Have a good day."

I approached the counter to get a refill and who came out of the restroom but Rita. "Oh, Rita. How are you? Did they interrogate you, too?" I glanced over at Madge, to watch her reaction at seeing Rita here, but she was scooting out the door in a hurry.

Tears filled Rita's eyes, and she shook back her hair. She opened her mouth to say something but lowered her head and said nothing.

I touched her arm. "If I can do anything to help, let me know. I'm truly sorry for your loss."

Again, she smiled weakly. Pain etched her face. She nodded then and walked to the counter and ordered a tall latte with the quietest voice I have ever heard. She paid for her order and edged down to the rounded corner of the counter to wait for the coffee to appear. She never once looked at me, although I hadn't moved. Virginia's death had apparently wounded Rita deeply—or she was putting on quite the show. But what would she have to gain by pretending to be devastated?

The server handed her the coffee order. She mumbled, "Thank

you," and left.

I couldn't help but wonder what she would do for income now that Virginia was dead.

Wait a minute. What was that?

I tossed my tea in the trashcan, rushed out the door, and caught up with her. "Rita, I couldn't help but notice the beautiful ring you're wearing. It's quite unusual. Was it specially made?" Virginia had worn that stunning ring, beautiful jewels encircling a bright ruby, on the night of the memorial for Jonas Whitworth. So why was her maid wearing it now?

Rita lifted her hand slowly and stared at the ring. "She gave it to me the day after Jonas' memorial. She was dying, you know, and passed out gifts like they were candy. She advised me to sell it until I could get another job, but I would never do that. It means too much to me that it's from her."

"I didn't know she was sick. What was wrong with her?"

"Cancer. She had a few months to live. I knew about it; she was gracious enough to tell me, so I could pursue other work. But I didn't. I wanted to stay with her until, you know, the end."

"Does she have any family?"

Rita blanched at my question and blinked several times. "I worked for her for over six months. I considered her my family. I believe she felt the same about me." Tears welled in her eyes.

I touched her arm. What was it with me today? Touchy-feely was not in my DNA. "I'm so sorry, Rita. I'd like to keep our coffee date, whenever you're ready. How about now? Do you have a few minutes?"

She shook her head. "I can't. I just, I'm sorry."

"Another time, then."

When she nodded, I smiled and started back toward the police department. Terri was sitting on the bench outside the double glass doors. I slipped onto the bench beside her.

"Who was that you were talking to?"

"Rita, Virginia's maid. She had Virginia's ruby-and-diamond ring on. From Jonas' memorial?"

"I remember it. Every woman there drooled over that ring. Did she steal it?"

"She said Virginia was dying from cancer and that it was one of several gifts from her. I wonder if Burke knows yet if Virginia had any heirs. There he is. Let's ask him." I needed to tell him about Edna's baby, too.

Burke parked, got out, and walked around the front of his car. "Hey. How did the interrogations go?"

I shrugged. "More of a conversation with a grumpy uncle. I sailed through mine."

Terri grunted. "Not me. I didn't know much, but the interrogator assumed I did. It was frustrating."

A car honked, and Burke turned his head toward the sound. A blonde in a convertible buzzed by and waved. "Hey, Burke!" Her singsongy voice carried over the other noises on the busy street. He lifted his chin—and his hand in a wave—and muttered, "Yeah, yeah."

He looked at Terri, then me. "Ladies, it's getting close to lunch, and I'm hungry. How about eating with me at Grannie Vee's? My treat."

I glanced over my shoulder at the beautiful blonde and her convertible, and at the very least, I wanted to grit my teeth and glare at her. But I didn't. So, Burke was making friends. Goody for him.

13

Grannie Vee's Kitchen was just a couple blocks away.

Inside one of the oldest houses in town, the restaurant was in the original downtown and was, by far, the most popular place to eat in Forman Falls. Great oaks hovered over the brick walkways; wrought iron benches sat every thirty feet or so; old-fashioned street lamps lit the way at night. A multitude of colorful flowers burst out of big clay pots lining the long brick sidewalk to the restaurant.

Terri walked in the middle of our threesome. "I hope we have time to finish our meal before the storm gets here."

"The storm? Is it supposed to rain?" I hadn't gotten any alerts about a storm, and then I remembered I'd turned my phone off just before my interrogation. I pulled it out, turned it on.

"Supposed to rain a lot, but what else is new?"

When we stopped in front of Grannie Vee's, Burke opened the door, and Terri stepped inside. I followed. Behind me, Burke said, "Three," to the hostess today, Grannie Dee, who was every bit of seventy-five, and at five-foot, was as wide as she was tall, just like her sister, Grannie Vee.

"This way," she said and guided us to the very back of the restaurant. Granny Dee knew what she was doing: our jaunt was for the entertainment of everyone sitting in the restaurant. A hush fell across the eatery as we strolled past, all eyes on us—or rather, on me.

When I sat, Granny Dee smiled at me and leaned over. "If I've ever done anything to make you mad at me, Sophie—" Her hearing loss had her practically shouting. "—I'm putting it on public record right now that I'm sorry and I'm hopin' you'll forgive me."

The gleam in her eye that followed her loud request told me she'd said that for the benefit of her patrons. A swell of chuckles and laughter, like a wave, swept over the restaurant. I laughed right along with them. "Well, shoot, I was so looking forward to adding you to my list, Grannie Dee."

Everyone laughed again and then settled down.

"Well done," Burke said, lowering his menu. Laughter wrinkles appeared around his eyes, the only part of his face showing above his menu.

Beside me, Terri raised her menu to hide her face. "Look who just walked in."

I glanced at the front door and gasped. My *mother?* What was she doing here? I didn't even know she was in town or, for that matter, where she lived these days. I raised my menu and whispered, "Terri, hide. We don't want her to—"

"Too late. She's coming this way."

I held my breath. I couldn't do this. The woman never talked. She just sat and did nothing. Sighing, of course—those horrible, disapproving sighs that spoke more than mere words.

"Wait, wait. She's pulling out a chair, Soph. No, a woman called her over to the other side of the room." Terri leaned over. "I can't see who it is."

"Great. We can make it out the back door. Come on."

"Oh, no."

I sat back down. "What?"

"Here she comes again. Someone must have told her you were over here."

"She wouldn't come see me if we weren't out in public."

"I know," Terri answered and touched my arm. "I'm sorry."

I groaned. My shoulders hurt from the stress of waiting for her arrival. A chair scraped on the wood floor when it scooted back. I could only assume that Burke had stood and tugged out a chair for her.

"Hello."

"Ma'am," Burke said.

Here goes.

163

I lowered the menu. My gaze crawled up my mother's simple gray dress, her bonnet strings, her unpainted mouth, and up to her unadorned green eyes. I offered her a weak smile. I tried to stretch it out to include the rest of my cheeks, but it would not oblige me. "Hello, Mother."

"May I sit?"

"Of course."

She sat.

Folded her hands on her lap.

And stared at her hands.

The plain life suited her. I assumed it was a low-key, quiet life where she probably didn't interact with many people, just stayed in her home or worked her five acres with Daddy.

"Mother." I indicated Burke with my hand. "This is Officer Maguire." No sense in telling her it was Burke Maguire, the cad who'd dumped me before my senior year. I'm not sure she even knew that my heart had been crushed. She had never been that interested in my friends or my life. "You know Terri Smaller."

She nodded and smiled shyly at Burke, at Terri, and then continued to stare at her hands. I didn't know what to do right now—should I speak and embarrass her, or should I stay quiet and cause discomfort for everyone around us?

"How are you and Daddy, Mother?"

"We're blessed. And you?"

I nodded quickly several times and thought of a bobbing head toy or maybe a wide-eyed little girl in pigtails, constantly in motion. That's the way I felt around my mother. I have always thought she disapproved of me and that I had to be someone else around her, someone quiet, like her. I had an overwhelming desire to whisper when I was near her.

"I'm well." I would never say 'I'm well', but I get around her, and I start talking like a cultured woman. "I'm fine." My gaze darted to Burke.

He lifted his brows in that look that says, "Yes, I remember."

I had never figured out why my mother couldn't seem to hold a conversation with me or with anyone else. Shyness, of course. Reserved. Introverted. I never understood how such a shy woman could have such a gregarious child. I know she didn't deserve me, but here I was. "How's the farm?"

She nodded quickly. "We're all fine."

The waitress, Shirley Sinclair, a great-niece to Grannie Vee, walked up cheerfully and said, "Hey! Y'all ready to order now?"

She had beautiful teeth. My gaze transfixed on how white and straight they were. "Oh, uh, no. We haven't—"

My mother stood straight up with her hands still folded at her waist. "I won't keep you." She dipped her head at Burke and Terri and left me with the word she'd greeted me with: "Sophie."

"Mother. Tell Daddy I said 'hey'."

"He sends his love to you." Then she turned and left.

But you don't.

I sighed oh-so-deeply and closed my eyes. I needed a moment to gather myself. I hated to admit that my whole body trembled like a leaf in a steady breeze, but that's my lot around my mother. She makes the people around her uncomfortable, as if she's on autopilot.

Terri finished giving her order to Shirley—a salad and no dessert. No wonder she was so skinny.

I opened my eyes and said, "I'll have the fried chicken with mashed potatoes smothered in white gravy with green beans and pecan pie."

Terri leaned over and carried the menu with her. "That extra ten will become twenty if you eat like that." At least she'd had the grace and good sense to lower her voice to me. Maybe Burke hadn't heard her.

"The ten looks good."

Yep, he'd heard. I eased my eyes above the menu to check his intent and found him grinning at me. He hadn't smiled at me like that since I'd re-met him.

"Eat, Sophie."

I folded the menu and handed it to Shirley. Burke ordered the special, a man's meal of steak and potatoes and ice cream for dessert.

I glanced past Terri, out one of the big glass windows lining this side of the restaurant. The sun was gone, and gray clouds covered the sky. I was surprised to see Samson's owner, Jim Peters, in the parking lot, leaning against an old green pickup with his ankles crossed, his arms folded across his chest, his cap pulled low over his eyes.

Was he looking at me? Or someone else?

I lowered my gaze and eased over to where he couldn't see me. "No, Terri. Don't move. Jim Peters is outside—no, don't look. He's staring at me or-or someone."

I glanced across the restaurant at my mother. She sat at a small table with two women who were not plain, with her gaze mostly on her water glass. A ghost of a smile played around her mouth while her friends laughed, gestured, chatted. She didn't seem to fit in with that trio either, but occasionally, she'd look up and smile or nod and then glance back down at her glass. I had no idea what to do with the woman.

"It's hard to believe it was just this morning that I found the blood in Virginia's house. Have y'all come up with anything, Burke?"

"No, nothing to report."

Terri elbowed me again. I glanced over at my mother. All three women were heading toward the exit. I didn't recognize the other two ladies. Since their visit in this restaurant had been just a few minutes, maybe they were going to another one where my mother would be more comfortable without my presence.

She walked behind her friends. Just as she entered the doorway, she stopped, turned toward me with a blank expression.

I looked at her with the same expression.

And she left.

A part of my heart ached. I wanted—oh, I don't know what I

wanted anymore. Her love and acceptance were beyond my reach. I looked out the window. Jim Peters was gone. My mother walked toward her friend's blue van. The restaurant glass between her and me could as well have been a fortress wall six feet thick. She was standing with her friends, but I couldn't hear them. I couldn't smell the air surrounding them. I couldn't feel the warm breeze that lifted her bonnet strings. A very old ache of yearning grabbed my heart and twisted it.

The van drove off, across the parking lot, and I lost sight of it. Not three seconds later, a loud crash caused me to jerk. Metal on metal. A scream. Then silence.

Burke jumped up and raced out the door. I grabbed Terri's hand and hurried after him.

On the main street in front of Grannie Vee's, the blue van seemed to have an appendage—another car—growing out of the driver's door. A man's gray head rested on the steering wheel as if it were a pillow, the back of his head facing us. His passenger, an older woman holding her forehead with blood streaming through her fingers, was screaming for help. I could hear her even though the windows were up.

My mother rounded her vehicle, her arm hanging limply at an abnormal angle. "Mother, are you all right?"

She presented me with another blank look. I grabbed my cell phone and dialed 9-1-1, but the operator said another caller had already notified them and that two ambulances were on their way to the scene.

I cleared my throat and glanced around for someone to rescue me from having to stand near my mother. Her friend, the driver of the van, opened the driver's door and said, "Esther, are you all right?"

Mother looked over at her friend without any sign of a grimace and said, "I think my arm is broken."

Why couldn't she have answered me that way?

I was—and still am, I presume—an embarrassment to Esther

167

O'Brion. When she chose to go the plain route my senior year in high school, I didn't want to go with her and Daddy to Kansas because I wanted to finish high school. At that point, both of them were an embarrassment to *me*. My friends thought they'd stepped off into the deep end of the cow pond, and I couldn't correct them, because I thought they had, too. Daddy had always been my rock and made up for the distance in my mother, but I felt he'd abandoned me when they left—not five months after Burke dumped me.

One of my older twin brothers—an editor for a scientific research group—lived with me so I could graduate. At least my parents had deeded their house to me. That was something.

But I could never figure out the deeper question of why? Why did my mother resent me? What did she shun me?

The EMTs gently placed Mother on a gurney and rolled her into the ambulance.

"I'll be right behind you, Mother."

She rolled her head away from me.

The ambulance doors shut. The other driver was loaded into the second ambulance; a bandage covered the head of the woman with him, and the EMTs helped her into the back with the man and shut the doors.

Both ambulances started out with lights flashing.

"I'm going back inside the restaurant. Anybody else hungry?"

Terri had silently stood with me, knowing how miserably uncomfortable I was with my mother. "I'm starving."

Burke held onto his duty belt and stared at me. He shifted his feet, looked over his shoulder, and slowly looked back at me.

"Are you hungry?" I repeated, a little edge in the question this time. I was so full of anxiety that I really didn't care if he came with us or not. I'd gladly pay the bill, instead of him, for a little peace and quiet.

Terri squeezed my arm and flicked her head. I followed where she was looking and spotted Frank Zagorsky coming out of a two-story, red brick house, 1940s style, with a wide porch and at least ten steps descending to the sidewalk. He walked down the steps, took a toothpick out of his mouth and flicked it away, and turned right.

Terri leaned toward me. "Whose house is that?"

Burke walked over to us as I shook my head, watching as Frank sauntered to the next block where a black SUV pulled up beside him. Without even looking at the driver, he opened the door and got in.

"Wonder what he's up to?"

Burke laughed at me. "He's a man with at least one friend who just picked him up. I'd bet my last—"

A piercing scream echoed from the house Frank had just left. Burke raced over and up those stairs as if he'd practiced that move all day. He pulled out his weapon, flattened himself against the wall, opened the door, and disappeared inside.

A shot rang out!

I fumbled my phone. With shaking fingers, I dialed 9-1-1 again. This time, I shouted, "Yes, an emergency on Maple Road, a house across from Granny Vee's Restaurant. A gun was discharged. Officer Burke Maguire is inside. Hurry!"

◆

Under overcast skies, Terri and I did as we were told: we got out of the way. Crouching behind an old storage building in the back corner of the parking lot next to Maple Road, brush and trees concealed us, but we could see out. Three patrol cars lined the street. Two policemen rested rifles with scopes on the tops of two cars, while two eased up to the house with their hands gripping their handguns, arms straight and poised to fire.

They made it to the screen door, opened it, and went inside.

I didn't know my heart could beat this hard and fast for so long. I held my breath and listened and watched, but nothing happened for several moments.

169

"Officer down," sounded over the shoulder mike of a cop near us. Burke!

I wanted to run inside and help him. "Why aren't they moving faster? What do they mean by 'down'? Is he alive? Badly hurt? Unconscious?"

"You're panicking, Soph."

"This calls for panic, Terri! What's taking them so long?"

In the stiff wind that had come up the last hour, EMTs ran up the sidewalk with a gurney, lifted it up the stairs, and disappeared inside. I let out a shaky breath.

Terri handed me a tissue.

I took it and wiped tears I hadn't known were rolling down my face. I stared at the front door. Where were the EMTs? Was Burke badly hurt? Was he—?

Terri gripped my arm just as the screen door opened. An emergency tech emerged, guiding the gurney onto the porch. Burke lifted a hand and waved.

"Oh. He's alive!" I hugged Terri, overwhelmed and relieved, and then I placed my hands over my face and sobbed.

"He's okay, Soph. He's okay." She handed me another tissue, and I sopped up the tears.

Wait a minute.

Wait just a minute.

My mother's accident happened right in front of a house where Frank Zagorsky was visiting? Was that a fluke? Or was Frank somehow involved in the accident?

Burke would probably laugh at such a notion and tell me to turn off the plotting mechanism in my brain, but I couldn't. "Is it a coincidence, Tare, that the wreck happened not fifty feet from Frank Zagorsky?"

"You mean, you think he pulled an invisible string and—"

I knew it sounded crazy, but it just seemed too much of a quirk of fate to have my mother in an accident so close to Frank. I needed to talk to the man or the woman in the other car. "I'm going to the hospital. Oh."

Burke lifted his head when they neared the ambulance. My heart ached with the pain I saw on his face. "Look at his leg." The bandage covering his left leg was stained with blood, lots of blood.

I gritted my teeth as we hurried toward the emergency vehicle. We stood back a little, buffeted by the wind that had picked up in the last thirty minutes. Burke's face was so pale, I wanted to go right over and hug him. He waved us over. One of the EMTs said something to him, but he shook his head and motioned us over again.

"What happened?" I asked, staring at the blood smearing his clothes, his hands, his face. My stomach sank to my knees, and I almost followed suit.

He reached for my hand and squeezed it. I let him hold it for a few seconds.

"Frank Zagorsky was messing around with the wife of the man who shot me."

The steel of the ambulance felt cool against my shoulder as I leaned against it. I thought of Miss Edna in the hospital, perhaps dying. "So much for the grieving boyfriend."

"The husband came in the back way, saw Frank leave, the wife screamed when her husband got his gun, and then he shot me, thinking Frank had come back to fight him." He lifted his head, studied his leg, and his jaw popped. "The bullet plowed a row in my flesh, but it's just a graze. He held the gun on me until I could talk him down."

"You're going to be all right?"

When Burke nodded, I added, "Good. That's so good." Time for a stab at my imagination. "I, uh, think it's strange that my mother had a wreck in front of that house with Frank Zagorsky inside."

One corner of Burke's mouth lifted. Oh, great. He's going to tell me to turn off my musings.

"I'd already thought of that. But I'm not sure how he could have

171

caused it.'"

Terri lifted her brows in a good-job-Sophie look.

I smiled at her and then turned to Burke. "Did you hurt the husband?"

"No. They're questioning him. He'll be out in a bit. His wife called 9-1-1 when he put his gun down."

I glanced around at Forman Fall's finest and their vehicles lining the street with lights flashing. "What are we missing here, Burke? Frank Zagorsky has an affair with a married woman. My mother has an accident across the street from him, and her arm's broken. Is any of this connected somehow?"

"I don't know." Burke lifted a hand when the EMTs started moving the gurney. "See you at the hospital?"

"I'll be there. I thought I'd talk to the driver of the vehicle that hit the van my mother was in or the woman with him and see if they know anything, saw anything." I winced, expecting another rebuke.

"Good idea." Burke closed his eyes, rested both hands on his midriff, and lifted one finger in a good-bye gesture as they pushed him aboard the ambulance.

Good idea? I glanced at Terri with an are-my-ears-deceiving-me look. Burke had just consented to my questioning the other driver or the woman.

"It's the blood loss," Terri offered, nodding and pursing her lips like a wise woman. "C'mon, Sophie, I feel raindrops. Let's get to my car and the hospital before this storm hits hard."

♦

An oxygen mask covered most of Edna Conroy's swollen and bruised face. Her skin was pale, even though bruises stained almost every part of her that I could see.

Bless her heart. I couldn't even imagine what it was like to be beaten so badly, especially if she knew her assailant, as Burke indicated. How could a person hurt an older woman like this?

I touched her forehead, bowed my head, and prayed for her. Someone—probably Terri—placed a hand on my back as I asked the Lord to heal Edna. When I said, "Amen," and a chorus of amens followed mine, I looked around and found Terri beside me and two women standing with my mother at the foot of Edna's bed—the same women from the restaurant.

I straightened, not quite sure what to say to any of them. Normally, I would have smiled and grabbed Terri's hand to leave, but that wasn't appropriate for this monumental moment: my mother praying with me.

Mother stared at Edna with what seemed like a genuine look of sadness. She patted Edna's foot with her left arm—the other one was in a cast held up by a sling—and walked around the other side of the bed, leaned over, and said something in Edna's ear. Then she prayed. When she opened her eyes and stared at Edna for another few seconds, I wondered what my mother's connection was to Edna. I wasn't even aware my mother knew her, much less that she'd be so affected by her misfortune. These were the actions of not just an acquaintance but a friend, an intimate, close friend.

Was Edna the reason my mother had come back to Forman Falls?

Mother looked up and found me watching her. Her facial expression didn't change a bit. She blinked three times at me and turned to leave. The smiles her two friends sent in my direction encompassed Terri as well when the three women left.

"Go." Terri nudged me with her elbow.

Wind whipping at the window drew my attention from the door my mother had walked through. Rain slashed in torrents against the glass. I shook my head. "She doesn't want me near her."

"But she knows Edna somehow. Maybe she has some information that could help with your case."

No, no, no. It was asking too much. I wouldn't force myself on anyone, not even—or especially not—my own mother. It was like asking me to do a backward flip; all it would produce is my humiliation and something broken.

"You're not pushing yourself on her, Soph. You're just asking some questions."

My answer was to lean over and kiss Edna's forehead. Where was all this mushiness coming from? I don't believe I've ever kissed anyone's forehead in my life. And here I was, smooching someone I hardly knew but someone I really felt sad about.

Little Miss Edna, with false teeth that were prone to slip or fall out, who has an outgoing and sometimes silly personality, had somehow captured the attention of an international man of mystery. How had that happened? And such a handsome man who could have any woman he wanted. What had Frank seen in her, to overlook her unsophisticated manner?

Better yet, what had Frank gained from having Edna's friendship?

I patted her hand and left, with Terri behind me. When I reached the long shiny hallway outside Edna's room, I was so shocked, I almost choked. There stood Burke on crutches, talking with my mother. I shoved Terri back into Edna's room and looked at my mother again. What could they be saying to each other?

Oh, please, Lord. Don't let her tell him how disappointed she is in me.

"He already knows you were an imaginative child."

"Stop it, Terri. How do you do that?"

She tilted her head and lifted a shoulder. "Logic. You were afraid when you saw Burke talking to your mom. The next step is you think your mother will tell him all the stuff you did as a child—although he knows about most of it. Heck, he was part of some of it. That's when I open my mouth and say, 'He already knows.' See? It's not too complicated."

"But he doesn't know that she hates me."

"Aw, honey, she doesn't hate you. She's just relationship challenged."

Burke laughed at something Mother said. Then my mother smiled, shook her head, made a big movement with her hand as if she described the world's largest watermelon, and she laughed with him. When Burke leaned closer, he said something that had her cocking her head and chuckling again. "Awfully chummy, aren't they?"

"I'd say, sister." Terri crossed her arms and nodded.

Still smiling and holding onto both crutches, Burke nodded toward a bench. If they sat, which was clearly their intent, then they would both be able to see me and Terri. I scooted back inside Edna's room, closed the door, and then opened it just a bit.

Well, weren't they cozy?

Mother turned toward him, crossed her legs—something she rarely does—and folded her arms over her waist with the casted arm on top. It was much more proper, she'd shown me many times, for a woman to cross her ankles and place her hands in an X over her lap. I had never seen her so relaxed with another person.

Burke and my mother continued to visit as if they were old friends. Burke was good; no doubt about that. Mother chatted on as if she'd known him for ages.

Someone's plump hand grabbed the doorjamb above my head. A nurse's frowning face appeared. "What is going on in here?" she said and shoved harder, moving me aside.

"I am so sorry." I stepped back and tried for sheepish, since that's the countenance most people respond to when I'm in trouble. The nurse brushed past us and walked toward Edna.

A quick glance down the hall revealed Burke and my mother staring in our direction. I backed out of their line of vision, but Terri didn't. She reported that they had started talking again.

The lights flickered a couple of times. "Whoa. What was that?"

"Storm's here. Haven't you heard that wind?" The nurse checked a dripping bag. "We're under a tornado watch. I'm moving this patient to the hallway, and I need you to evacuate or head to the basement. Just follow the signs."

175

"We need to go." I turned left with Terri right behind me and hurried the short distance to the stairs. I didn't care if my mother saw us leave. "Do you remember where you parked?"

"Across the parking lot in Section E. Maybe we should go to the hospital shelter."

"Terri, how many tornado watches have we lived through that we didn't see a tornado or even a hint of one?"

"Zillions."

As we opened the stairwell door, a voice said, "Attention, please. We are now under a tornado watch. Please—"

The door shut. The stairwell was dark. When we reached the first level and pushed on the steel door, harsh wind slapped us back a little. I looked outside.

Deep gray, rumbling clouds covered every bit of sky. Wind tossed and twisted the tops of trees. Paper flew in a twisting dance above some nearby cars. I tried to hold the door in place, but the wind gusted and slammed it into the brick wall.

Terri and I stepped out into the storm. Wind carrying heavy drops of rain whipped my hair and blouse and pants as I bent against it and followed Terri, weaving against the heavy gusts. Fighting to stand, Terri dug her keys out of her purse and pushed the key button. "Look for my lights!"

Rain pounded everything, including us. We both covered our heads with our purses and clung to parked cars as we searched for Terri's car.

"There!" I yelled, but I'm not sure Terri heard me—the wind snatched my words away. I grabbed her arm and aimed us toward her car.

I tugged on the passenger door. Squinting against the grit in the wind, I finally wrested the door open, stumbled into my seat, and worked just as hard to get the door shut. I leaned over and pushed on Terri's door. The wind almost landed her on her rear, but she held onto the door, slid inside, and then struggled to get her door closed.

Gasping for breath, I put my head back and watched the storm. Terri did the same. We were inside, we were drenched, but at least we were safe.

I looked outside. "Typical East Texas weather. I think maybe we should have stayed inside. Conditions look perfect for—"

Sirens sounded.

"Oh, no." In the distance, a thin funnel cloud dipped toward the ground then receded into the clouds. "Let's get to my house!"

"Do you want to drive, Sophie? I don't think I have the strength to fight this storm anymore."

"Sure. Crawl under me; I'll go over." I stretched a leg over the floor gear shift. The windows fogged up with our efforts to get past one another, but I finally landed in the driver's seat and Terri settled into the passenger seat, put her seat belt on, and watched the storm.

I turned the key, flicked on the wipers, and backed out in white rain. The wind kept the wipers from coming back down, and the downpour colored everything around us white. "I can't drive in this!"

A wave of hail pounded the car, and I thought the front window might burst. I couldn't see one thing around us. Then a howl, like a lion's roar, surrounded us. "Get down! Tornado!" I crawled into the backseat floorboard; Terri folded herself under the passenger dashboard. The wail of the storm grew louder. Hail hammered us. The ground shook, violently. Something crashed.

"Oh, God, help us!" I was so scared, my body shook. I covered my head with both hands and curled up as much as I could.

Another crash, right beside us!

Terri shouted something at me, but I couldn't make it out.

Then, the unthinkable happened. Terri's car moved! Slowly at first, then it picked up speed. It felt as if we were flying! I screamed just before we slammed into something. I flew up and hit the ceiling, and when I hit the floorboard again, I covered my head and waited. Metal screeching. Crunching sounds, crashing racket, creaking noises. And then it stopped.

I opened my eyes. Steady but heavy rain battered the car. I looked out the window and blinked at the chaos. Cars were upside-down on other cars. A pickup's front wheels sat on top of a small two-door car as if it had tried to crawl over it. Downed trees stretched across several parked cars. Vehicles were shoved up against other vehicles. I couldn't make out where we had flown to. "Terri, are you all right?"

She moaned, and then said nothing more.

"Terri! Come on. Wake up. Are you hurt?"

"Just my head. It feels like it's been blown up like a balloon and is just about to burst."

"What should we do? Stay here and be crushed to death or try to get out? Maybe someone needs our help, although I don't see another soul out here."

"We need to stay in here, Soph."

"Look, Terri! I think that's Virginia's Cadillac. It was parked at her house the day Burke and I went to see her. I've never seen one like it here in Forman Falls." The Cadillac hadn't flown anywhere. It was boxed in by a pickup and a white SUV. Who drove it here? I watched for movement in the car, but I saw none.

Something smacked the window behind me. I turned and faced Burke's frowning, wet face. Oh! He'd come to rescue us! I've never had anyone rescue me from anything, especially someone hurt and on crutches. It was worth going through this hair-raising storm to find out that Burke cared enough to find me, to help me.

He opened the door, and I backed out. I heard his crutches fall to the pavement as he turned me around and yanked me into his arms. A light rain now fell, and we were drenched.

"I thought I lost you."

His voice was raspy, and I heard the fear in it.

"I made it to a window just in time to see you and Terri get inside her car. Then the tornado lifted it." His arms drew me closer, if that was possible.

I wrapped my arms tighter around him. "I'm okay, Burke."

"I know."

My flight mechanism was pushing hard against my just-a-few-more-seconds wish to flow with this beautiful moment.

I mattered to him.

He mattered to me.

And we held each other tightly.

"Are you really okay?"

"I am." I stepped back. "Are you?"

"I'm fine. My car's right over there. I'll take you home." He pointed to a section of the parking lot that hadn't been affected by the quick tornado. Then he yanked the front door open and helped Terri out. "Are you okay?"

"I'm wet, I'm tired, and I need a cinnamon roll." Her soaked hair clung to her face as she reached inside the car and tugged out her purse. "Is anyone else out here?" She searched the area.

"I think they all ran inside. Even whoever was driving Virginia's Cadillac."

That got Burke's attention. "Where?"

"Over there. Isn't that her car?"

"Sure looks like it. Wonder who drove it here?"

"Maybe Virginia's not dead, Burke. Maybe she's in hiding like Farnsberry. Maybe she's visiting Edna."

"And maybe someone stole her car. A lot of maybes." He took out his cell phone and called Sheenen, talked for a few seconds, read him the license plate number, and hung up.

I grabbed Terri's hand. "C'mon. Burke's taking us home."

She looked at the pandemonium surrounding us. "How?"

"He's Superman. He'll figure it out."

We both watched him pick up his crutches. Terri whispered, "Superman doesn't use support aids."

I whispered back, "This one does."

14

"I'm so grateful that no buildings were damaged, and no one was killed, Burke. Thank you for helping my mother get to the storm shelter at the hospital."

Sitting at my breakfast-nook table that evening, Burke wore shorts and a T-shirt and nodded at me as he stretched his bandaged leg under my table. Moocher sniffed it and barked at it. Burke rubbed behind his ears, and Moocher settled at his feet, resting his chin on Burke's tennis shoe. "You're welcome. I didn't get in to see Miss Edna. How was she?"

I shook my head and placed a plate of cinnamon rolls on the table. "Not good." I sat across from him. "Was the Cadillac Virginia's?"

"Yes. We're going over it with a fine-tooth comb."

"What did you and my mother talk about?"

"Not much. She's a very quiet woman, a little shy."

"She's always been reserved. Even at home, she'd snap her fingers at me and my brothers instead of yelling at us. Anything on my case?"

Burke eyed his pastry. "We'll have the results on your car in the next week or so. Your arrest is certain." He took a bite.

"Arrest me for what, Burke? Farnsberry is alive and well. Ingrid talked to him."

Burke shook his head, licked his lips. "She received a call from Farnsberry's phone. We don't know if he was the one using it."

"Flint spoke to him after the accident."

"The word of a fugitive isn't reliable."

"Okay. *I* saw him. Terri saw him. At Virginia's. I can vouch that he's alive. He drove off with Ingrid."

"The word of the accused and her best friend don't amount to much either."

"I resent that, Officer." Terri came into the room with a towel around her shoulders. She rubbed the back of her wet head with it. "I wouldn't lie to save Sophie."

I whipped around and frowned at said best friend. Yeah, in the real world, I wouldn't want her to lie about anything, but this was my life we're talking about. I softened my stance. "You wouldn't?"

"I couldn't. The truth will prevail. Faith, remember?"

Burke said, "Toxicology came back on Sharon Farnsberry's hair. She was drugged. The killer didn't want her alive when he shot her. Sleeping is a lot like being dead. It made it easier for him to kill her."

"Which means it was personal, someone she knew. Did you trace the bullet?"

I loved seeing Burke's dimples when he smiled. When he smirked, as he did just now, they appeared but didn't twinkle at me. They sent me a shame-on-you look.

"Of course, I did. No match found."

"So, where are we? No, no. Let me recap. I'm accused of killing Yoda. The necklace, the bones, Sharon's grave. Jonas murdered. Yoda, alive. Garrett Flint, missing. Edna, beaten. Virginia loving Farnsberry, then she is killed or is missing. My mother's wreck. You're shot. The tornado. And before all of the above, Laura and Sharon murdered." I glanced at Burke and lifted my eyebrows, pretty pleased with myself.

"You left out a couple things. Farnsberry and Ingrid ran, and her coming to his house that week was planned. In putting this together, why did they run instead of letting law enforcement handle this? Who killed Laura and Sharon and Jonas and beat up Edna? Who is the connection between them? They're all pretty much around the same age."

"What do they have in common? UT Austin. Friendship. Marriages." I stood and paced from my refrigerator to my front window. "Laura and Sharon were married to Herman Farnsberry. Edna traveled to Europe and had her baby. Maybe—"

"Baby?" Burke sat up. "What baby?"

"Oh." Rather, uh-oh. I'd forgotten to tell him. "Edna was with child when she went to Europe. Madge Simmons told me today before lunch that Edna gave up her baby for adoption."

"Where did she—" Burke held up a hand as he stared at my kitchen table as if a troupe of vaudeville ants was dancing their way across it. "Someone's at your back door."

I jumped out of my chair, rushed toward the curtain, and moved it aside. Vivian, in early evening, stood there grinning at me. I opened the door. "Vivian, where have you been? We were all worried about you. Were you out in that storm?"

"I saw it at a safe distance."

I grabbed her skinny arm, drew her inside my kitchen, and gave her a warm hug.

She patted my shoulder and stepped back, a blush coloring her face. She probably wasn't used to such effusions from anyone. Her gaze wandered around the room. "Officer. Terri." She looked back at me and then eyed my coffee and donuts.

"Would you like some? Have a seat." I led her to the table and all ninety pounds of her sat beside Burke. I poured her a cup and shoved the plate of treats closer to her. "Eat and then tell us everything."

She bit into her donut, chewed for a couple of seconds, and swallowed a sip or two of her coffee. "Virginia Crane was killed or hurt after I left here. That breaks my heart. She was a good friend and would often sit with me in town at night, and we'd visit."

I sat opposite Burke with my fresh cup of brew. "What's her story?"

Vivian took another bite of donut. "Not sure how much is important now that she's gone. She once told me all her troubles started when she and Edna took a trip to Europe during college."

I glanced at Burke. Virginia went with Edna?

"Virginia was very vague about it, said holding those secrets had been the most difficult thing she'd ever done. There was a third person with them, but she wouldn't tell me his or her name. I do know that the third person ran into some kind of trouble in Europe."

"Third person? A man or a woman? Of course, that person could be long gone now or living in another country." I frowned at our resident tree climber and tried to think of people who might be friends with Edna. "Terri, did your mother ever say she went to Europe?"

She spurted out a laugh. "Are you kidding? She hates leaving her house, much less her country. It's strange, though, that one of the women who went to Europe is missing or dead; the other one, beaten badly."

I considered that. "Maybe the other person was Jonas, Edna's future husband. What did they see in Europe that was a threat to someone? Was it before or after Edna had her baby?"

Burke leaned forward and clasped his hands. "What else did you find out, Vivian?"

"I was at Virginia's house on Saturday. Frank Zagorsky was inside. They were yelling, but none of the windows were open, and I couldn't make out what they were saying. After he slammed out of the house, I went inside. She wouldn't tell me what they'd argued about. I left, and she went missing. Maybe he came back and finished her off."

"We don't know that she's dead. I could check with Chester County and find out what progress they've made on the case."

"We'd be in the know if she didn't live right outside our county line." I shook my head. "If Frank intended to kill her, why not do it when he was all riled up with motive and had opportunity? No one knew he was there. He could've killed her and left."

Burke nodded thoughtfully. "He wanted to get it right. Leave, plan it out, come back and execute his plan."

"Okay. Virginia said Frank looked almost identical to her dead husband. And, too, if you yell at someone, you probably know them intimately." When no one answered my observation, I asked: "Viv, you mentioned you figured out who the culprit was."

"I was wrong."

"So, we have nothing."

We all sat in silence. The wind brushed at my windows. Moocher snored at Burke's feet. The icemaker deposited ice in its basket. Soothing sounds of home. I covered up a big yawn as best I could. It had been such a long day, and I was bone tired.

Terri, the mind reader, slipped out of her chair. "I'm off." She placed her cup in the sink and said, "I'm too tired to think anymore." She leaned over and kissed me on the cheek. "I'll see you tomorrow. Burke, can I help you to your car?"

Bless my sweet friend, she was herding everyone out of my house. But I wanted to see a little more of Burke before he left. "Vivian, can I walk you home?" I reached for a bowl and stuffed it to the rim with donuts and handed it to her.

She took it and said, "I know the way. I'll talk to you tomorrow."

Terri and Vivian left. Burke struggled to his feet, leaned on his crutches, and walked to the kitchen counter. He coupled his crutches, secured them against the fridge door, and backed into the counter.

Then he held out his arms.

Oh!

It was the most natural thing in the world for me to walk into them. His arms were like big wings, stretching across my back, holding me securely, keeping me safe for the moment.

I wanted him to kiss me, but I didn't want him to kiss me. I trusted him more each day, but I couldn't get past the thought of his leaving me years ago. Right when I felt closer to him, my mind would go back to that horrible night, and all the terrible feelings would bombard me again, and I'd withdraw from him. But tonight was different. I felt his sincerity.

And he'd come to rescue me earlier today.

His arms tightened, and I heard a little moan from him. "I need to go." He nudged my ear and kissed it.

I nodded against his shoulder. It was the right thing to do. But I didn't want him to move for a few more moments.

He held me tightly, and then I stepped back.

"Walk me to the door." He settled onto his crutches and motioned with one of them for me to take the lead.

I stepped outside and held the screen door open for him. A cool breeze swept rain scents over me, and I took a deep breath of the sweetness as Burke passed me, stopped, and turned around. "I took a couple days off, Sophie. Will I see you tomorrow?"

"I hope so."

He nodded and left.

I cleaned my kitchen and went upstairs with Moocher close on my heels. The hall light revealed Yoda curled up like a pretzel on my bed. When I turned on the bedroom light, he didn't move. I put on my pajamas, brushed my teeth, crawled into bed, and thought of Burke and his wonderful hugs.

I had no trouble at all falling asleep.

◆

Terri called me the next morning. "They took the yellow tape down from Virginia Crane's house."

"Great idea."

"What idea?"

"Going over there and watching to see who shows up to go through her things."

"Exactly."

"Tonight, then. Around seven. Meet me here."

"You know what to wear, Soph, and use bug spray."

"Bug spray and I have grown very close lately." I chuckled. "We'll hide in her huge garden there on the east side. Make sure your phone is fully charged. I'll bring mine and video anything that happens."

"Be sure to turn the sound off, lower the brightness level."

"Of course."

"I'll pack the handgun Daddy gave me."

"A gun, Terri? Why?"

"In case someone evil finds us hiding in the petunias."

♦

We arrived at Virginia's house a little before dark and hid the car in the woods behind her house. It was still light enough to choose our position strategically amongst the flowers and growing things in her garden. "Oh," I said, "look at that beautiful trellis with honeysuckle." We walked through an arbor full of roses and discovered a spot where we could watch the front of the house and the back. I turned on the flashlight to check for mosquitoes and spiders. I hate spiders. I always shriek when I feel one crawling on me. Terri, on the other hand, squashes them between her fingers.

She is so brave.

"So, Tare. If a spider... you'll grab it, right?" A bit of a whine was in my voice. No matter how hard I tried not to be afraid of them, it didn't stick.

"Of course, I will. You know that."

She is so brave.

The evening was quickly becoming night, with lots of clouds. I thought to bring a blanket and imagined all sorts of scary bugs and things crawling on it. I spread it out and listened to the quiet night around us.

I wanted to talk. I wanted to tell Terri about Burke and the shaky bridge we'd crossed yesterday, that I was afraid of him because he was still capable of hurting me deeply, that I was on track for doing something really stupid—trusting him to the point that I would allow myself to think of *more* with him. I wanted to tell her that I didn't want more right now, that I liked being just friends with him, that maybe having him in my life as a friend was enough, that I didn't want to hurt *him* by not being able to give him the *more* he wanted.

I wanted to talk.

But the setting was all wrong.

Sharon Farnsberry came to mind. I wondered who took her necklace from my house. Had it been found? I thought of Samson, and I missed him. Burke told me that Jim had chained Samson in his back yard—which broke my heart—since the day a neighbor had complained that he'd taken his newspaper three days in a row. Poor Samson.

I wondered where Burke was tonight.

The lovely scent of honeysuckle surrounded us. A mosquito buzzed my ear, and I swatted at it.

Terri leaned toward me. "What?"

I could smell her perfume and hoped it wouldn't give us away to any murderers passing by. "Mosquito."

"Oh."

"Really big one."

"Mmm. Did you use bug spray?"

"Yes," I whispered. "I brought some with me, too."

"Then they won't bite you."

"What about spiders sniffing around?"

"Nope, not the same."

I heard her unzip something. "You brought your purse?"

"Here." Terri unwrapped a piece of candy, handed it to me. "It's peppermint. I brought a zillion." She dumped them onto the blanket. "Just sprinkle them all over. Maybe that'll stop the spiders. They hate peppermint."

I unwrapped the candies and methodically placed them four inches apart along the edges of the blanket and then sat back. "Thanks," I whispered to Terri. "That's a lot of peppermint."

"I came prepared for your whining."

"I don't whine."

"Yes, you do."

"Well, only about spiders."

"I know. Otherwise, you're a warrior."

187

A warrior? This little wimp? I snickered and listened to the cicadas singing, cloaking our soft voices. Virginia Crane's night light shone bright in front of her house. I don't know what I hoped would happen here tonight. Maybe Virginia would show up. I wondered if she'd attended church anywhere; she hadn't in Forman Falls. She rarely came into town, even at Christmas. Did she have family, brothers or sisters or close friends who would sort through her things?

I touched Terri's bony shoulder, and she jumped. "I never saw Virginia in town. Did you?"

"No. I heard once that she shopped in Milltree. It was closer for her."

"Did she go to church there?"

"I don't know."

A rabbit appeared in the light. It sat so still, I wondered if it had fallen asleep. Then its head twitched, and it hopped away.

The minutes rolled by. I was glad we had used bug spray, because I could hear the mosquitoes—the females—circling my body, scenting for blood for their broods. None of them lit on me. I stretched my legs, very quietly, and changed positions. As I did, a twig cracked, and the crack didn't come from me.

I gasped as quietly as I could and squeezed Terri's arm.

"Don't," she breathed.

I stopped squeezing, but I didn't let go of her arm. I needed the contact because my racing heart was choking the breath out of me.

Someone was nearby.

"Szzzzttt."

Vivian! How did she know we were here?

"Szzzzttt."

"Viv, over here."

She crept around the brush, stepped on a peppermint candy, and said, "What in the world?"

"It's peppermint," I told her. "For the spiders."

"You're afraid of spiders?"

188

"Aren't you?"

"I couldn't be, in my line of work." She joined us on the blanket. "What are you girls doing here?"

"Same as you." I stifled a yawn. "We wanted to see who showed up since the police tape was taken down."

"I figured the killer might rifle through her things in search of something that was worth killing her for. Or not. I'm just too nosy for my own good."

I chuckled. "Join the crowd."

"How did you get here? I didn't see any car lights."

"There's another entrance back of the lake. Virginia never used it."

We sat in silence for a few minutes. Vivian stood. "I'll get up this tree to a good vantage point. If I see anything suspicious, I'll try to warn you as quietly as possible."

"Okay," I answered and watched her climb up and disappear into the blackness.

Time crawled by like a did-I-eat-the-whole-thing ant leaving a July 4th picnic. Terri fell asleep. I wanted to, but I was told by a roommate in college that I snored. If I snoozed and the killer happened by, he'd hear me. My roommate said I had quite a freight-train snore.

Terri stirred.

"Terri?"

"Hmmm?"

"Do I snore?"

"No."

I looked up. I couldn't see Vivian. I wondered if she'd ever fallen asleep and dropped out of a tree. My eyes grew heavy. I gave in and...

♦

"I *told* you this was a bad idea. We shouldn't even be here."

Those whispered words caused my eyes to pop wide open. A

189

female. Was that Ingrid's voice?

"We at least have to look for it. You know that."

Was that Farnsberry? Look for what? Jewelry? Money stashed away?

I wanted to sit up and say, "Well, where have *you* been hiding, Farnsberry?" But good sense told me to be still. Terri moved beside me, placed a hand on my knee. She knows me so well.

Out of the black of night came a man and a woman. They crept beside the house, straight into the front light. The man was tall and thin. It was, indeed, Farnsberry. He held the woman's hand and seemed to tug her forward.

"How do you propose we get inside, Herman?"

"I know where she kept a hidden key. Now come on, Esther. Let's get this done."

Esther? My *mother*? *That* Esther? What in the world was she doing here with Herman Farnsberry? And where was Ingrid?

"She dropped them off and hid the car somewhere." This, from Terri, the mind-reader.

The couple disappeared around the corner, and I nudged Terri. "That was my mother, right? She's the only Esther I know."

"Szzzzttt!"

I looked up, although I couldn't see a thing. "Vivian, are you coming down?"

"I'm already down." She jumped soundlessly from the tree and joined us on the blanket. It was uncanny how skinny she was and how easily her legs folded to where her knees were in her face with her arms wrapped around her legs. "Why is your mother with Herman Farnsberry?"

"I have no idea. What could she want with anything that belonged to Virginia Crane? We need to call Burke. He should be here to see what they're up to."

Terri grunted. "Yeah, and we'll end up in trouble for being on private property."

190

"We didn't go inside. That's something."

Vivian shushed us. Someone else was coming. We all lowered our heads and looked toward the light in Virginia's front yard. I waited, breathlessly.

But nothing happened. "Viv, are you sure—"

She placed her hand on my knee.

A stocky man appeared in the front light. A fishing hat covered his face, and he carried a large shovel. The light behind him colored his face black. He jerked his head as if he'd heard something and stood as still as a deer on alert. I held my breath until he started moving again. He walked to the corner of the house and stepped off with long strides until he stopped at the edge of a window. I could hear him counting his paces. He made a perfect left turn and marched straight toward the flowers and growing things that hid us!

Three more steps. He stopped, placed the cutting edge of a shovel on the ground with his foot on its shoulder, and pushed. He tossed the dirt into a pile near us. We were so close, I could smell the overturned soil.

He did this several times. Then, he crouched, looked back over his shoulder, clutched the shovel's shaft, and ran off. I glanced toward the light again, but no one appeared.

From inside the house, a hazy glow moved around for a few seconds and then vanished. My mother and Farnsberry were still inside. I wracked my brain for any memory of Farnsberry and my mother or father through the years, but the only thing that rose to the surface was when I was in middle school, and my mother was called to the principal's office on several occasions because of some mischief I'd masterminded.

I was not aware of a friendship between Farnsberry and my parents.

The man with the shovel returned and continued digging. At one point, I thought he'd seen me, but he kept burrowing like a determined mole.

The shovel hit something. It reminded me of the night Burke and I found the jawbone, but this sound was more of a thud, like metal hitting wood.

The man bent over, let the shovel drop, and reached into the deep hole. Up he rose and with him, a small box. He walked to the front yard light, opened the box, and smiled. Then, it dawned on me. The man was my neighbor and Samson's owner, Jim Peters.

He reached inside the box and pulled out two books.

Was one of the books Sharon's diary? How did Jim Peters know where to dig?

Oh, I knew the importance of his find. It held Sharon's history and Farnsberry's as well. It might answer not only who was after Sharon, but who had returned from her past to kill Jonas and hurt Edna and Virginia.

But why was my mother here? Was she in the diary?

I tugged out my cell phone and the light came on. Jim whipped his head toward me, and quick as a lightning bug, came around the bushes and grabbed my arm.

I screamed.

Terri screamed.

"Wait. Wait."

Vivian screeched like a banshee as she landed right on Jim Peters' back.

They struggled, grunting and shoving. Jim Peters said, "Hold on. Stop it! Let me—" I jumped at him, too, and he shoved me away. I landed against a branch and bumped my nose. Tasting blood, I lunged and screamed and socked him right in the face.

Ow! I grabbed my hand, cradled it against my chest, and kicked him as hard as I could. Vivian pummeled his back and arms, and even Terri got into the fight by throwing dirt in his face.

Jim growled and rubbed his eyes. A big hand grabbed his upper arm. Burke! He shoved Jim to the ground, and then spun toward me and gripped my shoulders. "You're hurt! Where?" There was real panic in his voice.

"My nose." I swiped at the blood that dripped down my chin and onto my shoes and asked, "Where are your crutches?" just as Officer Sheenen handcuffed Jim and headed toward a patrol car parked in front.

"Let's get you inside," Burke said as I wondered where in the world that patrol car had come from.

♦

Burke, wearing shorts and a T-shirt, limped as he led us inside Virginia's home. He turned on all the lights, and I went to the bathroom and washed off the blood from my hands and face. My nose didn't look broken, but it sure hurt.

When I came out, Burke was waiting for me. "You were in danger, and you didn't even know it. You should have called me before you did this hare-brained thing."

"I considered it, but I knew what your answer would be."

"Then you should have listened to me even if I didn't tell you."

I frowned up at him.

"Okay. That didn't make sense." Resigned, he took my hand and led me to the room where my mother and Farnsberry were sitting side by side. My mother looked frightened and embarrassed. She wore jeans, tennis shoes, a black blouse, and no bonnet. She dropped her head and closed her eyes.

Farnsberry and my mother were handcuffed to their chairs.

Sheenen stepped forward and asked Mother and Herman questions that neither answered. My mother stared at the floor while Herman sat quietly, watching Officer Sheenen.

"Does your coming here tonight have anything to do with the trip you took to Europe with Edna and Virginia, Mrs. O'Brion? Were you there to help Edna with her baby?"

She gasped. Her eyes were so sad that I thought she might start

193

crying. She closed them and shook her head, not, it seemed, in answer to his question but as if she tried to block his question from her mind.

She was number three on the European adventure.

Sheenen held up the books. "Jim Peters dug up these two diaries, just outside this window. What are they going to tell us, Mr. Farnsberry?"

He didn't answer.

"Mrs. O'Brion?"

Not a word from her either.

I took no pleasure whatsoever in seeing my mother in such a predicament, handcuffed to a chair, being interrogated. Since she wouldn't offer up any explanations, I left the room and met Terri and Vivian in the hall. Terri opened her arms, and I walked into her hug. Vivian's arm wrapped around my back. Their friendship meant so much to me.

I wanted to cry, so I pulled back instead. "Do you need a ride home, Viv?"

"I have my car."

"What car? You don't own a car."

"I most certainly do. I keep it in my garage and drive it at night."

"But where is it?"

She playfully raised her brows. "I'll never tell. I have hiding places all over, so I can get around on foot, and no one knows I'm there."

The three of us walked outside. Vivian backed away and wiggled her fingers as she walked off into the night.

Two patrol cars approached and parked near the light pole. Two police officers I'd never met went inside the house and came back out holding the arms of Farnsberry and my mother and placed them in one of the patrol cars. I wondered if Ingrid was out here, watching all this. She was probably waiting in a getaway car, but there would be no getaway tonight.

One of the patrol cars holding Farnsberry and Mother drove off with two officers inside.

Burke appeared on crutches and motioned me and Terri over. I expected his rebuke. My mother had gone inside the house and had been arrested. I had stayed outside, which saved me from joining Mother in jail.

"You're going home, I trust."

"I am." I shrugged as innocently as I could. "If we hadn't been out here, you wouldn't have known Jim dug up the diaries."

"Maybe. We'll talk in the morning."

"Call me around ten. I should be up by then."

◆

My bones felt like mush, my muscles ached, and my brain needed to shut down. I tumbled into bed at *1:11* and fell into a deep sleep.

Until something crashed through my bedroom window!

I sat up, disoriented, and when another pane shattered, I screamed and jumped out of bed, absolutely terrified.

My first thought was "Run!" so I raced out of my bedroom, down the hall and the stairs in my bare feet, frightened beyond measure with no idea where I was going. Instinct had taken over. *Get away from the danger!* I paused at the bottom of the stairs, heard Moocher barking in the back yard, and then something flew against one of my big front windows.

Oh, dear God!

Another rock slammed into the large pane.

Then another, which broke the glass and sailed over my writing table.

I ran for the kitchen and the knife holder on my counter. Terri was right. It was stupid not to have a gun loaded and ready. I grabbed the largest knife, raced across the living room and down the hall, and ducked into the guest bedroom. Somewhere in my house, another window shattered, then a rock crashed through the window I stood beside. I slapped a hand across my mouth to stifle a scream. Shaking violently, I hunched over and tightened my hand on my mouth, so I wouldn't whimper and give away my location. My heart thundered against my ribs, causing me to pant.

My phone.

Oh, no. I'd left it upstairs in my bedroom. Stupid, stupid!

I tried to listen for any movement, inside or outside, but the pounding pressure of my frantic heart beat against my ears was all I could hear.

Until something creaked, like a floorboard. Outside this room.

Wide-eyed and panting, I rushed behind the door and tried so hard to be quiet, but holding my breath was impossible.

Then the unthinkable happened—the knob on the bedroom door turned!

Staring at it, I pulled the knife back and gritted my teeth. A figure all in black stepped into the room and quietly shut the door. He turned his masked face toward me and said, "Hello, Sophie."

I screamed and lunged at him, but he ducked, dodged, and then tried to grab me. I shoved him with strength I didn't know I had, dropped the knife, and ran out the door. As fast I could, I raced down the hall and up the stairs, but I could hear him right behind me! I was almost to my room when he grabbed my pajama top and yanked me to the floor.

"You're a feisty little thing. I like a girl with spunk." His voice was nasally, like he had a cold, but I didn't recognize it. When he leaned over me, I kicked him in the face as hard as I could. He stumbled back. I got up, ran into my room, slammed the door, and locked it. Panting, I stumbled to where I'd plugged in my phone, but it was gone!

The man knocked lightly on my bedroom door.

I froze, my eyes wide, my breaths trapped inside my chest, my whole body shivering. My heart slammed so hard against my rib cage that I thought I was about to pass out. Dear God, what is going on?

"Unless you have a second phone in there," the nasally male voice sounded muffled through my door, "or a gun, although I couldn't find one, then you have to make a choice, Sophie. One, do you want me to break down your door? Two, will you open the door and come with me? Or three, do you want me to go after your mother?"

What? My mother?

Oh, why hadn't I gone outside instead of back upstairs! Because someone was throwing rocks at my house, that's why.

What to do? What to *do!*

"I need an answer, Sophie."

I gritted my teeth at him for using my first name.

I frantically looked around for a way to escape, but there was none. I tiptoed to my balcony, knowing there was no way to crawl down, and it was too far to drop to the patio, but I opened one of the double doors anyway. In the glow of the streetlight, I could clearly see a hooded person in black standing in my yard, looking up at me. He waved enthusiastically.

My heart sank. I was trapped.

But, then... Ha! I waved back, took a deep breath, and did the only thing I could think of: I screamed bloody murder. A piercing scream. A long, horror-movie-quality scream. Lights turned on across the street. I screamed again. My neighbor, Morris Clayton, ran outside with a rifle and took a couple shots at the man in my front yard as he ran off. In a few seconds, another man ran down the sidewalk and followed the path of the first runner, although he couldn't catch up to him. Several popping sounds—Morris was firing away. And still I screamed until I no longer had a voice.

I heard a siren, but the first vehicle that careened around our street corner was a pickup. Burke! His truck skidded to a stop in front of my house, one wheel up on the curb. A patrol car with lights flashing parked behind his truck. Burke bounded out, leaving the truck door open, and ran toward the front of my house. Two officers hurried out of the patrol car and followed him.

I heard a loud crash and groaned. My front door.

197

I imagined the policemen downstairs, weapons drawn, searching my house quietly, quickly, efficiently. More silence. My doorknob turned, then rattled. "Sophie?"

"Burke!"

I couldn't get there fast enough. I opened the door and flew into his arms.

15

Burke tightened the hug and then pushed me back and looked into my eyes. "Are you okay?"

"Oh, Burke, I was so scared." The words came out a squeaky whisper. I tried to tell him what happened but fits of coughing interrupted every few seconds. "Careful, over there by those two windows, there's broken glass."

My head hurt, my heart was still beating too fast, and my throat was on fire. God help me, but I was stupid tonight. At the first sound of glass breaking in my bedroom, I should have called 9-1-1. Instead, I ran. Flight or fright, and I'd chosen flight—in the wrong direction.

I mouthed the words, "Burke, the chief was right. I am in danger. They intended to take me somewhere." I grabbed my throat. It hurt to talk. "They're after my mother, too."

"Who are 'they', Sophie? Can you describe them?"

I frowned and shook my head, wishing I could tell him more. I mouthed the words, "They said they'd go after my mother if I didn't come out. Black hoodies, average height, fast runners. Well, the one in my front yard was fast. The one inside had trouble catching up with his partner." Burke leaned over, positioned his ear next to my mouth. "The one inside my house was a man with a nasally voice, like he had a cold. The other one outside on my lawn also had a black hoody on. That's all I know."

"You're saying 'he'. Do you know for certain that both were males?"

"No. Just the one inside my house."

Officer Sheenen walked into the room. "Just got a call." He glanced at me, then at Burke. "Miss Edna just died."

I gasped and covered my mouth. Oh, no. I turned my back to both men and stepped a few feet away as tears filled my eyes. Poor

199

Edna. Poor, sweet Edna. She didn't deserve what hap—I gasped and spun around. "Did they kill her? Did she have any visitors today? Two men?"

Burke looked at Sheenen who said, "I'll find out," and walked into the hall.

"Someone's targeting the three women who went to Europe years ago, Burke. Edna's dead. Virginia's dead or missing. Now, they're after my mother, and me, obviously."

"Possibly because of the connection to your mother."

"Chief Johnston tried to warn me. Right now, you have to check on my mother, make sure she's all right."

Burke grimaced. "We released her."

What? I couldn't believe it. "Where is she? Where did she go?" Talking was playing havoc on my throat, and I rubbed it.

"We don't know. Would you like some water?"

I nodded. "Kitchen." I headed in that direction.

"Do you have any idea where your mother might go?"

"No. We're not chummy. I have to stop talking. Hurts too much." We reached the kitchen. I got Burke's attention and pointed to the broken glass. He handed ice water to me. The cold soothed my throat, and then I popped a lozenge.

"I'll start with the woman driving the van in the crash. Her name is on the police report."

I nodded, whispered, "You do that while I wake up George at the Door and Glass House and get him to replace my windows and front door in the morning."

"In the meantime, Soph, you need to stay with Terri."

"And I need to get somebody over here to put in a security system, ASAP."

♦

I awoke to a damp and cloudy morning and the whistle of a kettle promising tea. Terri's a tea person. Actually, she's a cream and sugar person who adds just a tad of tea to dilute the guilt. The whistling stopped as I sank deeper into my blankets. I didn't want to face the day yet. I heard Terri turn on the shower in the bathroom between our two bedrooms and wondered if I'd brought whatever had happened to me last night upon her by being here. I told myself that those men wouldn't come here; that would be stupid. The police were aware of them, were looking for them, but, still, no one could watch us 24/7. They could kill us both before Burke could get here.

I thought of George putting in my windows and my front door today, that I could maybe be home this afternoon. The bedroom door opened, and Terri walked into what I considered 'my room' because I always stayed in here when I spent the night.

She was carrying a gun.

She put it on my bed and sat beside it. "Daddy gave this to me because he didn't want me to live alone without protection. And now I'm giving it to you, just until this mess is over."

"I've never thought of myself as a wimp, but after last night, I have doubts today."

"You're no wimp, Sophie, not after that horrific scream. Everybody's talking about it. Where did that come from?"

"Probably built up from years of dealing with my mother." I tried to smile, but it wobbled just before tears flooded my eyes.

"Stop it. I'll start crying, too, and ruin my makeup." She grabbed my hand. "You were so smart. You faced a no-way-out situation, and you thumbed your nose at it."

"Next time, they'll put duct tape over my mouth so I can't—"

"There won't be a next time. Now wipe your tears. I have to get dressed. Call me any time today at work and don't go anywhere by yourself. You never know."

I sent her a no-truer-words nod and touched the gun. "I haven't shot one of these in a couple years."

"When I get off work, we'll go to the shooting range, get some practice in. I made hot tea if you want some." She started to leave and then turned back around. "What about your mother?"

"I don't know. Burke's looking for her. Call your mom, see if she knows anything. I'm going to call some friends and family. Maybe they've heard from her."

"You know I'd take off work if I could, but I can't. Please be careful today, Sophie."

"I will, I promise."

After a few minutes, I heard the front door shut.

I was alone, and I was suddenly terrified. I scooted out of bed and checked the front door locks. Terri had three: a regular lock, a sliding lock, and a heavy-duty bolt latch lock. In quick order, I made sure all three were secured.

I'd written scenes where the female protagonist was alone, afraid, and thinking of ways to get out of an impossible and deadly situation, but the reality of it was that I didn't know, firsthand, what I was writing about. I'd never been as afraid as I was last night in my own home.

At least I would be a better writer when all this ended.

I glanced outside. A light rain fell. It was a perfect day to spend in bed. I picked up my cell phone, crawled back under the covers, and started making calls about my mother. I'd left instructions with George to call me when he was finished. I'd go home and try to figure out how to live alone again with a gun, a dog, and a cat. Maybe a couple more dogs were in my future, big dogs with deep, threatening barks and teeth that could munch on an intruder until the police arrived.

◆

The rain finally stopped. Burke called me that evening while I was coming up to a stop sign to tell me they hadn't located my mother. The overcast day only added to the stress of not knowing where she was or if something horrible had happened to her. I popped a lozenge and said, "I've called everyone I know. Maybe she's on her way back to Kansas. She doesn't have a cell phone, y'know, or email."

"Her friends in the van haven't heard from her. She could be anywhere by now."

"Or those two men took her. Burke, do you think they're the ones who beat Edna and killed Jonas? How do they fit into the picture? The pieces aren't coming together at all."

"It's an ongoing investigation, Sophie. I checked your house. Your windows and front door have been replaced."

"George called me with the 'all clear'. He said the security system people were there, too. They just called and gave me the password to the system and told me how to set it. Pretty easy, actually."

"I'll need that password."

"I'll give it to you."

"Even with the security system, I don't like you being by yourself until we find your mother. Are you still at Terri's?"

"No. I left this afternoon. I just finished shopping, and I'm headed home. I wouldn't mind some company while I get my things together. All I took with me last night were my pajamas and my toothbrush. I can give you the password then, and you can tell me what you're not telling me."

"Ongoing investigation, Soph. I can't tell you everything."

"Then, you do know something?"

"Ongoing investigation, Soph."

Hmmph.

My house lay in pitch black. I didn't remember turning off the automatic lamp in my living room. Maybe the electricity had gone off—it wasn't too unusual for that to happen in Forman Falls—or maybe one of George's crew had turned the lamp off and forgot to turn it back on.

Burke opened the front door. "I hear Moocher."

My voice was coming back, but I could only manage a whisper. "I put him outside since I was going to be gone all day. Watch me do this." I put in the security password and reset the alarm.

"Got it."

We stepped inside the dark living room. I imagined someone sitting in one of my chairs, a gun across his lap, waiting to kill both of us. With shaking fingers, I turned on the lamp and there sat Yoda, with no gun in sight. I snuggled him and walked to the kitchen to let Moocher inside.

"I'll check the rest of the house," Burke said. "Stay in there."

As lights came on, the tension eased a little from my shoulders. I opened the back door to a squirming Moocher and scratched behind his ears. "You okay, sweetie?" I made sure the backdoor lock was secure.

Burke appeared in the doorway. "Let's go upstairs and get your things."

"I'll make it quick; you need to get home. You've had a long day, too."

Even though light preceded us as we walked upstairs, memories of the last time I'd been up the stairs flooded back, and I felt as if the man was right behind me again. I glanced over my shoulder and hated that I felt weak instead of strong. I had won that skirmish, but it sure didn't feel like it.

On the top landing, I glanced both ways, rushed toward my bedroom, and put Yoda in his bed at the foot of mine. Everything looked as it did before the attack. No broken glass anywhere. I picked up my overnight bag and stuffed it with essentials.

"Almost done?"

"You won't laugh, will you, if I take my Teddy with me? I've had him since I was five." I plucked my brown and orange teddy bear off the shelf of stuffed animals. "I even took him to college with me." I held him up, face to face with Burke. "He can be ferocious if I'm in trouble."

"Oh, I can see that." Burke chuckled.

I unlatched the pet door so Moocher could go outside, made sure the back door and the front door were secure, and joined Burke in his patrol car.

♦

Terri lived on the first floor of the Hampton-Wade Apartments. To get to her place, we had to walk through the main door and down the hall on the right to number 137. I didn't ring the doorbell; she knew we were on the way over, so I walked inside.

She was sitting on the sofa with her hands clasped in her lap. She stared at me and offered no greeting. Had I spoiled plans with Stan?

My bag slid to the floor. I held out Teddy and said in a silly, tinny voice: "Hey, Terri. I'm sorry I'm coming over so late."

She didn't move. Her eyes seemed larger than usual. She stared at me for maybe two more seconds, then looked to her right slowly as if her eyes were shoving weights toward her bedroom door. Twice.

Was that a signal?

Burke saw it, too, grabbed my arm, and said, "Don't I get a good-bye kiss?" And then he kissed me. I was shocked. He acted as if it meant nothing to kiss me—all just part of the job. I wanted our first real kiss to mean something, but I knew he was playing a part, so I slapped his chest. "Burke, stop it. Oh!" He kissed me again, and then we wrestled as he tugged me toward the door. To Terri, I said, "He can be such an animal sometimes." To Burke, I said, "Would you stop?" I actually conjured up a giggle. "You're embarrassing me."

Once we were out in the hall, he grabbed my hand and jogged to the main door. He punched his shoulder microphone and called in the emergency. While he waited for backup, he looked at me. "Good job. You were very convincing in there."

"And to think I flunked acting in high school." But I was worried. Who was in the other room?

Within two minutes, patrol cars arrived, parking a block away. An ambulance appeared within five minutes. Policemen with guns drawn quickly surrounded the apartment building. Three followed us inside and down the corridor to Terri's apartment.

Burke had already briefed me on what to expect.

If ever there was a time for me to act convincingly, it was now.

Burke and the other officers flattened themselves against the wall, their weapons pointed up. He nodded toward Terri's apartment.

I was on.

I opened the door. Terri wasn't sitting on the sofa. "Hey, girl. I'm back. That man is so smoochy tonight. Are you ready for some cinnamon rolls?" Good. That was cheerful, unsuspecting. "I'll just get my things."

Her bedroom door opened. Terri stood in the doorway, her eyes wide and filling with tears.

"What is it, honey? Did Stan do something stupid? Men. The training never stops, does it?"

Terri walked out rigidly with an I'm-so-sorry look on her face.

My mother came next, wearing pretty much the same expression. Thank God, she was alive. Jim Peters followed my mother.

Wait a minute. Jim Peters? What was he doing here?

They all walked to the sofa, sat, and huddled together. And then she appeared, Rita what's-her-name, Virginia Crane's maid, with a gun aimed right at me.

I had to let Burke know that Rita was in here with a weapon. The door was still open behind me. "Rita, what are you doing here? Is that gun real?"

"Shut up, you stupid woman!"

And that's all it took. Officers moved toward the door. I shouted, "Get down!" and Mother, Terri, Jim and I dropped to the floor and covered our heads.

Rita did not.

"Freeze!" Burke yelled, pointing his weapon right at her. "Put the gun down!"

Rita swung her gun towards Burke and fired, but he was faster.

She screamed, clutched her shoulder, dropped the gun, and fell to her knees. My mother grabbed the revolver, set the safety, and slid it across the floor to Burke. He took it, holstered his gun, and handcuffed Rita.

I grabbed Terri's hand. "Are you okay?" She shook like a grasshopper in a stiff Texas wind. Or was that me?

"I'm fine."

"Mother, are you hurt?"

Instead of staring at me, she said, "No, I'm not." Wow. A whole sentence. She turned to Jim Peters. "Are you all right, Jimmy?"

Jimmy?

He looked at my mother with tears in his eyes. "I'm okay. Are you?"

Tears? From Jim Peters? Macho, tough boy Jim Peters?

My mother grabbed his hand. "I'm fine, sweetheart."

Okay. I was so ready to toss my supper. What was I missing here?

Rita gritted her teeth at Jim. "It's all his fault! He killed my mother!"

Her mother?

"I did not, and you know it, Rita." Jim glanced at Burke. "This ends right here, right now."

"I'll need your statement." Burke handed Rita over to Officer Sheenen and said to Jim, "Let's get out in the hall."

EMTs and a police officer took Rita to the hospital while several officers interviewed Jim and the rest of us individually. After I'd given my statement, Burke approached me and said he'd drive Terri and me to my house.

Terri said, "My mom's coming over to pick me up. I'll stay at her house for a while and come into town tomorrow."

"I'm going to miss you," I said. "Call me."

"I will. You know you can come, enjoy some country living for a change."

I glanced at Burke. Nothing about tonight made sense, and I

needed answers to the questions swirling in my head before I could walk away. "I know." I hugged her again.

Burke said, "Let's go, Sophie. I have to get back to the station."

"We can take her home," Terri offered.

"I want to check out her house, make sure she's safe."

I frowned at Burke. "But Rita's in jail now. I'll be safe."

"I still want to take a look, make sure."

I looked around for my mother, but she was nowhere in sight. Terri's face brightened when she saw her mother; she ran and hugged her. Oh, to have that kind of connection with mine.

Burke and I walked to his car. "I found out where Laura and Herman Farnsberry lived when Laura disappeared, and I contacted PD earlier. Although they never found her body, they have DNA from Farnsberry's home. Just thought you'd like to know the latest."

"DNA? That's good news."

"We have DNA here in Sharon's case, too, but no matches."

♦

It seemed appropriate somehow that Samson was sitting on my porch when Burke drove up to my garage. I was so glad to see him and to know that Jim had finally let him off the chain.

Neither Burke nor I reached for the door handle to get out.

The light rain had stopped. It was nice sitting in his car with the windows down, allowing the sweet scents of the recent shower inside. He leaned back against the headrest and closed his eyes. After a few seconds, he rolled his head towards me. "We do eventually have to get you inside."

I nodded, unconvinced.

There was something about tonight that bothered me, but it didn't have anything to do with Rita or the gun she'd pointed at me or the tears I'd seen in Terri's eyes.

Burke had kissed me, twice.

Our first real kisses in twelve years. I knew they were in the line of duty, but those kisses reminded me that we were good together once upon a time.

He didn't move. I think he was wanting, like me, to sit here in the dark and enjoy the quiet, to have a few moments where no one needed our attention, no responsibilities were calling us, no bad guys around to catch or to even think about. After a few more minutes, he got out, walked around the car, opened my door, and offered me his hand. I placed mine in it.

Samson danced and nuzzled as he welcomed us home. Moocher was barking a welcome from inside the house.

"Nothing about tonight makes sense, Burke. But if Rita's the culprit and she's in jail, then I might be able to get some sleep with Moocher in my bedroom."

"I hope you do, Sophie."

♦

Moocher barked and woke me up, but it wasn't 5:45 in the morning. The sun was up, and I wasn't. I rolled over and smelled coffee through my open window.

Mmm. There's not another smell in the world so inviting after waking up from a good night's sleep. I smiled and snuggled down into my comforter and thought about Burke and the kisses he'd given me last night. I couldn't help the long sigh that—

Wait a minute.

Coffee?

I didn't set the timer.

I glanced at my door and blinked at it as if it had answers to how coffee had been made without my help. I threw off the covers, grabbed my robe, slid into my slippers, and eased the door open.

Listening, I heard nothing.

I tiptoed down the hallway and started down the stairs, stopped, listened. I didn't hear a thing. Gripping the banister, I eased down two more steps and leaned over until I could see my kitchen.

A note was on my sliding glass door, stuck on the outside.

I glanced around and cautiously moved toward it.

"We brought coffee and hope you'll join us on your back patio. Herman and Ingrid Farnsberry."

I moved the curtain. There they sat, sipping coffee as if they had a right to be on my patio. But I couldn't be angry. I wanted answers, and they were apparently ready to give them to me.

When I stepped outside, Farnsberry stood and touched Ingrid's shoulder with the back of his hand. "Good morning, Sophie."

Ingrid rose as well and turned toward me with a warm smile. "Good morning. I hope you slept well?"

I must have looked like a buffoon, staring at them with my hair sticking out in every direction and sleep still pinching my eyes. I glanced around my back yard to make sure I was still on my property and hadn't been plucked into another dimension.

"I did, thank you." I didn't move as I stared at Farnsberry. There was so much I wanted to say, but I couldn't think of where to begin. I was surprised that I could even *think* lucidly before I'd had my two cups of coffee.

He looked a little sheepish and said, "You must be wondering why we're here. We brought a thermos of coffee if you'd like some."

"I would. Thank you."

Farnsberry poured me a cup, walked around the table, and pulled out a chair. "Would you sit with us, please, and let us explain what's been going on?"

I sat across from them.

Farnsberry took a seat as well and reached across the corner of the table for Ingrid's hand. She smiled at him and turned her gaze on me when Herman began.

"Now that Rita has been arrested, we came out of hiding." He glanced at Ingrid, who slowly nodded. "We wanted to let you know a bit about our history, Sophie. I'll start at the beginning. My parents divorced when I was very young. My father remarried, had another family. My mother married Ingrid's father when I was fourteen and Ingrid was twelve. We're step siblings." His expression softened when he looked at her. "It was love at first sight, for both of us. Here." He leaned over, tugged on his wallet, and pulled out an old black-and-white photograph of a young man and woman. "That's us, when I went away to college."

"You could be sisters with Laura and Sharon, Ingrid." To Herman, I said, "You chose these women because they looked like Ingrid?"

"Subconsciously, not intentionally." He stared at the picture and then put it away. "Our parents saw what was happening between us and forbade it. They didn't have the resources to send me away to school, or they would have. We lived in the same house but were never allowed to be alone." Here, he chuckled, as did Ingrid. "But we managed to see each other when we could."

Ingrid turned to me. "We grew up, went away to different colleges, and lived with heavy guilt because we loved each other. I married. Herman didn't, until his thirties when he married Laura, a friend from college. She disappeared a few months into their marriage. I divorced and remarried. Herman married Sharon, and she also disappeared. It was horrible, not knowing what happened to them."

"Did you have an affair with Sharon's sister?"

Farnsberry shook his head. "No. She was like a very needy little sister. I didn't even have an affair with my wife, I'm ashamed to say." He patted Ingrid's hand. "Not too long ago, Virginia Crane contacted me about her maid, Rita. She'd worked for Virginia for a couple of months and felt an unnaturally strong sense of loyalty to her employer. She'd occasionally ask questions about Virginia's life, where she went to college, her college friends, details about her life. With a little prodding, Virginia opened up about Laura, Sharon, your mother Esther, Edna, and Jonas. One day, Rita asked about me—Virginia was

211

my secretary for several years, and we thought that was the reason for the questions. But that day, Virginia called to tell me she suspected Rita thought I was her father—"

I lifted my brows. "Her father?"

"Which would be normal, of course," Ingrid interjected, "because of the paperwork. But," she glanced at Herman, "I'm getting ahead of the story."

"Virginia said that Rita knew things she couldn't possibly know. Are you aware, Sophie, that Esther, Edna, and Virginia traveled to Europe during their college years?"

"Yes. I recently figured out that my mother was the third woman in the trio."

"Yes, she and Edna were pregnant."

What? "My mother was pregnant?"

He nodded. "Esther and Edna were raped by the same man at a college fraternity party. At the time, they didn't know the name of the culprit nor had they seen him the dark night of the attacks."

My mother was *raped?* The shy, reserved woman who shut out every person who loved her was *raped?*

"I'll tell you this, Sophie: something died in your mother the day she gave away her baby." Herman shook his head. "I don't believe she ever recovered."

Raped, pregnant, alone, and having to give away her baby. It's no wonder she had difficulty recovering. My poor mother.

Oh, no.

"You're going to tell me Rita is my sister, aren't you?"

"No. Jim Peters is your brother."

Jim Peters? Samson's owner and my neighbor? *That* Jim Peters? "My half-brother lived down the street from me for two years?"

Farnsberry nodded. "He found out about the orphanage when his adoptive mother was dying and researched—*hacked* is a better word—into their computers. He moved here a couple years ago and only approached me once. I told him I was not his father, that I couldn't

212

divulge his mother's name, and he never bothered me again."

I shook my head. "So many secrets."

"There are more. Rita came to my house and accused me of, in her words, 'throwing her away'. When I told her I wasn't her biological father, she asked me about her mother. I wouldn't tell her, and she struck me over the head, enough to draw blood. I passed out. I think she thought I was dead."

"Why would she think you're her father?"

"Because when Edna and your mother had their babies in Europe, I traveled there to help my friends out and took their babies to a small orphanage that catered to Americans wanting quick adoptions where no questions were asked and a good amount of money was exchanged for the care of the babies until they were adopted. I refused to divulge their mothers' names, as promised, and I alone signed the papers. Virginia was there and paid for everything."

He sighed, deeply. "Our best guess is that Rita hacked into the orphanage computer, saw my name, and came here to find out the name of her mother."

"Did she have anything to do with killing your wives, Laura and Sharon?"

"She would have been sixteen or so when Laura disappeared. That's a bit young, to my way of thinking, but if the pathology is there to kill, then maybe she did." He lifted a shoulder and shook his head. "After Sharon's disappearance, I didn't marry again." He glanced at Ingrid and smiled. "Until two months ago when our mother passed away."

"I'm sorry for your loss."

Ingrid nodded. "Herman and I had to get away because Rita was after Herman. It's our guess that she killed Laura and Sharon because she didn't want him to be happy. We were afraid she might find out that Herman had married again and come after me. So, we ran."

"Why not call 9-1-1- and get help?"

Herman shook his head. "We felt our story was too convoluted, that if we contacted the police about Rita, then the disappearances of my wives would come up and lead to me. We had only one option and that was to leave and hide."

Herman took Ingrid's hand. "By the way, the reason I couldn't help you the night you found me at Virginia's is because I had promised Edna and Esther that I would never tell about their babies. It was simply too complicated to tell you. I figured that, eventually, Rita would find out that Virginia went with Edna and Esther to Europe and kill her, too. I was trying to protect you, Sophie."

My mind swirled with all this information. I tried to make sense of it, but all the pieces didn't quite fit.

"This is probably a little late, but you're welcome to keep Yoda if you'd like. Thanks for taking care of him."

I nodded slowly. "Why did you accuse me of killing him?"

"I didn't. Rita started the rumor. She discovered the names of the two women who gave up their babies—"

"How?"

"Research. Asking questions. Hacking. She told me the night she tried to kill me that her adopted mother told her the name of the orphanage, and she found me in the paperwork. She uncovered the names of my friends at the university. It wasn't difficult for her to narrow down the names to Edna and Esther, since friends knew of their trip across Europe. I didn't ask Burke Maguire to watch my house; Rita got someone to ask him as me. I didn't bury any bones; Rita did, and she placed a cross on the burial site. Samson brought me the bone; I didn't know what to do with it, and I left it on my back porch. Rita found it, buried it, and thus started the Sophie-killed-the-cat story."

I nodded. "Garrett Flint told me you knew Sharon was buried in the national forest."

"Knew?" He shook his head. "Guessed. When Samson began bringing bones to my house, I thought they might be Sharon's and that she was buried nearby. The national forest abuts my back yard."

"The diary." Ingrid prompted.

Herman nodded. "Ingrid and I knew you had been in my house, and Ingrid discovered that Sharon's diary was missing, and we went to your house to retrieve it."

"I never found the diary."

He nodded. "We know that now. But at the time, we thought you had it, so we tried to retrieve it. Ingrid hit you over the head in your kitchen."

She turned, stretched out her hand to me, and I took it. "I was protecting Herman. If anyone read Sharon's diary, he would be incriminated for Laura's murder. I'm sorry I hit you, Sophie. You startled me, and I reacted. I'm so sorry."

I slowly nodded and let go of her hand. "You could have asked me for it."

Herman leaned forward. "We didn't know for sure if you had it, and we didn't want to involve you in all this any more than you already were."

"Fair enough. Did Rita use my car to hit your car?"

Herman nodded. "She called me to meet her out on Highway 22. She drove up in your car, told me to get out. She rammed my car and then left me there. I called Ingrid. She came to get me. That night, Rita came to my house, hit me over the head, and we went into hiding. It was Rita's plan for you to be arrested."

"She was after *me*?"

"For a short time, she thought your mother was her mother, and she resented the fact that Esther had kept you and not her. Then she found out Edna was her mother."

"Did she beat her?"

"That's what we think."

Ingrid nodded. "I stayed here in Forman Falls to find out as much as I could about Rita. I was taking a chance, being Herman's stepsister, living in his house with a madwoman after him. I had a gun with me at all times."

215

Ingrid reached for Herman's hand. "We're here to clear the air with you. We hope you can forgive us for everything."

"Consider yourselves forgiven, but I have two more questions, Herman. First, do you know who hit Burke Maguire on the head in your back yard?"

"No."

I didn't know how to ask the second question, but Jim was my brother, and I wanted to know. "Do you have any idea who raped my mother, who Jim's father is?"

Herman sent a questioning look to Ingrid. Even though she nodded, he looked frustrated as he shook his head and sighed. He really didn't want to say.

"Who?"

He looked up. "My half-brother, John Clarke Farnsberry."

Clarke of Laura and Clarke?

"He also went by the name Clarke Zalensky and Frank Zagorsky. Criminals change their names at will."

Virginia was right. Clarke and Frank were one and the same. "But I was told that your brother died several years ago."

"We all thought he had, until recently."

"Does Burke Maguire have this information?"

"We don't know. We'll make sure he gets it."

"And what about Virginia? Do you know what happened to her?"

"We don't know if she's dead or alive."

They left then. I called Burke and told him about their visit and that my mother and Edna had been raped by Clarke Farnsberry, who was the Clarke of 'Laura and Clarke' and was one and the same with Frank Zagorsky.

Burke said. "This investigation just got interesting, didn't it, Sophie?"

"Do you know where Frank slash Clarke is?"

"We're looking for him. Are you coming to the station to sign your statement?"

"I'll get dressed and do that, but when I get home, I'm doing nothing for the rest of the day. I'm relieved we found the perpetrator, and she's behind bars. Now, you need to find Clarke Farnsberry."

◆

After signing the papers and returning home, I got into my pajamas again and started a good book I'd picked up a couple weeks ago. A sort of peace settled over me. Rita was in jail. The Farnsberrys were happily married. I felt as if a huge weight had been lifted from my shoulders.

I fixed myself some lunch, fell asleep a couple of times with Moocher and Yoda, and continued reading. I didn't talk to a soul, except my pets, and I didn't work on my next book.

I vegged and read all day.

When I finished the book, I showered and dressed and went downstairs to start cleaning my living room. I put on ear buds and dusted while music filled my soul, humming along as best I could. I'm not a singer as much as I'm not an actress. Although, after my stellar performance last night at Terri's, I'd have to re-think my acting abilities.

Something touched my arm. I screeched, whipped around, and faced a snickering Jim Peters. He said something, and I tugged off the ear buds. "Sorry, I didn't hear you."

"I knocked a couple times. Your door was open."

Well, shoot. I'd forgotten to set the security system *again*.

"Yes." Okay. What should I say to a new brother several years older than me, a neighbor that I had been suspicious of for two years? "So." Ahem. "How are things?"

"Great. Great. I like your mother." A nervous laugh came out of him. He shifted his feet. "Our mother."

Yikes. What was that feeling? I wanted to punch him. Hard. My mother liked him, and she hated me. What was I supposed to do with that? "Would you like something to drink?"

"Naw, I'm okay. Just wanted to, uh, to come by and say hey to my little sister."

Okie-dokie and all righty. I'm just not there, Big Brother. I glanced at my front door, wishing Burke would pop over right...now. "Well, I'm glad you did." This relationship would take time. We could aim for acquaintanceship for now, or maybe friendship, and eventually, siblingship.

"I've, uh, noticed that you like Samson. He's yours, if you want him. Kind of a thanks-for-the-family gift."

"If I want him? Of course, I want him. You don't?"

"I think it's more that he wants you."

"Thanks, Jim. I appreciate it."

Jim nodded and looked outside. "That night at Jonas' house? The night he was killed? It wasn't Jonas who stood on the porch and called Garrett Flint a fool. It was Frank Zagorsky. He grabbed Flint and dragged him into the house. The four of us decided to play some poker. Jonas didn't like Garrett Flint, a wanted man, coming around his house. I thought Flint was harmless, but Frank liked having him around, so he could take what little money Flint had in poker. Frank thought Jonas was cheating, and he shot him. We all scattered after that."

"Did you tell Burke Maguire?"

"Oh, sure. Some time ago."

Some time ago? Why hadn't Burke mentioned this to me?

"That's my boy."

I spun around at the voice behind me, in my kitchen. Frank Zagorsky stood beside my refrigerator, smirking. The hand in his pocket slowly slipped out.

And in it was a gun!

"Always telling the truth, boy. You were raised right, and that's good." Frank circled the room, holding the gun on me as well as his gaze. He hadn't blinked yet. His wide eyes made him look crazy. "So,

218

this is the little tramp you told me about."

My heart stopped.

"Frank, you—"

"Ah-ah-AH-ah." Frank shook the gun at Jim. "I told you I don't like my boy calling me 'Frank'. I'm your dad, so call me 'Dad'."

Dear God. I was facing the man who raped my mother!

I shook like a leaf. I wanted to be brave, but my knees were giving out, and I needed to hold onto something. I could hardly get a breath of air into my lungs. I didn't want him to see me as easy prey, so I lifted my chin and gritted my teeth and prayed, prayed, prayed.

Jim sent me a quick glance and then looked at Frank. "What are you—"

"Don't interrupt me, boy." Frank cocked the gun and pointed it right at me. One corner of his mouth lifted in a sneer, and I honestly thought I might slip to the floor from sheer terror. "Here I thought I had you, little lady, the other night, chasing you in your house. But you're not getting away this time. I'm going to enjoy you just like I did your mama."

My mind went blank with fear.

Frank smirked. "You need better security, honey. I had no trouble at all getting in here. And you should get out more, buy yourself some nice, girlie panties. Make yourself more appealing to the man about to take you."

I shivered, more afraid than I ever thought I could be. I glanced at Jim. He looked at his feet and didn't offer even a hint that he would come to my aid if I needed him.

"You go on home now, son. I've got plans for your little sister. Go on, now."

Jim didn't bother to look at me as he shuffled to the front door. And left! My brother left me with this monster!

"I've set up a little place for you and me in that empty house across the street, honey." Frank's features hardened. "Let's go."

Frantically, I looked around for anything to grab and hit him, but I

219

was near the front door and there was nothing.

"Move."

I couldn't believe this was happening. My entire body shook as I stepped onto the porch. Surely someone will see me and come to my—

Frank turned off my porch light.

I tried to swallow but couldn't. This was real. There was a man behind me with a gun. His intent was to rape and kill me. *God? Father? I need help. Please send me help.*

I glanced around. It was dark. The nearest streetlamp was three houses down. No one was about. I couldn't scream; I didn't have enough spit in my mouth and, besides, I knew Frank would kill me the second I made a sound. I needed to make a run for it, but he grabbed the back of my blouse and shoved me across the street.

"Around back."

I stumbled across the lumpy yard, frantically looking for a way to escape this nightmare.

"Up the stairs."

My mind was racing, and I couldn't stop it long enough to *think.*

"Open the door." The barrel of his gun jabbed my back.

I looked around for Moocher. Where was he? Where was Samson?

"*Now*, girl, or I'll just shoot you and have my fun with you, dead or alive."

Dear God! My hands were shaking when I clutched the knob and turned it. The door opened with a squawk. He shoved me inside. A blanket lay on the floor. *Oh, God. Please.*

"Your luxury suite, madam." He chuckled.

I had to act quickly, or I'd never get out of this alive. "Why did you kill Edna, Clarke?"

He raised his brows at me, a surprised expression on his face.

"Did she find out you'd raped her in college?"

His smile was quick.

"Did you tell her?"

He sent me an I'm-so-proud-of-myself smirk. "It was beyond exhilarating to watch her face while I told her." His eyes glinted. "She had to die. It was—" He looked up at the ceiling. "Well, I'll have to use the word 'exhilarating' again. It was exhilarating to beat her to death."

Dear God, he's going to kill me. I had to stall him, but would Burke—would anyone—even think to look for me in the vacant house? I needed to calm down, to think of a way out of here.

"You were leaving Virginia when your car exploded."

I'd surprised him again. His brows lifted, and he slowly smiled.

"She thought you died that day."

"That's what she was supposed to think."

"You changed your looks. Plastic surgery?"

He squinted at me.

"You were in the clear." The door we'd just come through wasn't locked. "Everyone thought you were dead." I could jump out and run. "So why risk coming here?" He's old and won't be able to keep up with me. "What could have induced you to come here?"

I screamed and shoved him hard, opened the door, and jumped down the steps in one leap. I knew he'd fallen on the floor. I only had a few seconds to reach Farnsberry's gate.

I could hear him behind me! I tried to open the gate with shaking hands. Oh, God, help me. Help me.

A shot sounded!

Ducking, I opened the gate and slammed it closed. Flying from tree to tree, I made it to the other side of Farnsberry's house. I hid in the shadows, grabbed the hem of my blouse, and covered my mouth to quiet the sound of my frantic breathing.

I listened, heard nothing, and eased back against the tree. My heart was racing, racing.

"He's coming, Sophie."

I jerked at the whispered words. Virginia Crane stepped into the light with a gun in her hand. "What are you doing, Virginia?"

"I'm going to kill Clarke Farnsberry."

What? "Where have you been? We found your Cadillac at the hospital and thought someone—?"

"Misdirection. I parked it there, walked through the hospital, out the other side, and made my way here. I've been inside Herman's house the last two days, waiting for my chance to end Clarke's life. I knew that piece of scum was spending time with his son, Jim Peters, and I waited. I'll kill him this time."

Uh…

"Hello, Virginia."

She spun toward Frank. I backed up a couple of steps.

He was breathing heavily, but the gun in his hand was surprisingly steady. "I'll answer your question now, girl. Why did I come here? To meet my son."

Virginia's eyes flashed with pure hatred. She gritted her teeth while the hand holding the gun on Frank trembled. She was positively on fire with rage. "I thought I killed you a long time ago, Clarke, but you got away. Not today. Not today! Sophie," she said, breathing heavily without taking her gaze off Frank. "We're both dying of cancer. It's what we deserve. He raped my friends in college, then he targeted and married *me!* When he told me a few weeks after our marriage, I was livid. All I could think about was ridding the world of him. I planted a bomb in his car with a timer. You saw my shock at Jonas' memorial dinner when I discovered I'd failed. Who died in the car explosion, Clarke?"

He chuckled. "Some homeless man. He was thrilled when I gave him my car. You must have been proud to have put your chemistry degree to good use."

I thought I heard her growl.

"Killing you isn't *enough!*" Her hand was shaking so much, I thought she might drop the gun. "You should be hanged, drawn, and quartered—"

I put up both hands. "Wait. Maybe we can settle this—"

"We're way past that, Sophie." Virginia took in a long, shaky breath, her fierce gaze still on Frank. "He told me he found the orphanage's paperwork in Herman's safe and went there. He paid them a lot of money to find out what had happened to his kids. When he was diagnosed with cancer, he came here to meet his son. He'd already met Rita and convinced her to come here, too. After telling me all this, he tried to kill me, but I pretended to be dead and then got away."

"You always were a tad too... *rigid* for me, Virginia."

"You snake!" She fired.

Frank did, too.

I screamed and stepped back as both of them stared at the other and then slowly fell to the ground.

"Sophie!"

Burke's voice. "Over here!" I was so relieved to see him peering around Farnsberry's house with a gun. His gaze moved from Frank to Virginia to me.

"Are you okay?"

"Yes."

Another gunshot!

Burke's head snapped back, and he groaned the worst guttural sound I've ever heard as he grabbed his chest.

I screamed, "Nooooo!"

His fingers relaxed, and his gun slipped out of his grip and dropped into the grass a second before he slowly fell. I lunged toward him, but Frank held his gun on me now.

"I didn't tell you to move, girl." Lying on the ground, blood stained Frank's shirt and his hand covering the wound. "He got what he deserved, as will you."

I gasped as Jim Peters came around Farnsberry's house, gun drawn and pointing right at Frank. "Put the weapon down," he said. When Frank moved his arm, Jim shot him. Frank stared at him for a moment, then his eyelids slowly closed as if they couldn't hold back impatient sleep. Jim lowered his weapon. He touched Burke's neck, said something to him, then moved to Frank and Virginia and did the same. He tugged out his phone, punched in some numbers, and waited. "Yeah, Jim Peters here."

"J-Jim?" I breathed the word. I was falling apart, and I could hardly speak. "Burke's been sh-shot." *Oh, God. Don't let him be dead. Please don't let him—*

I gasped, nauseous and on the edge of hysteria. I stepped around Frank and studied Burke's body, hoping for any movement that told me he was still alive. But he just lay there, not moving. *Please, God.* "Oh, please, please." I heard Jim in the dark behind me, still talking on the phone.

I began to sob. My stomach literally churned as I stumbled toward him. "Please, God. Not Burke. Not Burke."

Suddenly, Burke groaned and rolled to his back. "Ouch. That really hurt."

What? How—?

Oh! I was so relieved to see him alive and moving to his knees—where I needed to be right now, thanking God that he wasn't dead—that I burst into blubbering tears. "Oh, B-B-Burke."

He reached for me. "Come here," he said and tugged me into his arms. I sobbed even harder.

"Everything's okay now, Sophie. No need for tears."

No need for tears? Was he kidding? This was the perfect time for tears! When I burrowed into his chest, he moaned, and I jerked back. "Are you okay? Are you hurt?"

"I'm okay. Bruised and feeling stupid. I know better than to walk toward a man holding a gun when I haven't verified he's been taken down." Burke picked up his handgun and holstered it as Jim walked toward him.

"I checked on those two. They're both dead."

"Thanks for warning me about Frank. You're good at undercover work, Jim, and a great actor." Burke extended his hand. "Help me up, buddy."

I stood as he tugged him to his feet. Burke sucked in a breath through his teeth, groaned, and said, "Getting shot in a vest hurts like the dickens."

I brushed the tears off my face. "What do you mean 'undercover work'?"

"Jim's been helping us since Jonas was killed. He's a retired police officer on disability from Austin. Look, I need to call this in. Give me a few minutes." He walked slowly to the gazebo and sat.

"He's in a lot of pain."

Jim nodded at me. "At least the vest stopped the bullet."

"Jim, how did you find out about Rita?"

"Frank told her I was her half-brother, and she approached me one day about helping her and our father get rid of the three women who'd given us up for adoption. I played along, contacted Burke, told him everything. We came up with a plan for me to befriend Rita, so I'd stay in the loop."

"How did you find out about the diaries and where they were buried?"

"When Virginia received the news that she was dying of cancer, she told Rita where she'd buried her diary and Sharon's."

"But why bury them? Why not put them in a safety deposit box?"

"I asked her that. She said Virginia didn't want any record of them. I think Virginia thought Sharon's might incriminate Farnsberry in his wives' deaths; she was protecting him by burying them. Rita thought they had more information about our history, our adoptions. I convinced her to tell me where they were buried, that they would be safe with me. The last time I talked to Rita she told me about Frank's plans to get you, Sophie, 'just for the fun of it, as usual'. His words."

"Fun? He thought the evil he did was fun?" That made my stomach churn even more. I didn't want to think about Frank or Virginia or Rita anymore, but I was sure they would have starring roles in my nightmares for the next few weeks.

I glanced over at Burke. He motioned Jim and me over. With help from Jim, Burke eased out of his vest. Just below the center-left of his chest was a huge red-and-purple bruise. No wonder he'd passed out; the bullet had barely missed his heart. He looked at me as several police officers hurried into Farnsberry's back yard. "I'll brief them on what happened and then you two can give your statements to them. I need to get to the hospital. Might have a broken rib or two."

Jim said, "I can take you."

"Appreciate it, but I've got a ride." Sirens sounded. "And there it is."

16

The late afternoon sun hid behind the tall trees lining my quiet neighborhood as Burke and I strolled down the middle of Elm Street. Beside me, Moocher wagged his tail and barked. I thought he might be calling his brother Samson to join us, but Samson was nowhere in sight. "I'm glad—relieved—that Sharon's funeral is over and that she finally has a proper resting place. Whatever happened to the necklace?"

"Farnsberry found it in his mailbox, sold it, and started a scholarship fund for our high school graduates who want to go to college or to a trade school."

Jim waved at us from his garage. I lifted a hand, grateful he didn't intercept us on our long overdue and very peaceful walk. I was indebted to him. If he hadn't watched Frank take me to the vacant house the other night and then called Burke, I would probably be dead right now.

"Sophie, we have a match from the DNA results from Laura's crime scene and Sharon's."

"And?"

"You'll be surprised when you hear—"

I nudged his shoulder. "Just *tell* me, Officer Maguire! It's Rita, right?"

"No. Virginia Crane was at both murder scenes."

"Virginia?" I was shocked beyond measure.

"Apparently, Virginia couldn't live with the thought of Farnsberry married to anyone but her. Her diary wasn't much help. Didn't mention the trip to Europe, Clarke Farnsberry, or killing Laura and Sharon, but she wrote in detail of her love for Farnsberry. She also wrote about a gold necklace with a cross and two pendants that she had given Sharon. She even mentioned burying it with her. I think it was Virginia who returned it to Farnsberry as an act of contrition for everything she'd done to him."

"But Virginia told me she and Sharon were soul mates." I shook my head. How could she murder her soul mate? That was like me killing Terri. Heavenly days, I couldn't even go there.

"Maybe they were, but she loved Farnsberry more, in a convoluted way. You were right about her killing them."

I basked in the glow of his words for a few moments. "Virginia Crane was one very sick woman. She'd make a good case study on how to compartmentalize your life, to appear normal to everyone even though you're a murderer. This is such a mess. Virginia killed Laura and Sharon and then Frank Zagorsky. Frank killed Jonas and Edna and Virginia. And Rita didn't kill anyone."

"She assaulted Farnsberry, wrecked your car and Farnsberry's—by the way, the paint came back a match, which was no surprise. Rita also tampered with evidence, plotted to kill your mother, assaulted a police officer, shot at a police officer, and held several people hostage."

"Assaulted a police officer?"

"It was Rita who hit me from behind in Farnsberry's yard. Frank was inside the house."

"Farnsberry told me she was out to get me until she realized my mother wasn't her mother."

"In Rita's mind, your mother was just as guilty as her mother, Edna, for giving her up for adoption. It was Frank and Rita at your house that night, Frank inside and Rita, the rock thrower, outside."

I nodded. "One loose end is Garrett Flint who didn't do anything but love Sharon. No one's seen or heard from him in a while. He probably knows who killed Sharon now. Maybe he'll find some peace and move on with his life."

"He won't leave Vivian," Burke added. "I saw something between them."

I smiled. "I did, too. And I finally heard from my father. Mother is with him in Kansas. I hope she's happy now that her baby is back in her life. Actually, Daddy told me Jim is moving to Kansas soon to live on their property and help out."

"I hope it works out for all of them. Another loose end is the man who sent you the package on your back porch."

"I never heard from him after we found Moocher at that ramshackle shed." I playfully nudged Burke and expected him to feign a stumble or something, but the nudge didn't rock him at all. The man was built like a tank.

"Also, the dentals on Frank Zagorsky match Clarke Farnsberry."

"No surprise there. Well, hello there." Samson's entire body wagged when he caught up with us. Barking playfully, he jumped up and licked my face. Ugh! "No licking, Samson."

Burke poked his side to get him down and then picked up a stick and threw it. Samson and Moocher ran after it, snarled and fought over it, and Samson the Conqueror proudly brought it back to Burke.

"Oh, I've solved the problem of Samson and our neighbors' newspapers. I put him in the backyard at night and let him out after ten in the morning. Most of the papers have been picked up by that time."

Burke nodded. "A simple solution."

We passed Vivian's house and, heavenly days, she was outside working in a new garden. "What's this, Vivian? You've taken up gardening? In broad daylight?"

She flapped a hand at me and laughed. Mrs. LeGraff stepped out of Vivian's house wearing a gardening hat and gloves and carrying a trowel. Vivian lifted her eyebrows at me and sent me a with-a-little-help-from-my-friend grin.

And Vivian was wearing shoes. Would wonders never cease?

Another surprise came out of her house: Garrett Flint, wearing a cowboy hat and work gloves. He dipped his head at us, his gaze squarely on Burke, who acknowledged his greeting with one of his own.

Well, good for Vivian and Garrett! I sent her a big smile and a wave. She held up her left hand with her fingers splayed. On her third finger rested a wedding band. "Oh, Vivian, congratulations!" I ran up and hugged her and then Garrett. Vivian giggled as Garrett draped an arm around his wife's shoulders.

"I'm so happy for you two!"

"We are, too." When Vivian looked at Garrett and he smiled at her, she was beautiful with love.

I decided right then to throw a wedding shower for Mrs. Flint.

We left and reached my next-door neighbor's house. A FOR SALE sign was in the front yard. After Jonas' funeral, his nephew came and set things in motion to get everything in his uncle's life sold. Hopefully, a family with children would move in. Our neighborhood needed more children.

We approached my driveway and turned toward the old vacant house. Samson disappeared around back with Moocher close on his heels. A few kids were on the front porch, playing jacks. The vacant house was the only playground for several streets, and kids came to Elm Street to play in its back yard or on the stoop in front.

Burke nodded toward the old eyesore. "The vacant house is going to be burned down next week."

"Really?" I stared at the house that had initiated solving my first mystery with Burke, when Samson gave me Sharon's necklace. The vacant house was a big part of my life growing up, my 'go-to' for emotional outbursts and crying bouts and wars with my Nerf guns. It was also a sweet spot for my time with Burke. Maybe burning it down will usher in a new era for me, one not so reclusive. Or maybe not. I liked where and who I was right now. Mostly.

"Someone bought the land and plans to build a house there."

"Do you know who?"

Burke chuckled. "Me."

"You, Officer Maguire? We're going to be neighbors?"

"I was raised on this street, and it's the only available lot." He nodded at Jonas' house. "I heard someone's put earnest money down.

You'll soon have new neighbors moving in."

"Who?"

"No idea. Happened earlier today. That's all I know."

"When will you start construction on your new house?"

"A month or so."

I nodded, smiling. "Neighbors. I like that. If a monster comes into my house, I'll scream, and you'll come a-runnin', right?"

"Right." He chuckled. "Everyone knows you can sure scream."

Samson ran out from around back of the vacant house with a piece of white paper in his mouth.

"What's this, buddy?" Burke leaned over and plucked it out of his mouth. "Looks like something you'd write, Soph." He handed it to me.

I gasped.

A page from my latest book!

I'd printed a copy of it just this morning for a final read-through. How did it get out here? I groaned. "Oh, no."

"What?"

"This is my book! Check the back yard. See if more pages are there!" I dashed up my driveway and inside my house. At the fastest clip I've ever made, I topped the stairs and raced into my room. "No." My desk was bare, and my book was gone. "No, no, no."

I whimpered when I grabbed the computer mouse and moved it. "Come on. Come on!" My computer woke up. My hand shook as I clicked on the working copy of my book, sitting as bold as you please on my desktop.

It didn't come up. "No, no, no." I clicked on a document with a made-up name—a hidden version of my book. The document opened, and it only had the words, "You should have gone out with me when I bought you the tickets" on it.

"Burke." My voice wobbled. I could hardly breathe. "Burke!"

By now, my whole body was shaking. This psycho had been in my house! I went into my email. I'd sent a copy to my account as a safe measure, so I wouldn't lose any of my writing if my computer crashed. But the file I put it in was gone!

"Burke!"

I heard him talking downstairs. He was on his cell phone when my life was falling apart?

I searched my SENT file. That email was deleted, too.

I checked the Recycle Bin. Gone!

Someone had stolen my book. I opened the locked compartment on my desk and reached for my memory stick. It wasn't there.

"Burke!" I screamed as loudly as I could. "Burke, where *are* you?" I've been violated! I've been robbed! Someone is out to get me!

Just when I thought things had settled down, a *thief* appears.

"Buurrrrkke!"

Loud footsteps pounded on my stairs. Burke ran into my bedroom, frowning and holding a stack of papers. "What is it? What's wrong?"

"My book. Someone stole my book. Someone deleted everything and stole the copy I printed this morning."

"Don't you have a backup system?"

"No. I don't trust them."

"Uh, twenty-first century, Soph?"

"Exactly why I don't trust them. Twenty-first century hackers, Officer?"

Burke took a moment to look around my room and then guided me toward the door. "This is a crime scene now, Soph." He slipped on gloves. "Let's get you outside."

"But—"

He slid a hand into one of his pants' pockets and pulled out some gum.

Oh, this man.

I unwrapped it and popped it into my mouth. As I led the way down the stairs, Burke called in the burglary. I stood in the foyer, trembling like a nervous foot.

232

When he finished the call, he opened the front door.

"What do I need to do?"

"Stay out of my way."

"Stay out of—? If you think a stick of gum is enough to bribe me out of your way, Officer Maguire, then you haven't learned much about me the last few weeks." I stepped outside in the best huff I could come up with.

He chuckled and followed me, pulled the door shut. "I've learned plenty about you. You're courageous, stubborn, generous, and kind. At least stay with Terri until I get this crime scene cleared."

Oh! I'm generous and kind?

"And beautiful."

Beautiful, too? "Thank you, Burke." I decided to let him have his way. I learned something about me just now: I can't be bribed with gum, but compliments work. I glanced around my neighborhood as Burke walked to his car. Mrs. LeGraff stood with Vivian and Garrett in Vivian's front yard, none of them moving a muscle as they stared in my direction. Then Mrs. LeGraff lifted a cautious hand and fluttered it at me. I waved and sent her a thumbs-up to reassure her that things were under control.

Burke stooped to look in the gutter, carefully picked up something small, and held it up. "Is this yours?"

Oh! My memory stick! I hurried over to him. "My book is on that. He must have dropped it." I reached for it, but Burke withdrew his hand.

"Fingerprints, Sophie. Let's get inside and see what's on it."

"We can use my laptop downstairs on the dining table." I wanted to dance a jig, I was so happy. "Come on."

A patrol car pulled up in front of my house. Officer Sheenen got out, grabbed a backpack, and shouldered it as he rushed toward us.

"Upstairs, the bedroom on the right," Burke told him. "I'll be up there in a few minutes."

I hurried to my laptop, inserted the memory stick, and breathed a sigh of relief. "It's all here. I'd like to save a copy to my desktop, Burke."

"All right. I can't leave you alone with the evidence, so get that done and get outside. When Sheenen's finished, we'll figure out how he broke in."

We? Hmmm. I liked the sound of that, although I was sure he meant Sheenen, not me. I smiled warmly at him. "We're bull dogs, aren't we, Burke? Tenacious and ferocious. We'll get this guy."

"Bull dogs?" He grinned. "I do feel the need to nibble on something."

"Bull dogs don't nibble, Deputee. They bite." I bared my teeth and chomped at air, my teeth clicking in the quiet room.

"I like the direction this is going." He reached for me, tugged me close.

I leaned back to say something, and he captured my mouth in a soft, just-go-ahead-and-melt-my-toes kiss. His arms tightened. His mouth became more insistent, and I leaned in and gave as much as he did. It was all so familiar—and all so new. Our first not-in-the-line-of-duty kiss.

He stopped, brushed my lips lightly, and said, "I could do this all day, but right now, let's get to work and catch this guy."

Let's? As in, 'let us'? So, he *did* mean me? "Okay," I said in my most professional voice, although I wanted to wiggle my eyebrows and grin like a possum. "Where to, first?"

From Tamara:

I hope you enjoyed *The Vacant House!* Sophie's adventures aren't over; they're just getting started, because Book 2 will be on its way soon. Until then, come join me in East Texas for a series of three novels that are suspenseful, exciting, and difficult to put down.

Book 1, *Who Killed Brigitt Holcomb?*

Marianne is ecstatic when she inherits her uncle's remote ranch in the Texas panhandle. Little does she know that with her inheritance comes a very dangerous (and very deadly) threat. The Brothers of Texas trilogy is a romantic suspense series that readers like you have called "excellent mysteries," "full of suspense," and "with just the right amount of romance." Join the Texas brothers on their quest for love—and survival—in this exciting series you won't be able to put down.

Grab your copy of *Who Killed Brigitt Holcomb?* and dive head-first into this engaging trilogy today.

If you enjoyed *The Vacant House,* please leave a review on the review site of your choice. Reviews are so important for authors! Thank you!

Books by Tamara G. Cooper

SERIES

Brothers of Texas
Who Killed Brigitt Holcomb?
Rosie Won't Stay Dead
Deception at Fairfield Ranch
Brothers of Texas Trilogy

Sophie O'Brion Mysteries
The Vacant House
The New Neighbors (Coming soon!)

Learn more about Tamara and her books at her website:
authortamaragcooper.com

Have a question or comment?
Send Tamara an email at: tamaragcooperauthor@gmail.com

About the Author
Born and raised in the great state of Texas, Tamara G. Cooper lives with her husband, three sons, and five dogs in a small town in East Texas. Her two older sons have left the nest. A homeschooling mother, she enjoys fishing, swimming, hiking, camping trips, reading, and, of course, writing.

Manufactured by Amazon.ca
Bolton, ON